ACES

CURSE OF THE RED BARON

Shannon Eric Denton • G. Willow Wilson

Curtis Square Briggs

AiT★PLANET LAR

SAN FRANCISCO

Aces: Curse of the Red Baron

by Shannon Eric Denton, G. Willow Wilson, and Curtis Square Briggs

published by
Larry Young and Mimi Rosenheim
AiT/Planet Lar
2034 47th Avenue
San Francisco, CA 94116

First Edition: May 2008

10 9 8 7 6 5 4 3 2 1

Book Design by Shannon Eric Denton and Patrick Coyle

ISBN-10: 1-932051-52-X
ISBN-13: 978-1-932051-52-0

Printed and bound in Canada by Imprimerie Lebonfon, Inc.

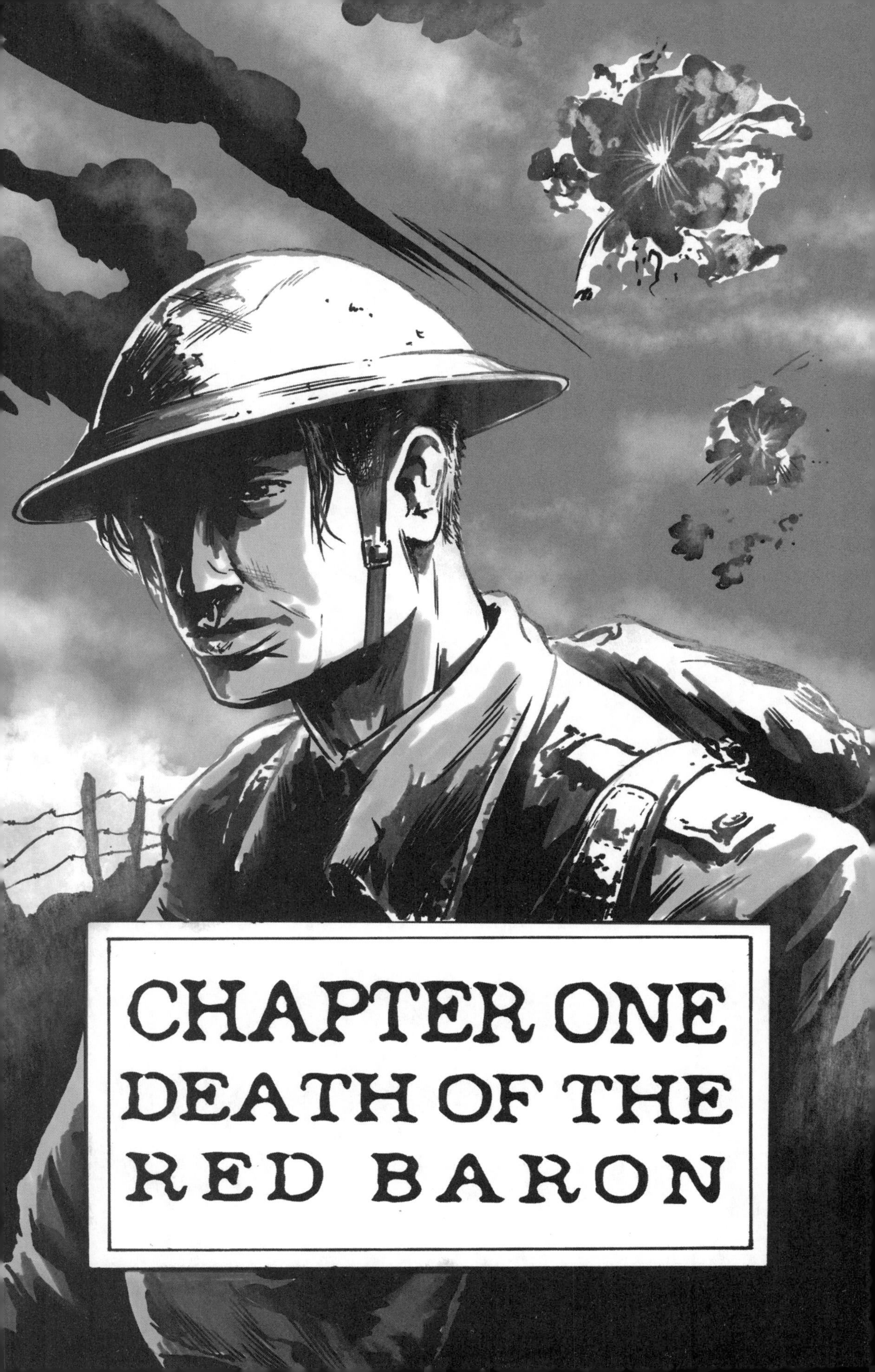
CHAPTER ONE
DEATH OF THE
RED BARON

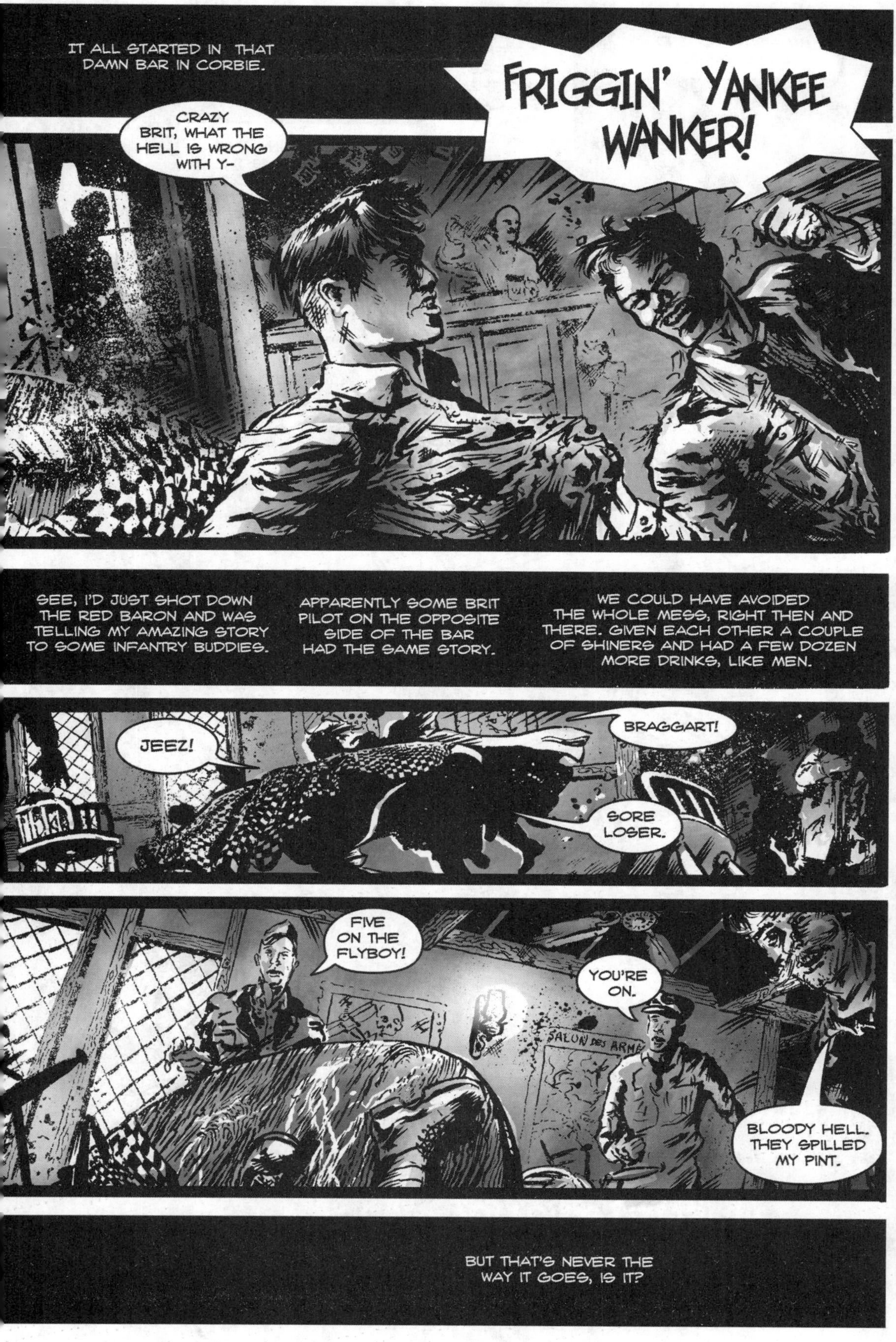

IT ALL STARTED IN THAT DAMN BAR IN CORBIE.
FRIGGIN' YANKEE WANKER!
CRAZY BRIT, WHAT THE HELL IS WRONG WITH Y-
SEE, I'D JUST SHOT DOWN THE RED BARON AND WAS TELLING MY AMAZING STORY TO SOME INFANTRY BUDDIES.
APPARENTLY SOME BRIT PILOT ON THE OPPOSITE SIDE OF THE BAR HAD THE SAME STORY.
WE COULD HAVE AVOIDED THE WHOLE MESS, RIGHT THEN AND THERE. GIVEN EACH OTHER A COUPLE OF SHINERS AND HAD A FEW DOZEN MORE DRINKS, LIKE MEN.
JEEZ!
BRAGGART!
SORE LOSER.
FIVE ON THE FLYBOY!
YOU'RE ON.
SALON DES ARMES
BLOODY HELL. THEY SPILLED MY PINT.
BUT THAT'S NEVER THE WAY IT GOES, IS IT?

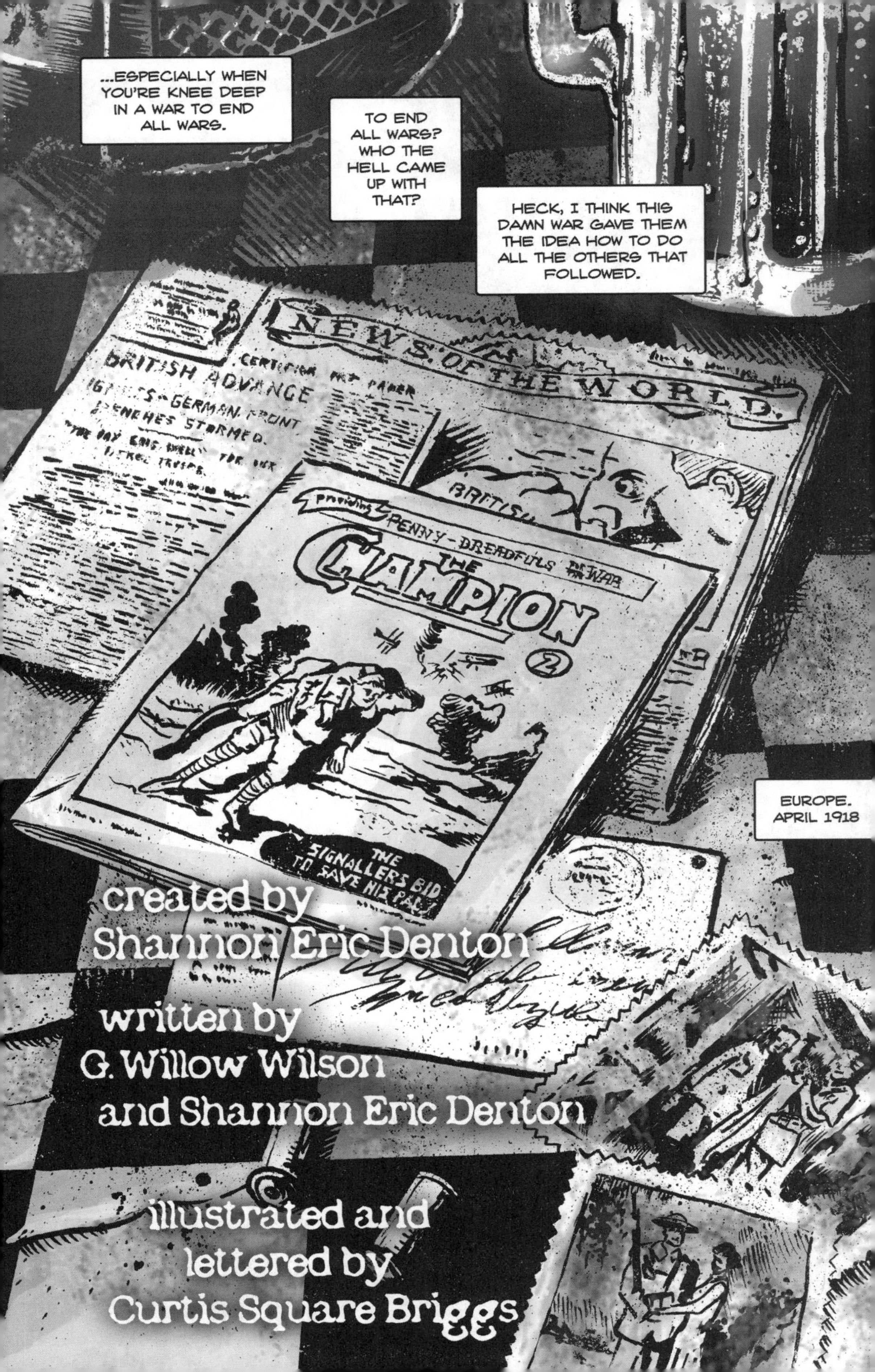
...ESPECIALLY WHEN YOU'RE KNEE DEEP IN A WAR TO END ALL WARS.
TO END ALL WARS? WHO THE HELL CAME UP WITH THAT?
HECK, I THINK THIS DAMN WAR GAVE THEM THE IDEA HOW TO DO ALL THE OTHERS THAT FOLLOWED.
NEWS OF THE WORLD
BRITISH ADVANCE
PENNY-DREADFULS OF WAR
THE CHAMPION
2
THE SIGNALLERS BID TO SAVE HIS PAL!
EUROPE. APRIL 1918
created by
Shannon Eric Denton
written by
G. Willow Wilson
and Shannon Eric Denton
illustrated and
lettered by
Curtis Square Briggs

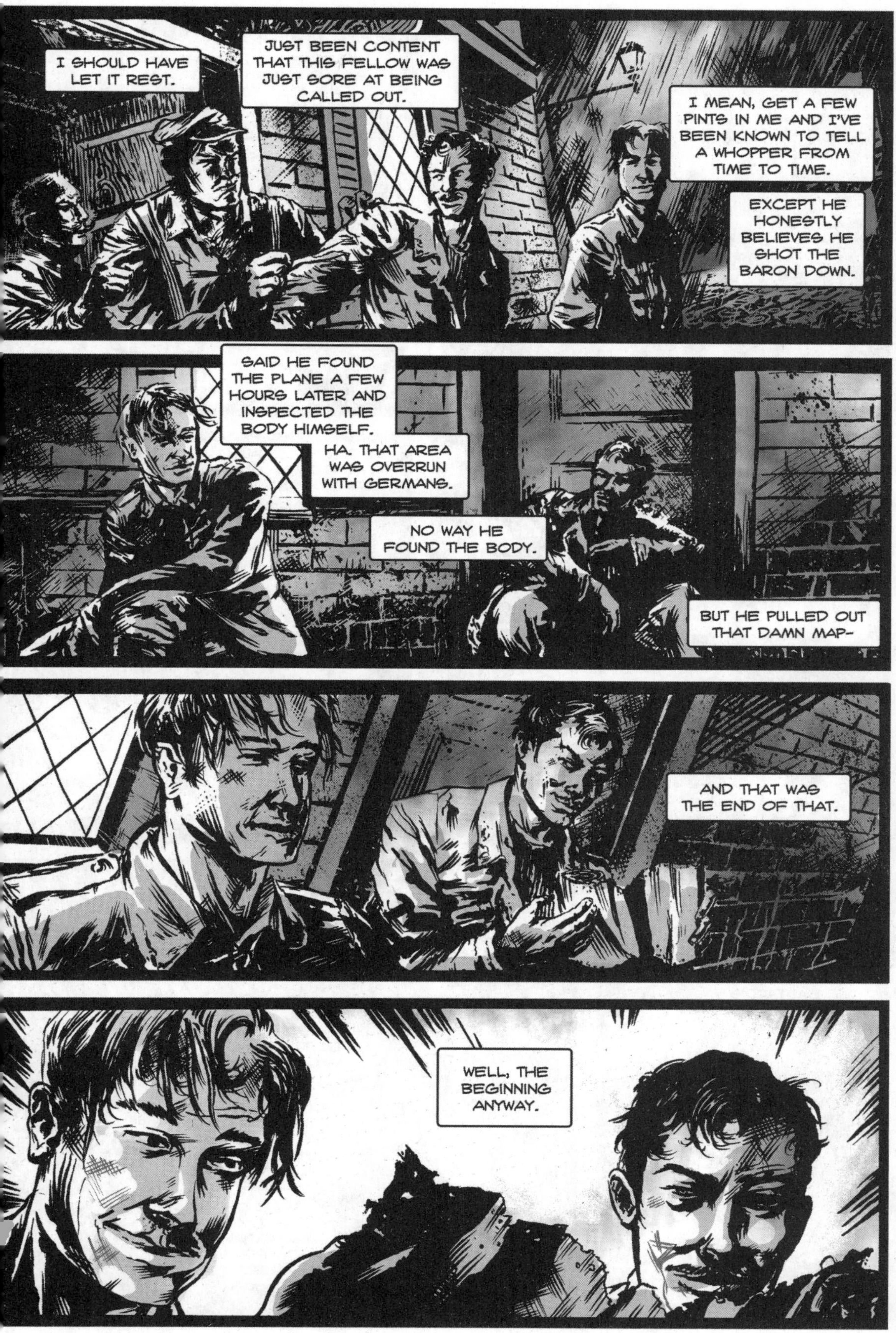
I SHOULD HAVE LET IT REST.
JUST BEEN CONTENT THAT THIS FELLOW WAS JUST SORE AT BEING CALLED OUT.
I MEAN, GET A FEW PINTS IN ME AND I'VE BEEN KNOWN TO TELL A WHOPPER FROM TIME TO TIME.
EXCEPT HE HONESTLY BELIEVES HE SHOT THE BARON DOWN.
SAID HE FOUND THE PLANE A FEW HOURS LATER AND INSPECTED THE BODY HIMSELF.
HA. THAT AREA WAS OVERRUN WITH GERMANS.
NO WAY HE FOUND THE BODY.
BUT HE PULLED OUT THAT DAMN MAP-
AND THAT WAS THE END OF THAT.
WELL, THE BEGINNING ANYWAY.

THAT PUTS THE ISLAND SOMEWHERE NEAR THE SCANDANAVIAN COAST. CAN'T TELL EXACTLY WITHOUT A NAUTICAL MAP.

I S'POSE THAT EXPLAINS WHAT THE RED BARON WAS DOING SO FAR INTO ALLIED TERRITORY.

SO DO YOU *HONESTLY* THINK IT WAS *YOU* WHO SHOT HIM DOWN?

I'M TELLING YOU, HE STARTED TO TALKSPIN THE INSTANT AFTER I FIRED.

S'FUNNY, BECAUSE FROM WHERE I WAS STANDING HE CAME DOWN AT AN ANGLE YOU COULD ONLY GET AT WITH GROUND FIRE.

YOUR GROUND FIRE, OF COURSE.

OF COURSE.

LET'S NOT START THIS AGAIN. WHEN WE GET TO THE ISLAND WE WON'T CARE WHO SHOT THE BARON,

WE'LL BE SWIMMING IN THE BASTARD'S LOOT.

PROVIDED HE REALLY HID TREASURE LIKE THIS MAP IMPLIES.

SERIOUSLY, ARE ALL YOU CHAPS SO GLIB?

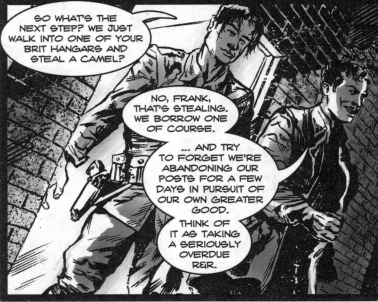

SO WHAT'S THE NEXT STEP? WE JUST WALK INTO ONE OF YOUR BRIT HANGARS AND STEAL A CAMEL?

NO, FRANK, THAT'S STEALING. WE BORROW ONE OF COURSE.

... AND TRY TO FORGET WE'RE ABANDONING OUR POSTS FOR A FEW DAYS IN PURSUIT OF OUR OWN GREATER GOOD.

THINK OF IT AS TAKING A SERIOUSLY OVERDUE R&R.

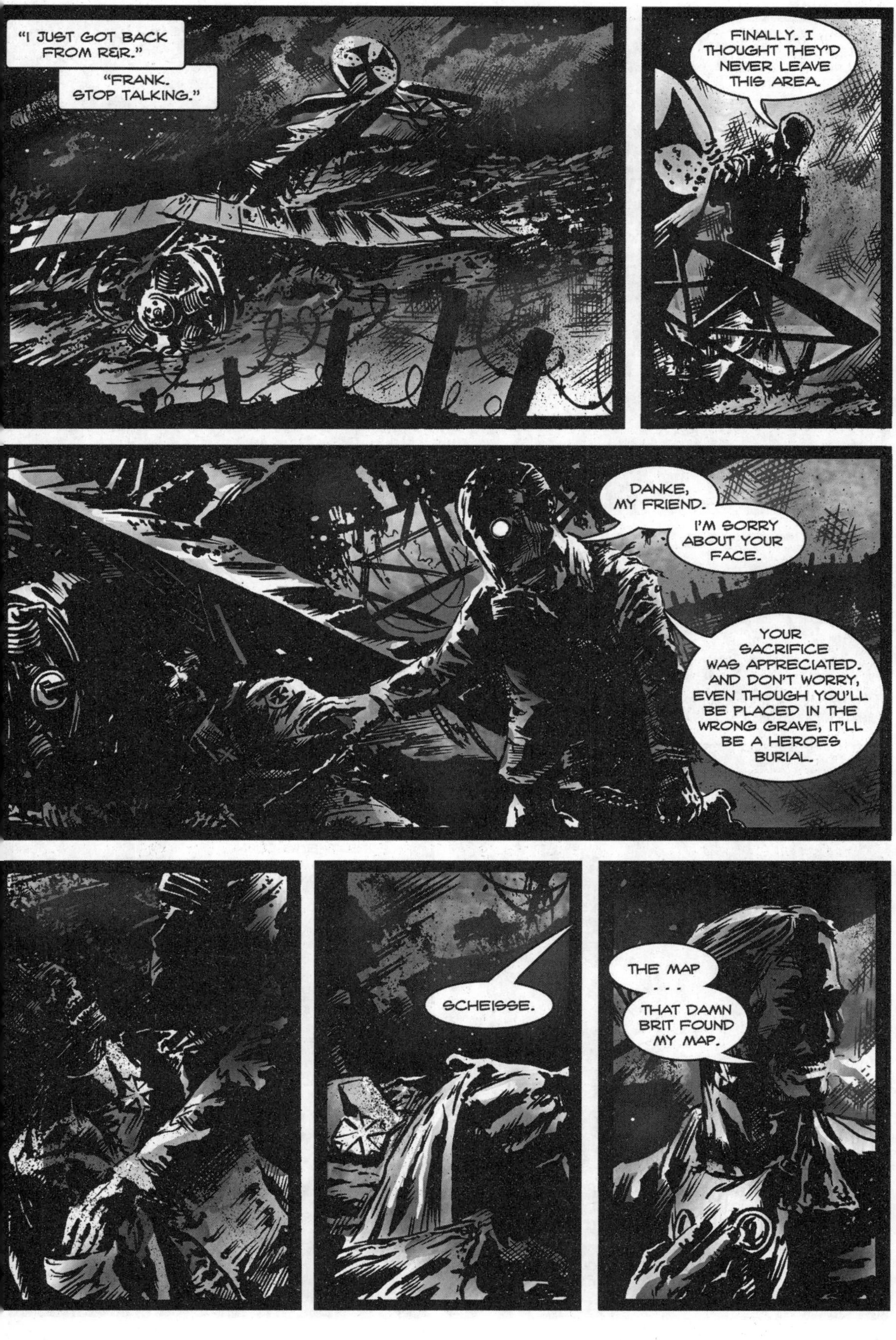
"I JUST GOT BACK FROM R&R."
"FRANK. STOP TALKING."
FINALLY. I THOUGHT THEY'D NEVER LEAVE THIS AREA.
DANKE, MY FRIEND.
I'M SORRY ABOUT YOUR FACE.
YOUR SACRIFICE WAS APPRECIATED. AND DON'T WORRY, EVEN THOUGH YOU'LL BE PLACED IN THE WRONG GRAVE, IT'LL BE A HEROES BURIAL.
SCHEISSE.
THE MAP . . .
THAT DAMN BRIT FOUND MY MAP.

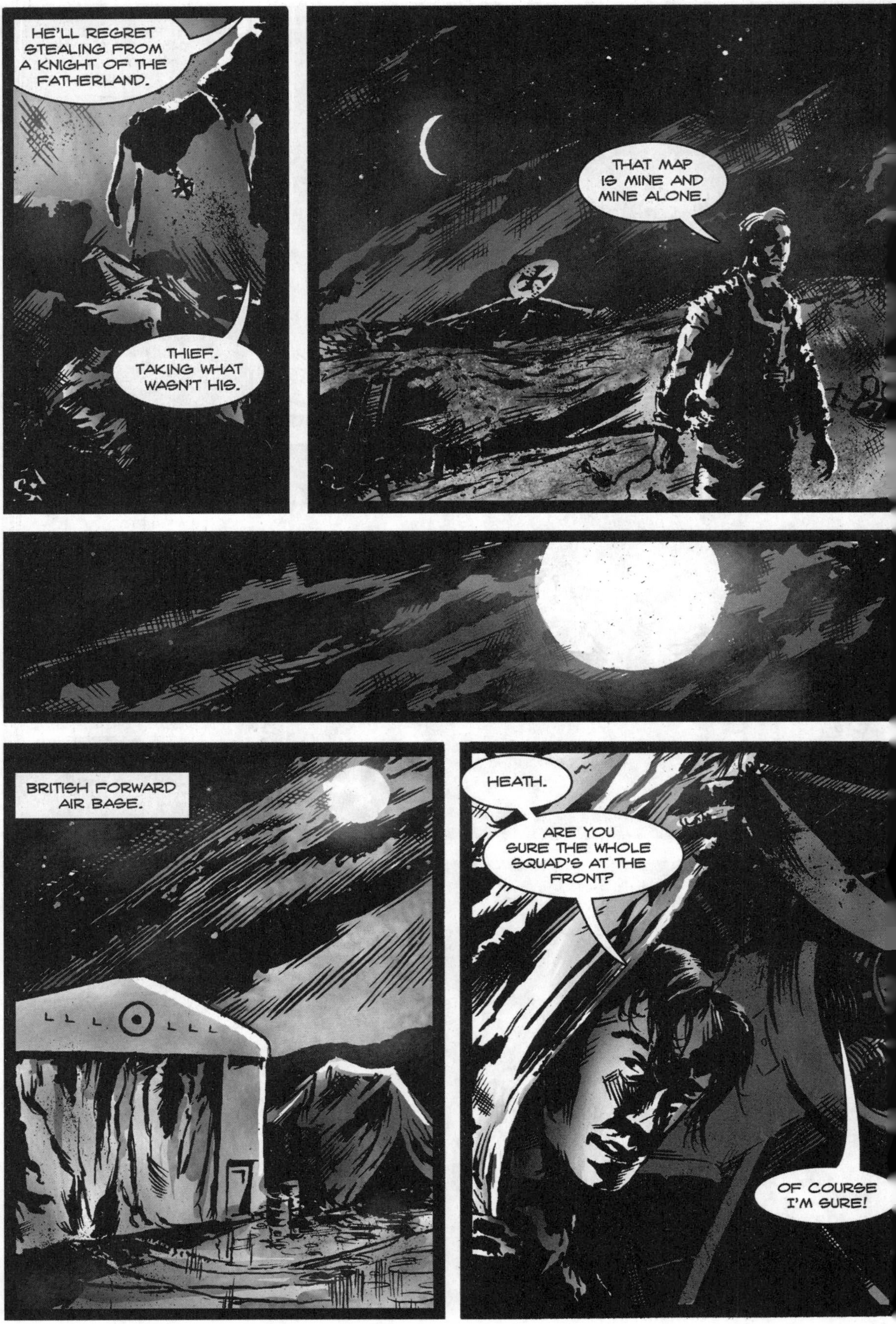
HE'LL REGRET STEALING FROM A KNIGHT OF THE FATHERLAND.
THIEF. TAKING WHAT WASN'T HIS.
THAT MAP IS MINE AND MINE ALONE.
BRITISH FORWARD AIR BASE.
HEATH.
ARE YOU SURE THE WHOLE SQUAD'S AT THE FRONT?
OF COURSE I'M SURE!

ALL RIGHT, THAT'S DONE IT. OPEN UP THE HANGAR

"WE NEED TO HIT THE SKIES."

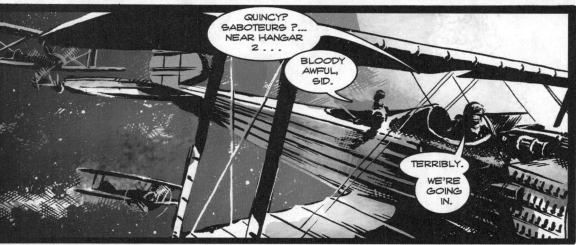

QUINCY? SABOTEURS?... NEAR HANGAR 2 . . .

BLOODY AWFUL, SID.

TERRIBLY. WE'RE GOING IN.

OI! ALL ABOARD!

YEAH, YEAH. I'M HURRYING.

SHOOT.

SHOOT? SHOOT WHAT?

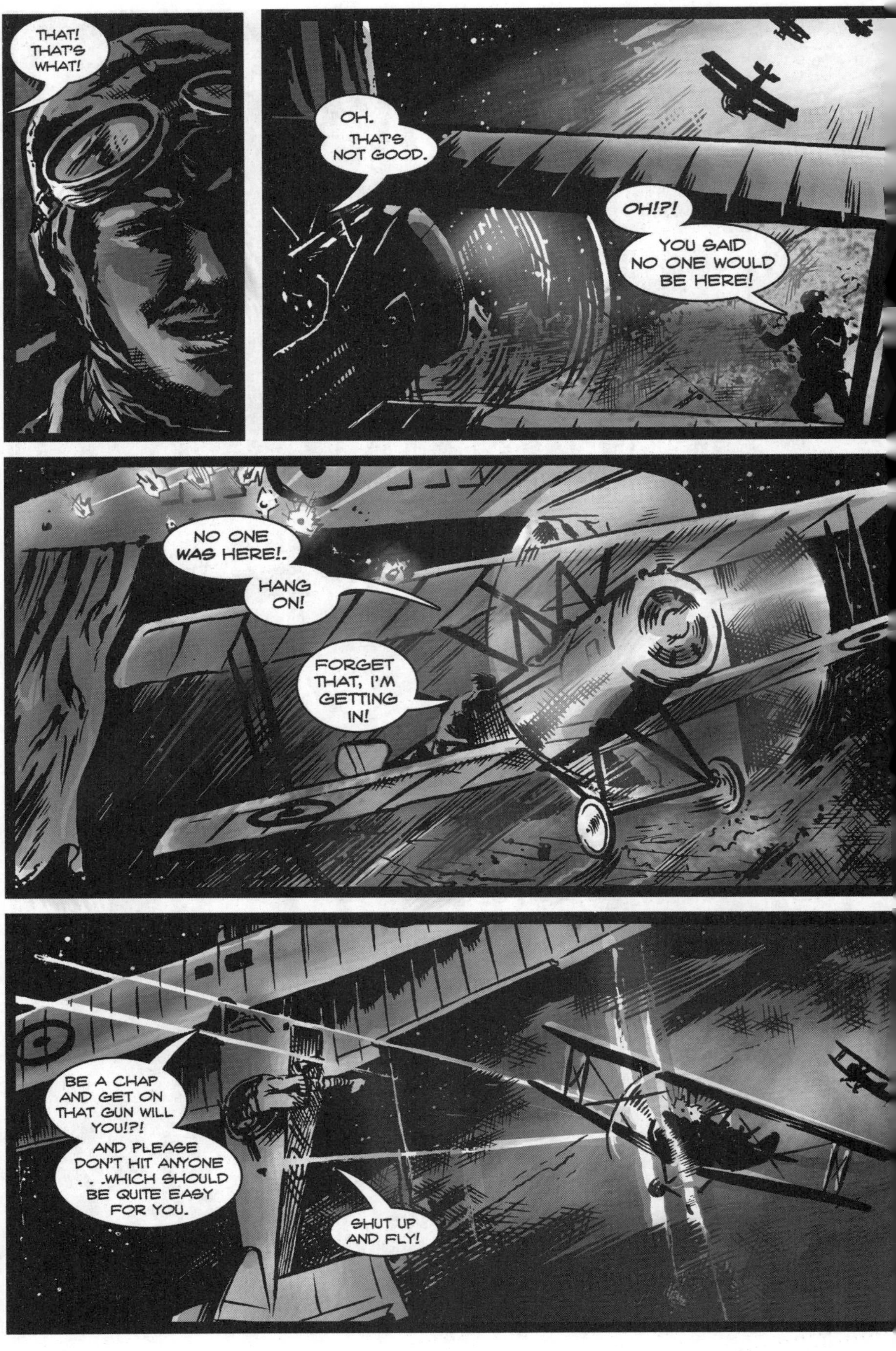
THAT! THAT'S WHAT!
OH.
THAT'S NOT GOOD.
OH!?!
YOU SAID NO ONE WOULD BE HERE!
NO ONE WAS HERE!.
HANG ON!
FORGET THAT, I'M GETTING IN!
BE A CHAP AND GET ON THAT GUN WILL YOU!?!
AND PLEASE DON'T HIT ANYONE . . .WHICH SHOULD BE QUITE EASY FOR YOU.
SHUT UP AND FLY!

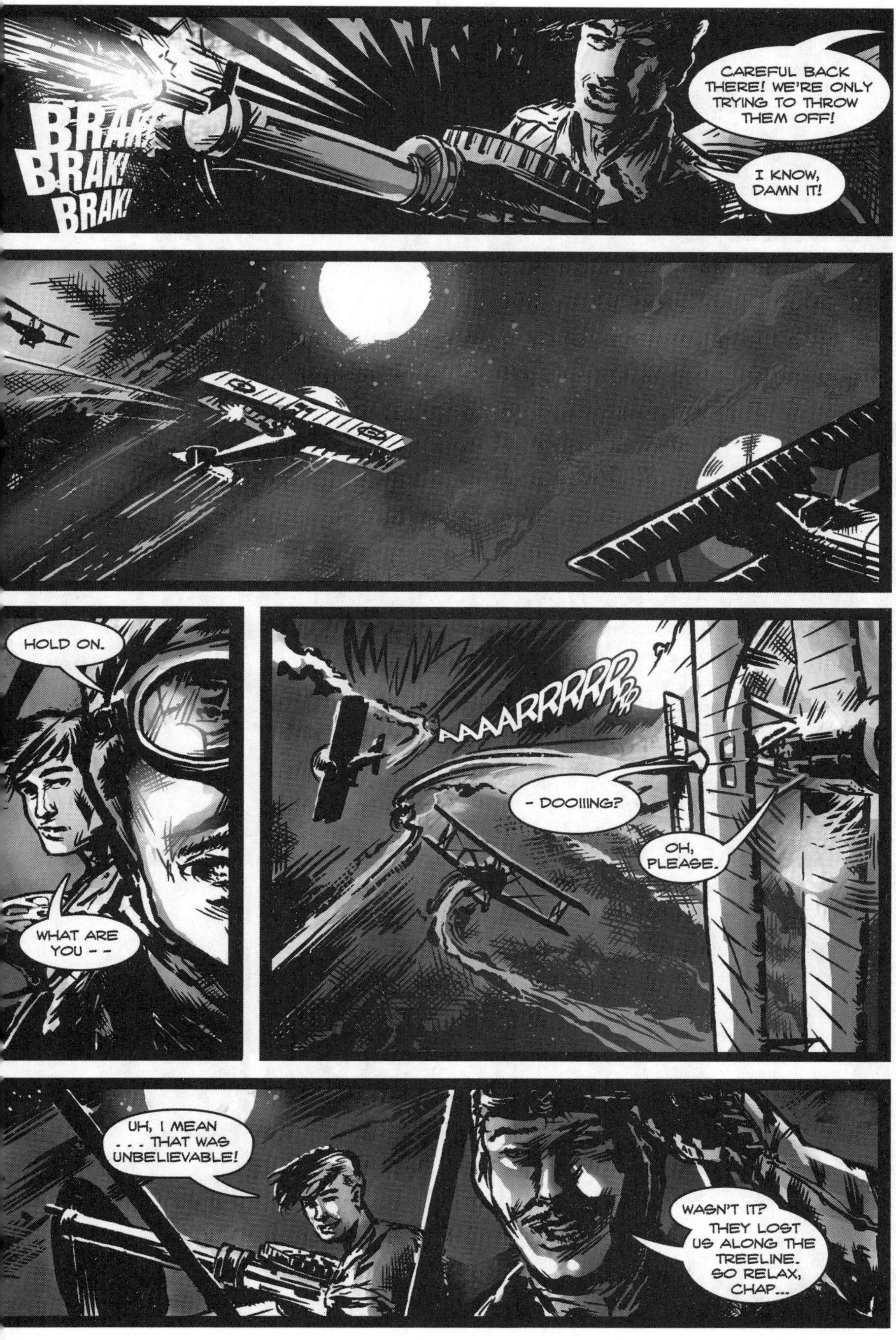
BRAK!
BRAK!
BRAK!
CAREFUL BACK THERE! WE'RE ONLY TRYING TO THROW THEM OFF!
I KNOW, DAMN IT!
HOLD ON.
WHAT ARE YOU - -
AAAARRRRRRR
- DOOIIING?
OH, PLEASE.
UH, I MEAN . . . THAT WAS UNBELIEVABLE!
WASN'T IT? THEY LOST US ALONG THE TREELINE. SO RELAX, CHAP...

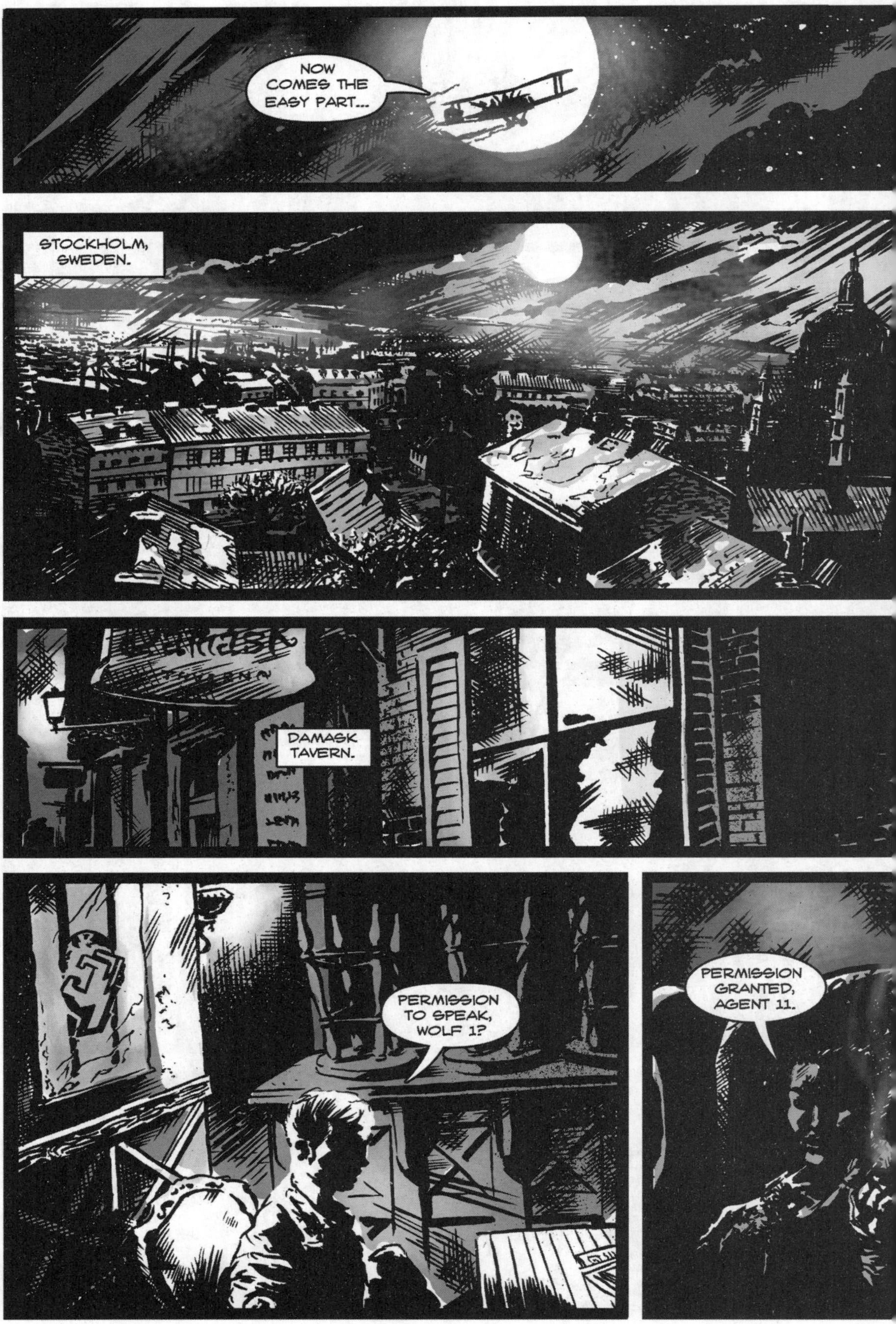
NOW COMES THE EASY PART...
STOCKHOLM, SWEDEN.
DAMASK TAVERN.
PERMISSION TO SPEAK, WOLF 1?
PERMISSION GRANTED, AGENT 11.

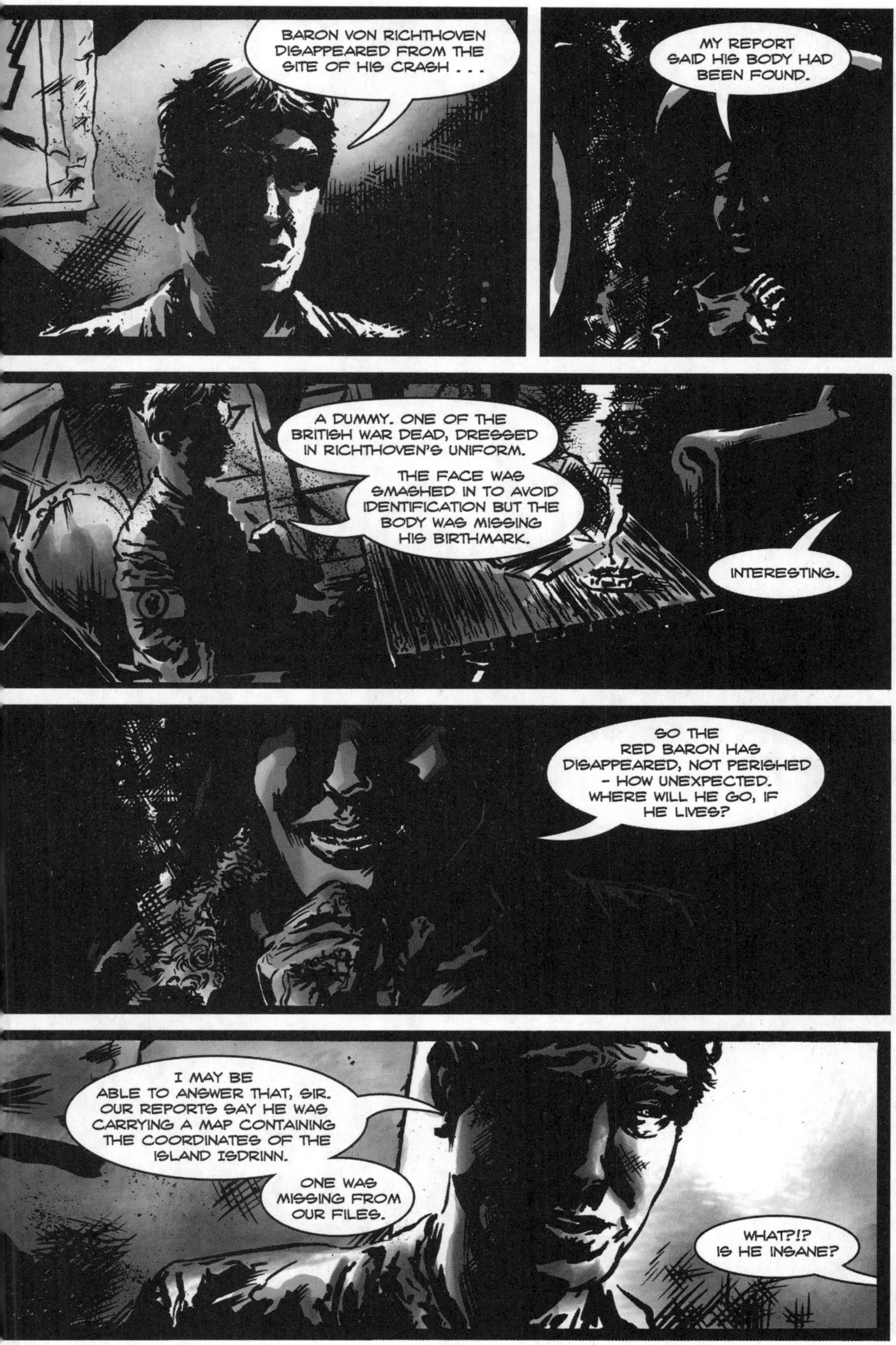
BARON VON RICHTHOVEN DISAPPEARED FROM THE SITE OF HIS CRASH . . .
MY REPORT SAID HIS BODY HAD BEEN FOUND.
A DUMMY. ONE OF THE BRITISH WAR DEAD, DRESSED IN RICHTHOVEN'S UNIFORM.
THE FACE WAS SMASHED IN TO AVOID IDENTIFICATION BUT THE BODY WAS MISSING HIS BIRTHMARK.
INTERESTING.
SO THE RED BARON HAS DISAPPEARED, NOT PERISHED - HOW UNEXPECTED. WHERE WILL HE GO, IF HE LIVES?
I MAY BE ABLE TO ANSWER THAT, SIR. OUR REPORTS SAY HE WAS CARRYING A MAP CONTAINING THE COORDINATES OF THE ISLAND ISDRINN.
ONE WAS MISSING FROM OUR FILES.
WHAT?!? IS HE INSANE?

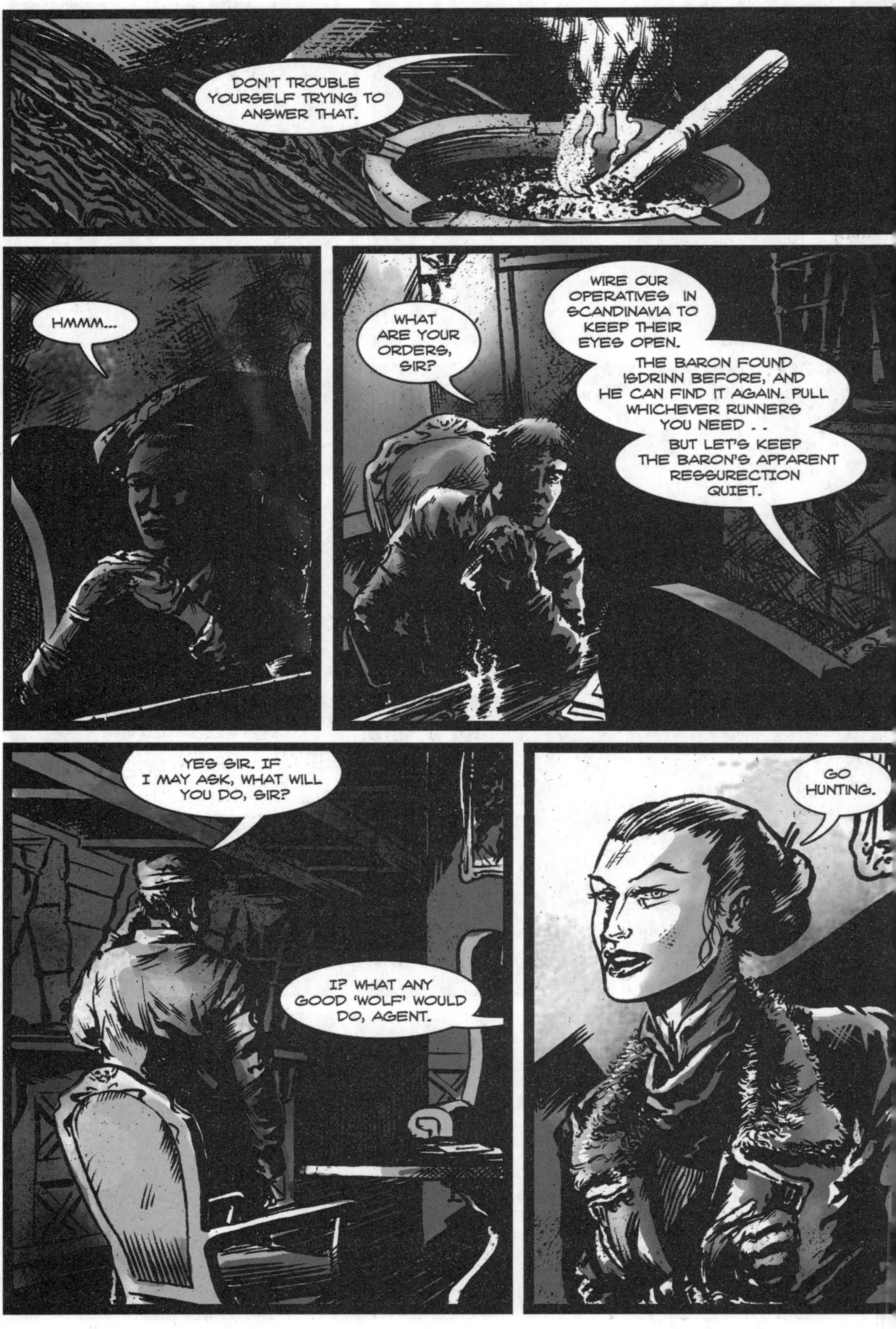
DON'T TROUBLE YOURSELF TRYING TO ANSWER THAT.
HMMM...
WHAT ARE YOUR ORDERS, SIR?
WIRE OUR OPERATIVES IN SCANDINAVIA TO KEEP THEIR EYES OPEN.
THE BARON FOUND ISDRINN BEFORE, AND HE CAN FIND IT AGAIN. PULL WHICHEVER RUNNERS YOU NEED . .
BUT LET'S KEEP THE BARON'S APPARENT RESSURECTION QUIET.
YES SIR. IF I MAY ASK, WHAT WILL YOU DO, SIR?
I? WHAT ANY GOOD 'WOLF' WOULD DO, AGENT.
GO HUNTING.

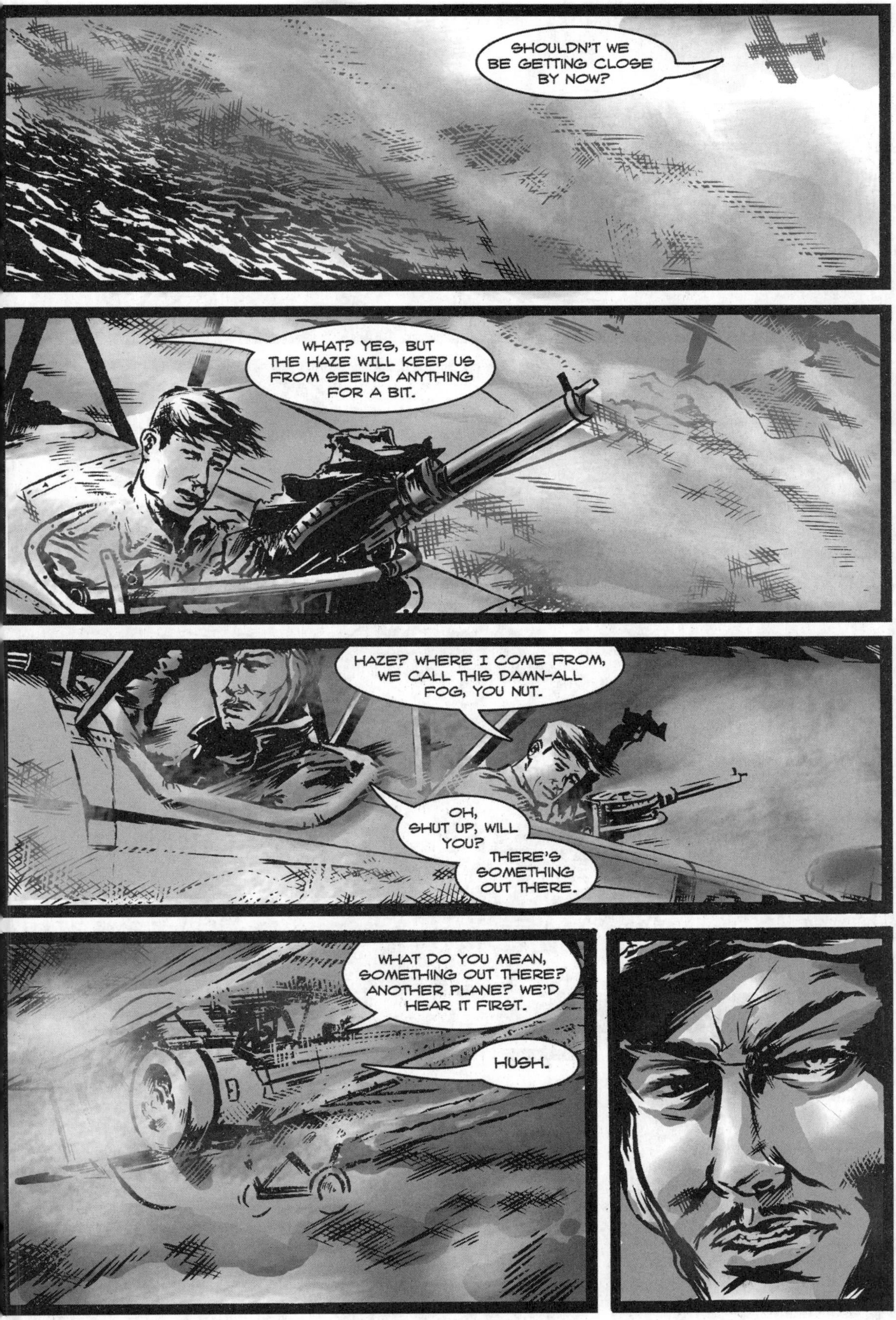
SHOULDN'T WE BE GETTING CLOSE BY NOW?
WHAT? YES, BUT THE HAZE WILL KEEP US FROM SEEING ANYTHING FOR A BIT.
HAZE? WHERE I COME FROM, WE CALL THIS DAMN-ALL FOG, YOU NUT.
OH, SHUT UP, WILL YOU?
THERE'S SOMETHING OUT THERE.
WHAT DO YOU MEAN, SOMETHING OUT THERE? ANOTHER PLANE? WE'D HEAR IT FIRST.
HUSH.

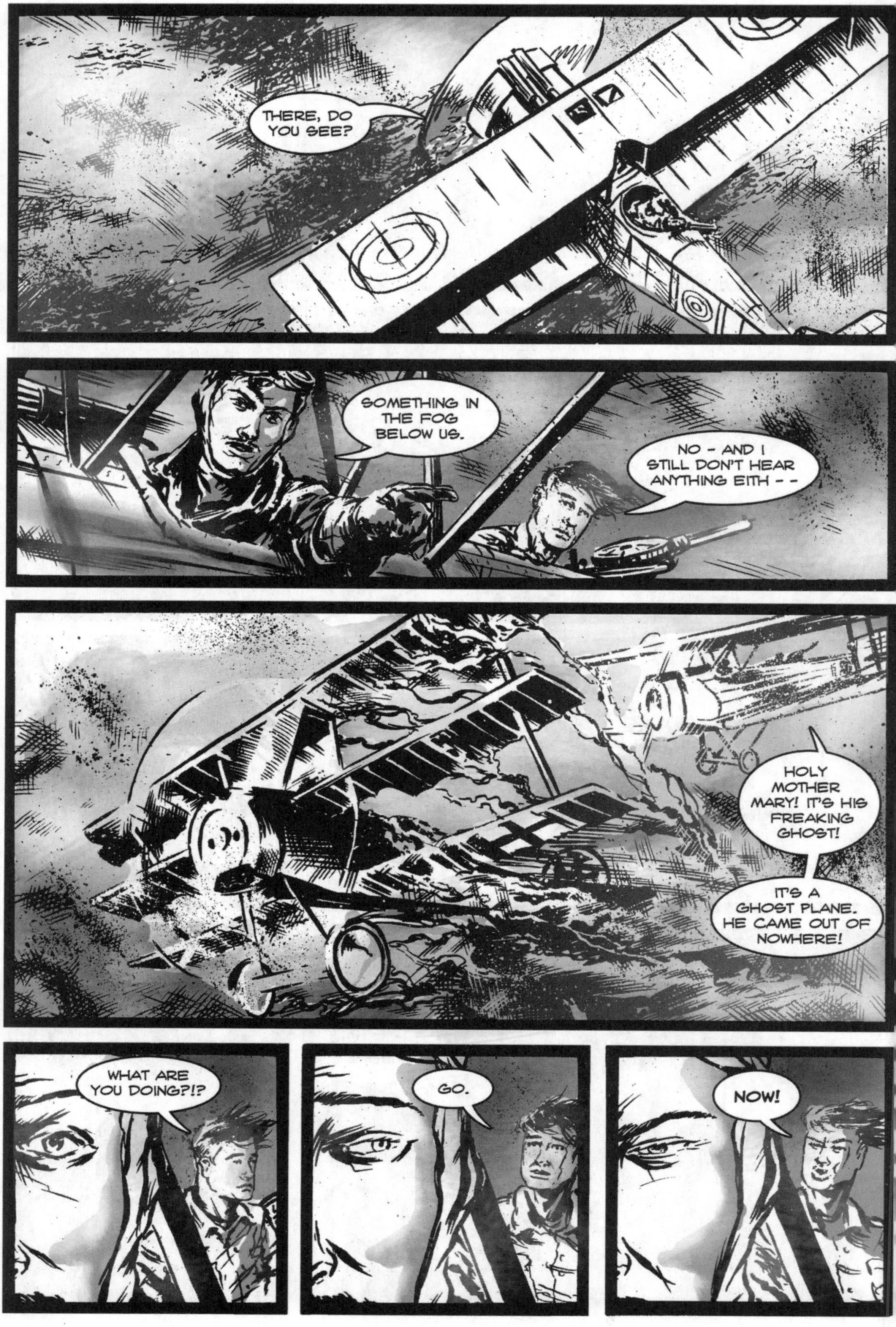
THERE, DO YOU SEE?
SOMETHING IN THE FOG BELOW US.
NO - AND I STILL DON'T HEAR ANYTHING EITH - -
HOLY MOTHER MARY! IT'S HIS FREAKING GHOST!
IT'S A GHOST PLANE. HE CAME OUT OF NOWHERE!
WHAT ARE YOU DOING?!?
GO.
NOW!

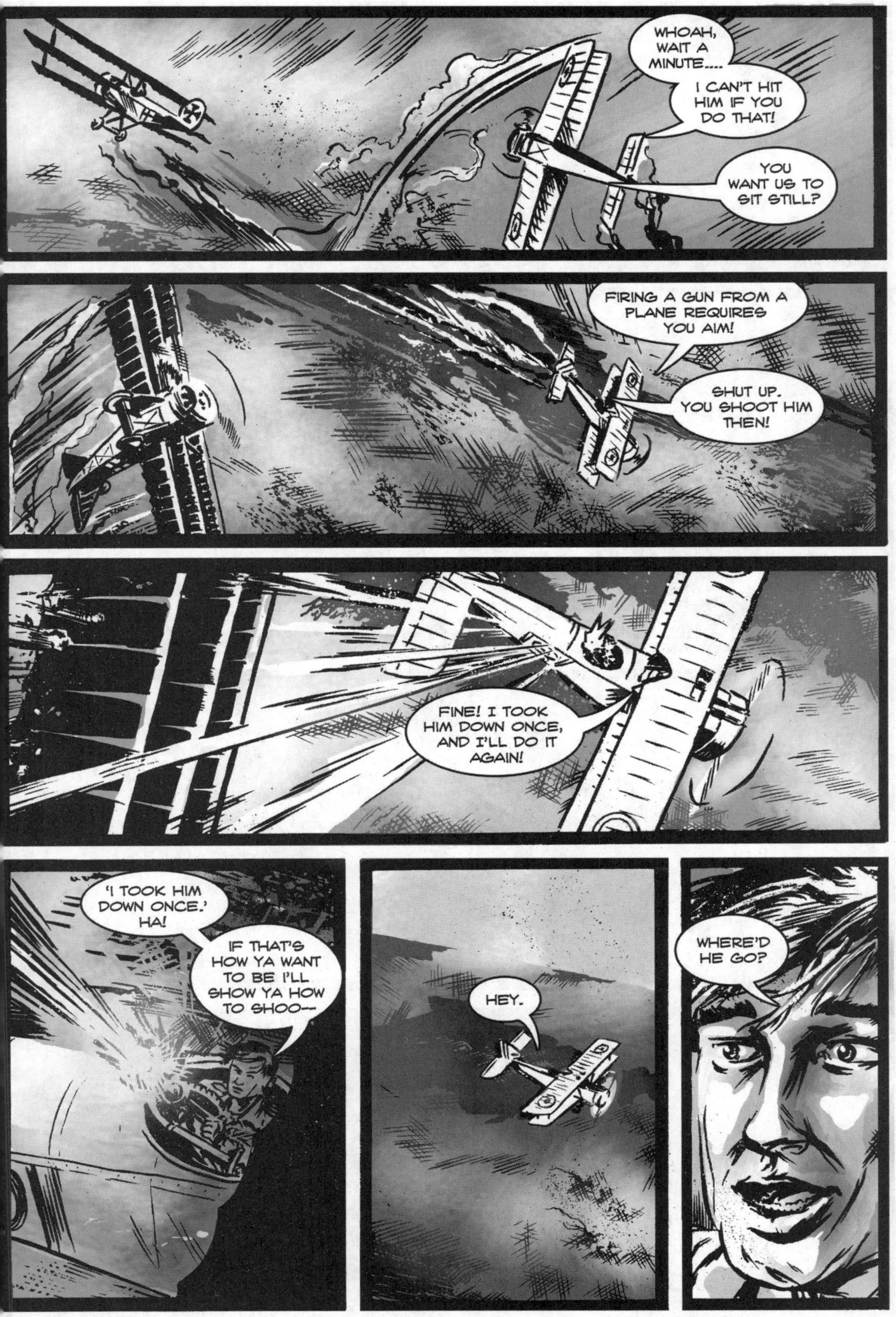
WHOAH, WAIT A MINUTE....
I CAN'T HIT HIM IF YOU DO THAT!
YOU WANT US TO SIT STILL?
FIRING A GUN FROM A PLANE REQUIRES YOU AIM!
SHUT UP. YOU SHOOT HIM THEN!
FINE! I TOOK HIM DOWN ONCE, AND I'LL DO IT AGAIN!
'I TOOK HIM DOWN ONCE.' HA!
IF THAT'S HOW YA WANT TO BE I'LL SHOW YA HOW TO SHOO—
HEY.
WHERE'D HE GO?

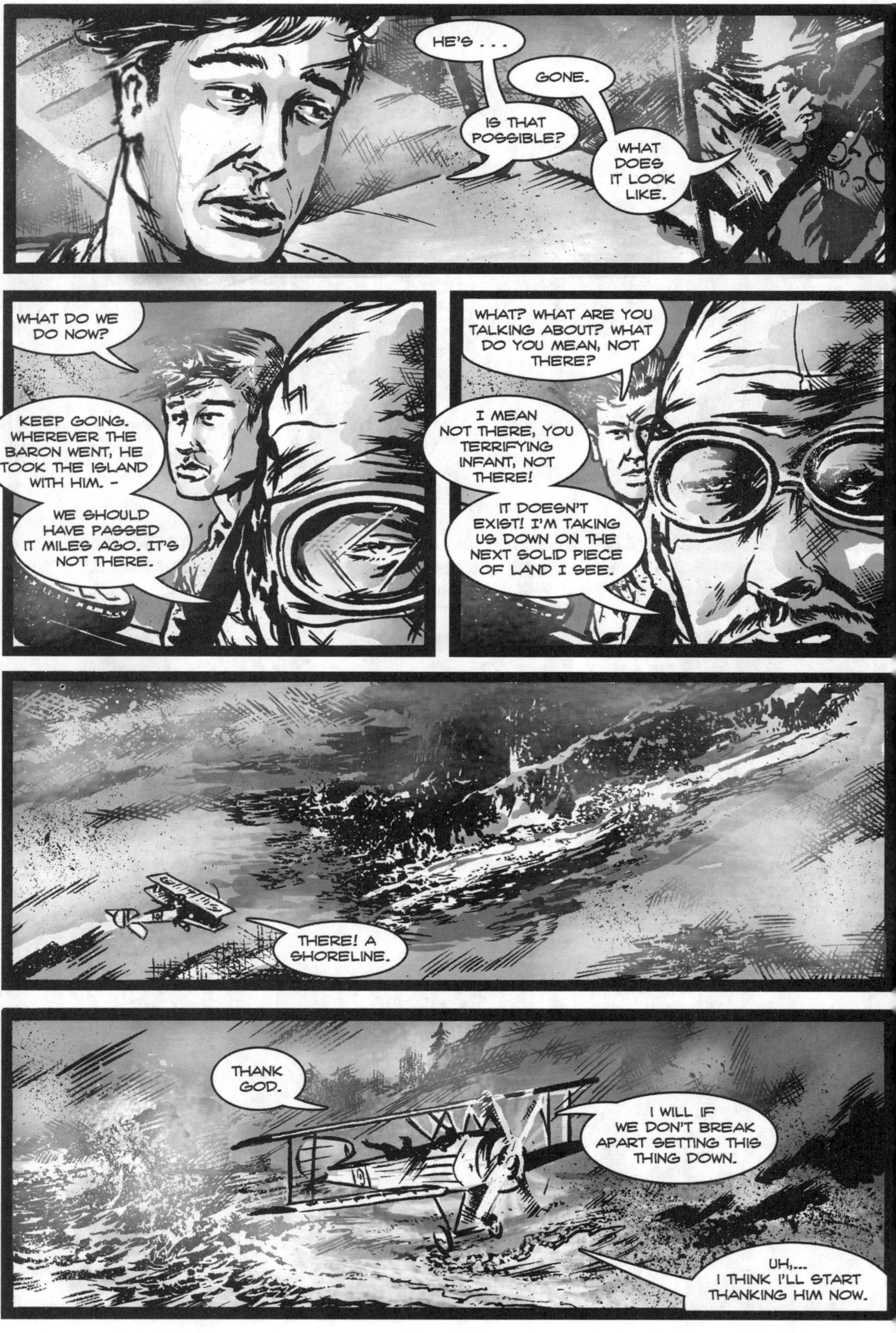

HE'S . . .
GONE.
IS THAT POSSIBLE?
WHAT DOES IT LOOK LIKE.
WHAT DO WE DO NOW?
KEEP GOING. WHEREVER THE BARON WENT, HE TOOK THE ISLAND WITH HIM. -
WE SHOULD HAVE PASSED IT MILES AGO. IT'S NOT THERE.
WHAT? WHAT ARE YOU TALKING ABOUT? WHAT DO YOU MEAN, NOT THERE?
I MEAN NOT THERE, YOU TERRIFYING INFANT, NOT THERE!
IT DOESN'T EXIST! I'M TAKING US DOWN ON THE NEXT SOLID PIECE OF LAND I SEE.
THERE! A SHORELINE.
THANK GOD.
I WILL IF WE DON'T BREAK APART SETTING THIS THING DOWN.
UH,... I THINK I'LL START THANKING HIM NOW.

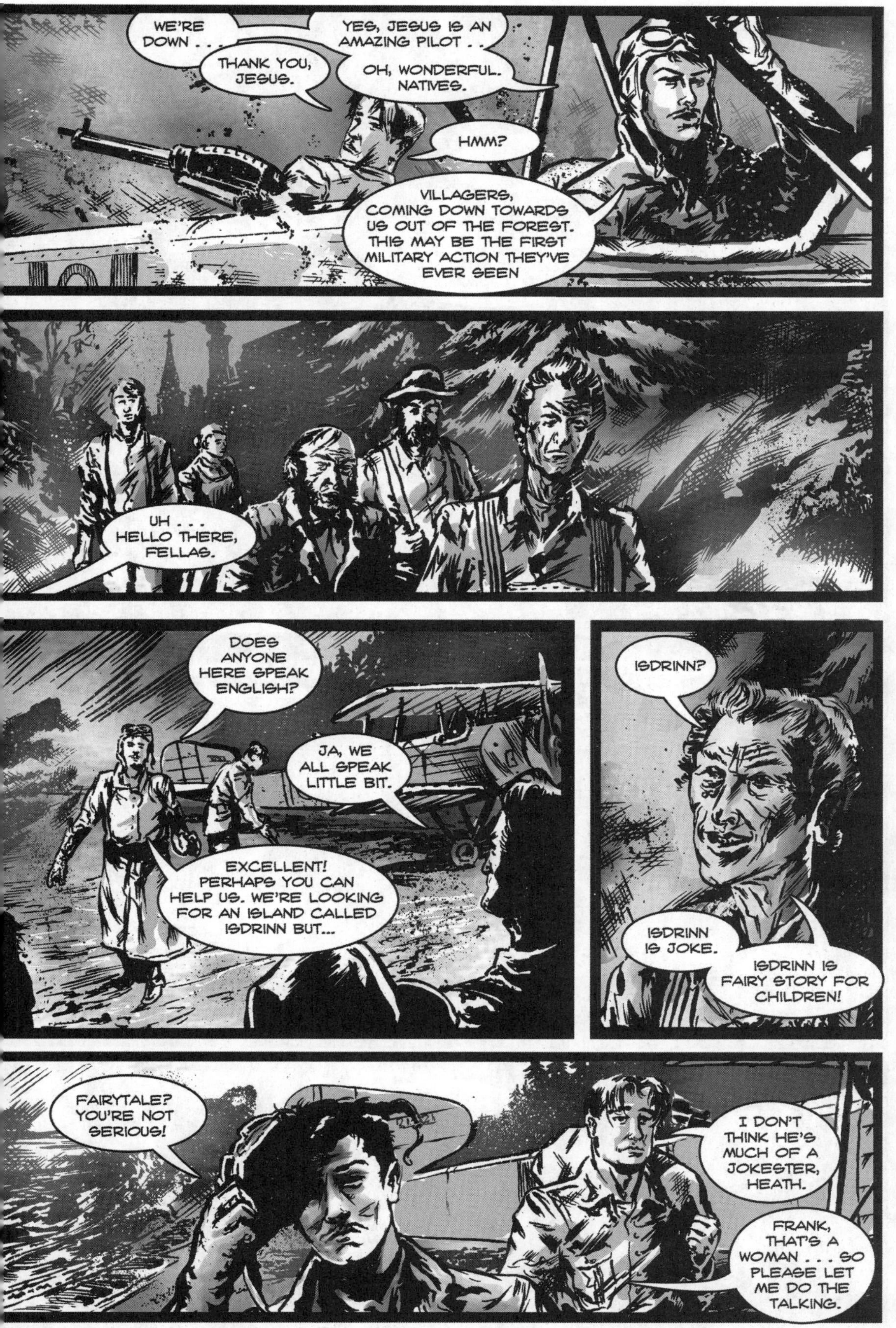
WE'RE DOWN . . .
THANK YOU, JESUS.
YES, JESUS IS AN AMAZING PILOT . .
OH, WONDERFUL. NATIVES.
HMM?
VILLAGERS, COMING DOWN TOWARDS US OUT OF THE FOREST. THIS MAY BE THE FIRST MILITARY ACTION THEY'VE EVER SEEN
UH . . . HELLO THERE, FELLAS.
DOES ANYONE HERE SPEAK ENGLISH?
JA, WE ALL SPEAK LITTLE BIT.
EXCELLENT! PERHAPS YOU CAN HELP US. WE'RE LOOKING FOR AN ISLAND CALLED ISDRINN BUT...
ISDRINN?
ISDRINN IS JOKE.
ISDRINN IS FAIRY STORY FOR CHILDREN!
FAIRYTALE? YOU'RE NOT SERIOUS!
I DON'T THINK HE'S MUCH OF A JOKESTER, HEATH.
FRANK, THAT'S A WOMAN . . . SO PLEASE LET ME DO THE TALKING.

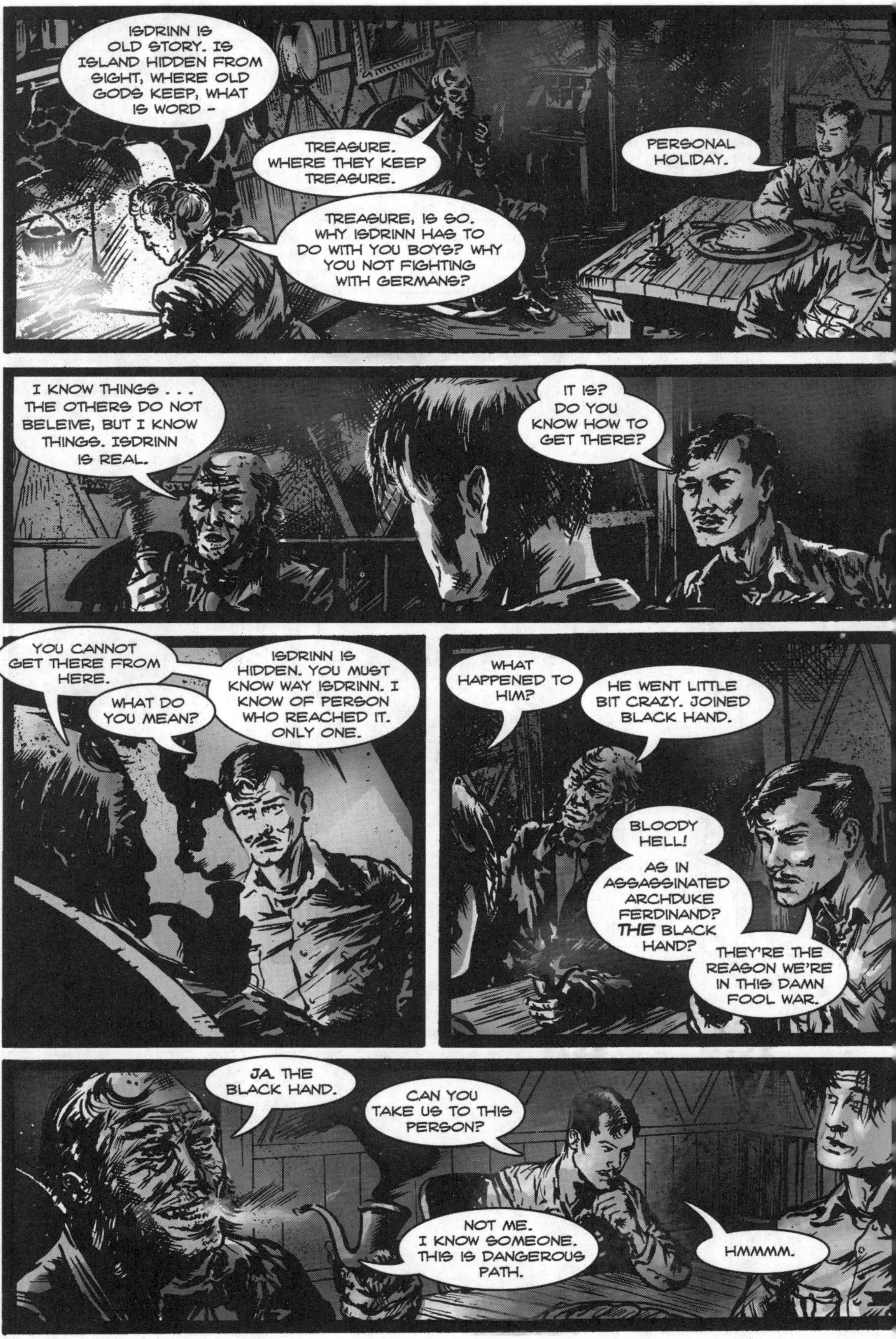
ISDRINN IS OLD STORY. IS ISLAND HIDDEN FROM SIGHT, WHERE OLD GODS KEEP, WHAT IS WORD -
TREASURE. WHERE THEY KEEP TREASURE.
TREASURE, IS SO. WHY ISDRINN HAS TO DO WITH YOU BOYS? WHY YOU NOT FIGHTING WITH GERMANS?
PERSONAL HOLIDAY.
I KNOW THINGS . . . THE OTHERS DO NOT BELEIVE, BUT I KNOW THINGS. ISDRINN IS REAL.
IT IS? DO YOU KNOW HOW TO GET THERE?
YOU CANNOT GET THERE FROM HERE.
WHAT DO YOU MEAN?
ISDRINN IS HIDDEN. YOU MUST KNOW WAY ISDRINN. I KNOW OF PERSON WHO REACHED IT. ONLY ONE.
WHAT HAPPENED TO HIM?
HE WENT LITTLE BIT CRAZY. JOINED BLACK HAND.
BLOODY HELL!
AS IN ASSASSINATED ARCHDUKE FERDINAND? THE BLACK HAND?
THEY'RE THE REASON WE'RE IN THIS DAMN FOOL WAR.
JA. THE BLACK HAND.
CAN YOU TAKE US TO THIS PERSON?
NOT ME. I KNOW SOMEONE. THIS IS DANGEROUS PATH.
HMMMM.

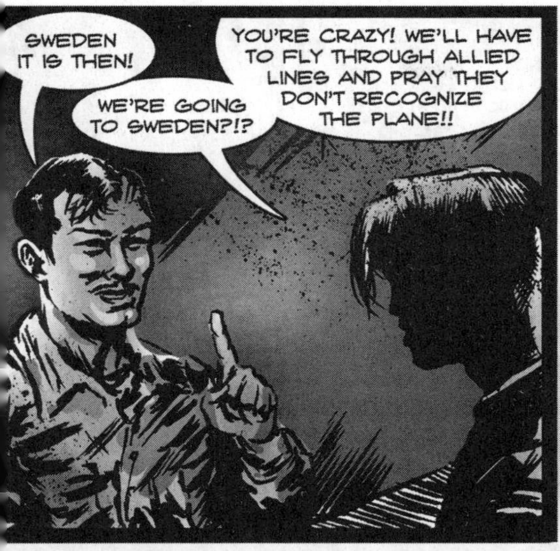
SWEDEN IT IS THEN!
WE'RE GOING TO SWEDEN?!?
YOU'RE CRAZY! WE'LL HAVE TO FLY THROUGH ALLIED LINES AND PRAY THEY DON'T RECOGNIZE THE PLANE!!

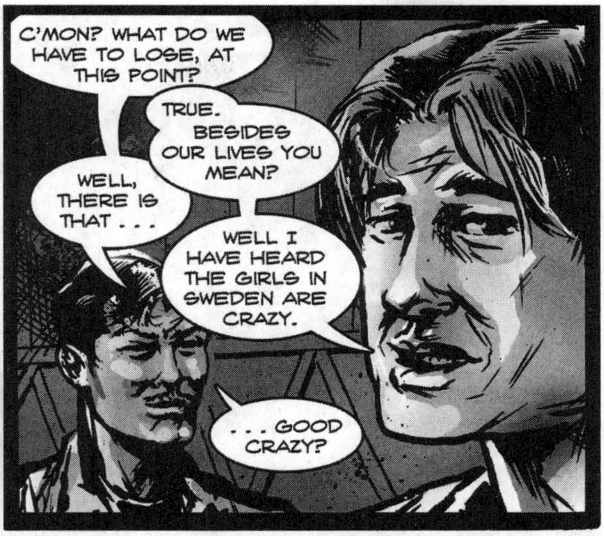
C'MON? WHAT DO WE HAVE TO LOSE, AT THIS POINT?
TRUE. BESIDES OUR LIVES YOU MEAN?
WELL, THERE IS THAT . . .
WELL I HAVE HEARD THE GIRLS IN SWEDEN ARE CRAZY.
. . . GOOD CRAZY?

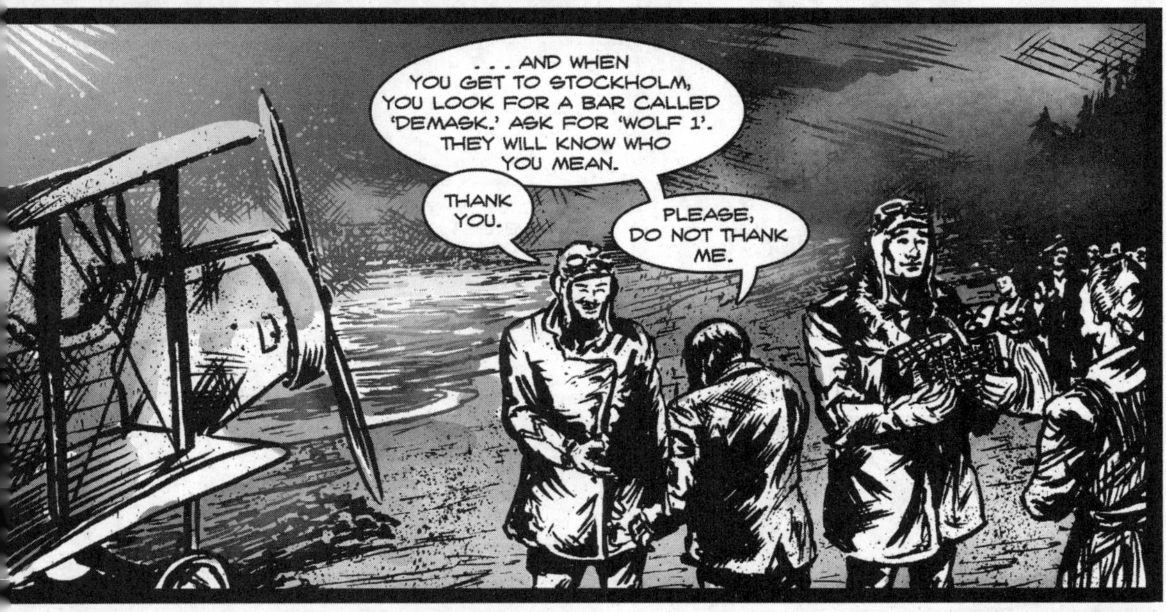
. . . AND WHEN YOU GET TO STOCKHOLM, YOU LOOK FOR A BAR CALLED 'DEMASK.' ASK FOR 'WOLF 1'. THEY WILL KNOW WHO YOU MEAN.
THANK YOU.
PLEASE, DO NOT THANK ME.

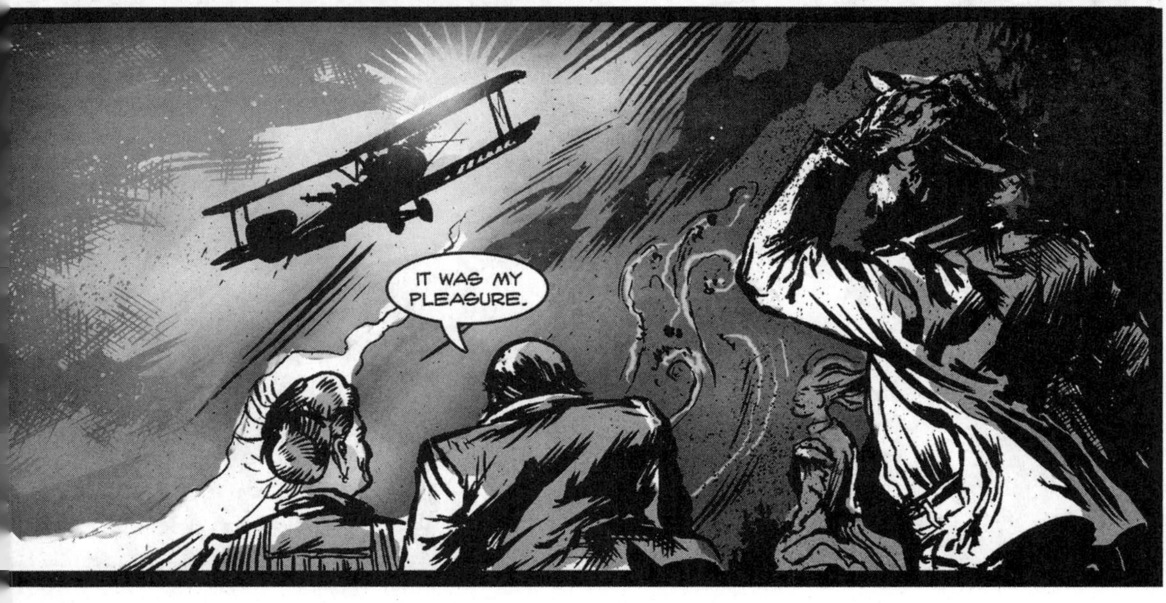
IT WAS MY PLEASURE.

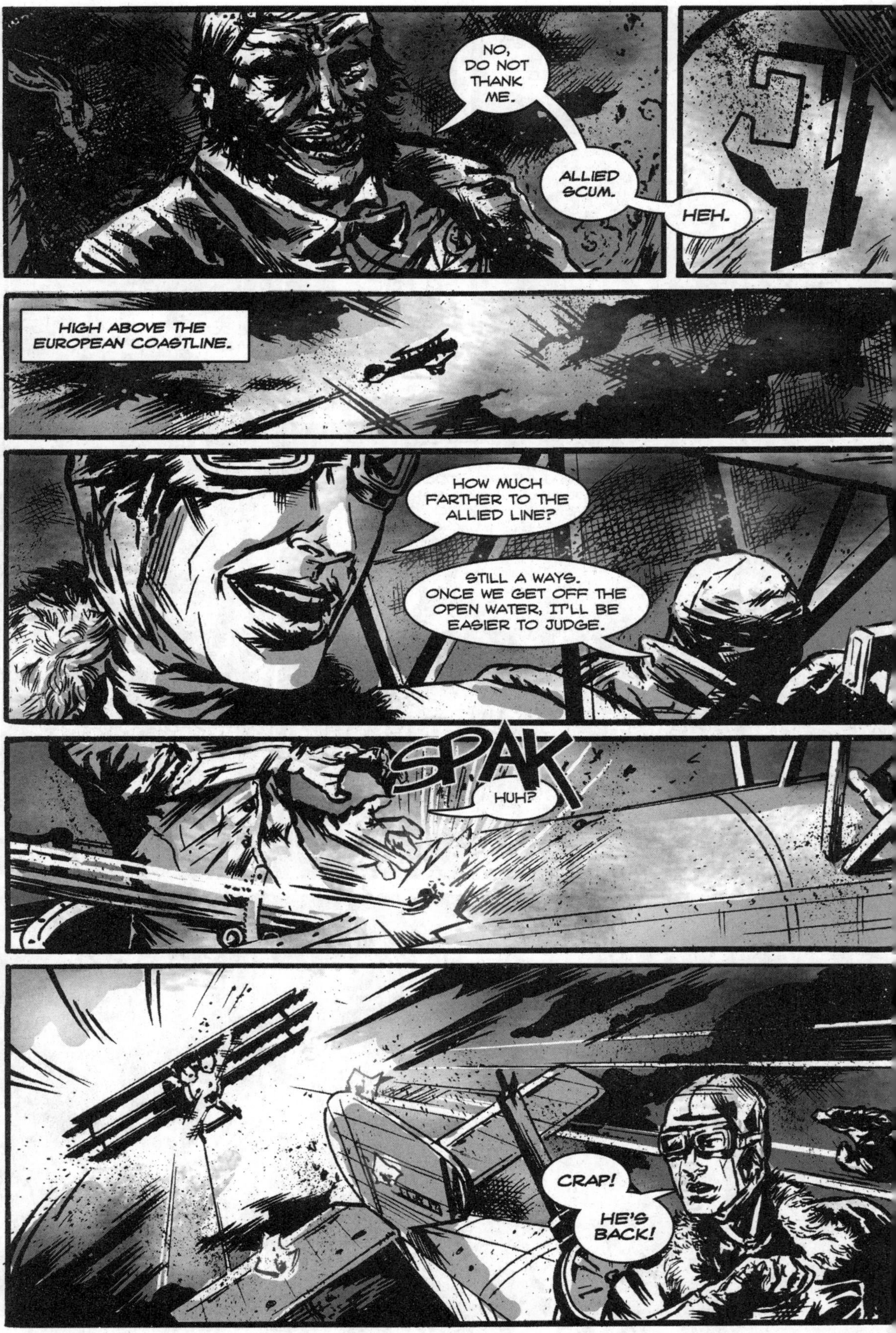
NO, DO NOT THANK ME.
ALLIED SCUM.
HEH.
HIGH ABOVE THE EUROPEAN COASTLINE.
HOW MUCH FARTHER TO THE ALLIED LINE?
STILL A WAYS. ONCE WE GET OFF THE OPEN WATER, IT'LL BE EASIER TO JUDGE.
SPAK
HUH?
CRAP!
HE'S BACK!

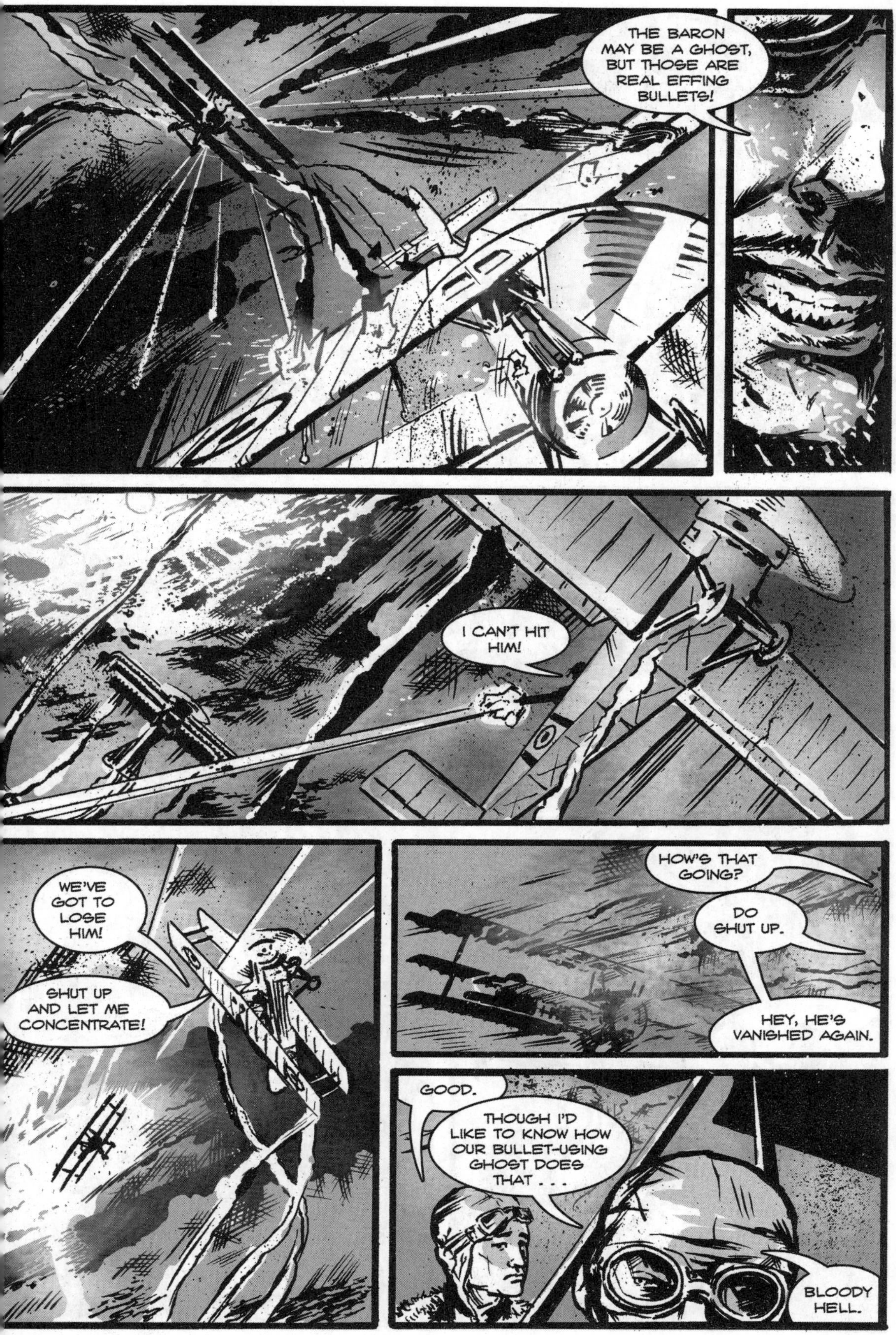
THE BARON MAY BE A GHOST, BUT THOSE ARE REAL EFFING BULLETS!
I CAN'T HIT HIM!
WE'VE GOT TO LOSE HIM!
SHUT UP AND LET ME CONCENTRATE!
HOW'S THAT GOING?
DO SHUT UP.
HEY, HE'S VANISHED AGAIN.
GOOD.
THOUGH I'D LIKE TO KNOW HOW OUR BULLET-USING GHOST DOES THAT . . .
BLOODY HELL.

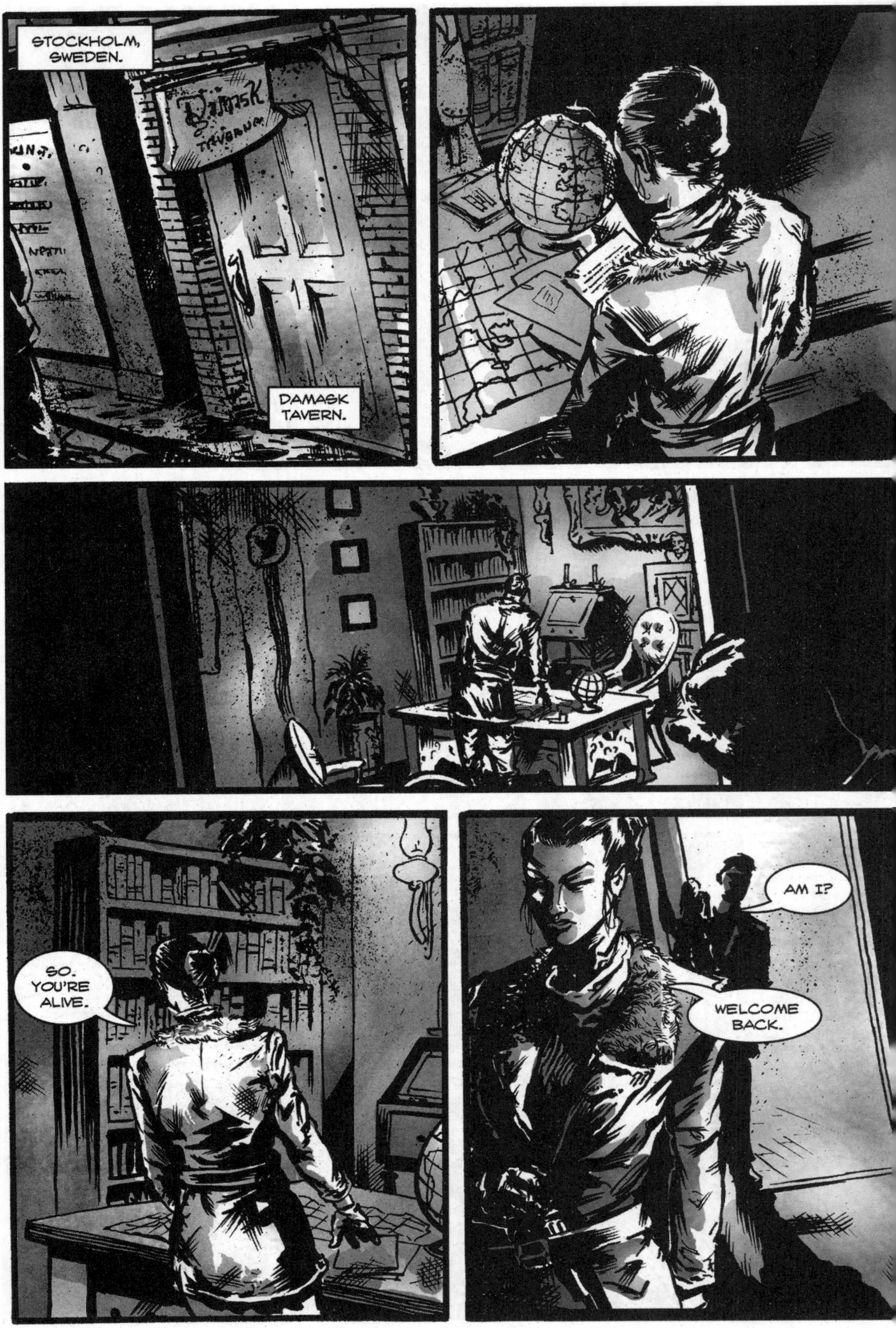
STOCKHOLM, SWEDEN.
DAMASK TAVERN.
SO. YOU'RE ALIVE.
AM I?
WELCOME BACK.

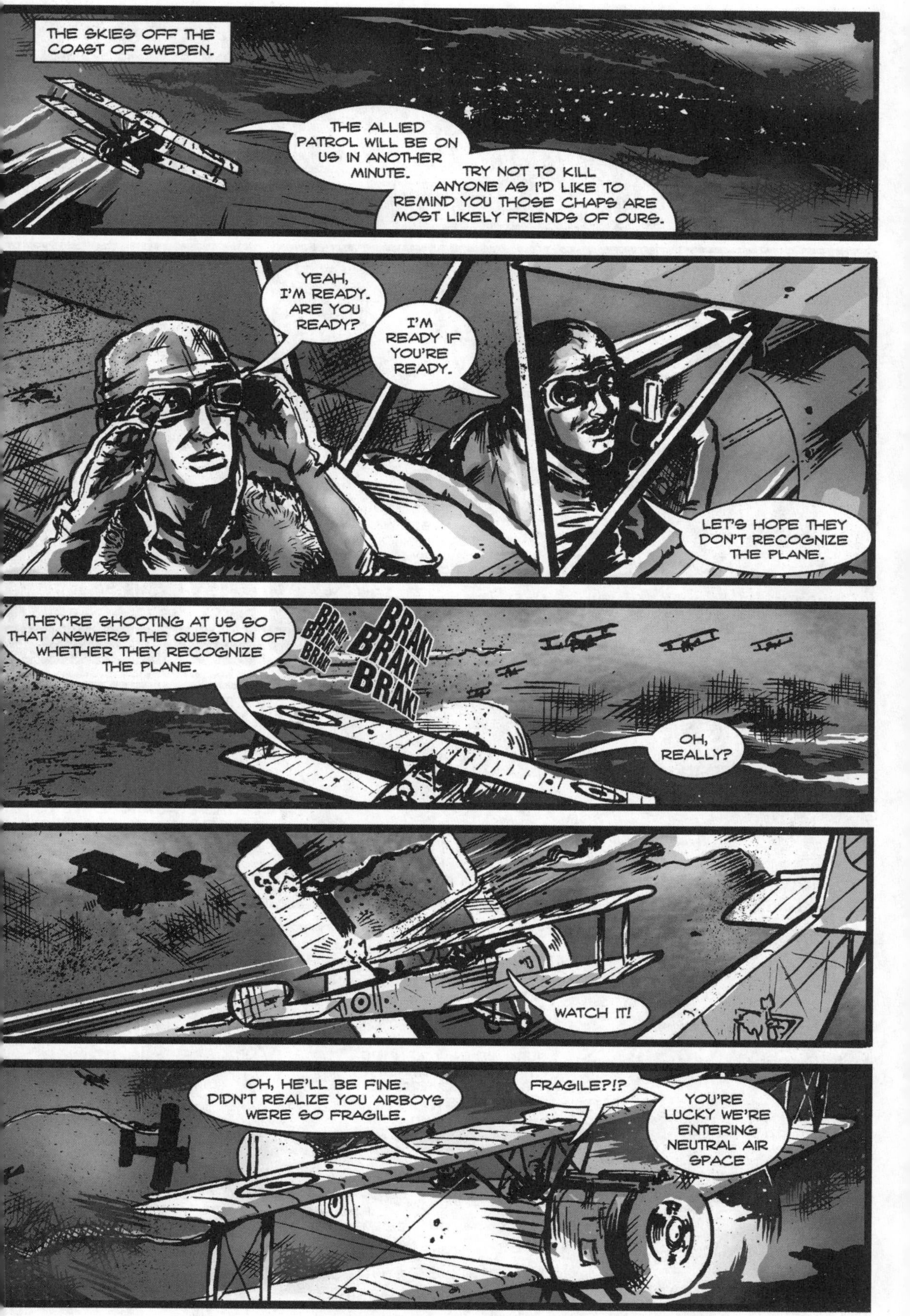
THE SKIES OFF THE COAST OF SWEDEN.
THE ALLIED PATROL WILL BE ON US IN ANOTHER MINUTE.
TRY NOT TO KILL ANYONE AS I'D LIKE TO REMIND YOU THOSE CHAPS ARE MOST LIKELY FRIENDS OF OURS.
YEAH, I'M READY. ARE YOU READY?
I'M READY IF YOU'RE READY.
LET'S HOPE THEY DON'T RECOGNIZE THE PLANE.
THEY'RE SHOOTING AT US SO THAT ANSWERS THE QUESTION OF WHETHER THEY RECOGNIZE THE PLANE.
BRAK! BRAK! BRAK!
BRAK! BRAK! BRAK!
OH, REALLY?
WATCH IT!
OH, HE'LL BE FINE. DIDN'T REALIZE YOU AIRBOYS WERE SO FRAGILE.
FRAGILE?!?
YOU'RE LUCKY WE'RE ENTERING NEUTRAL AIR SPACE

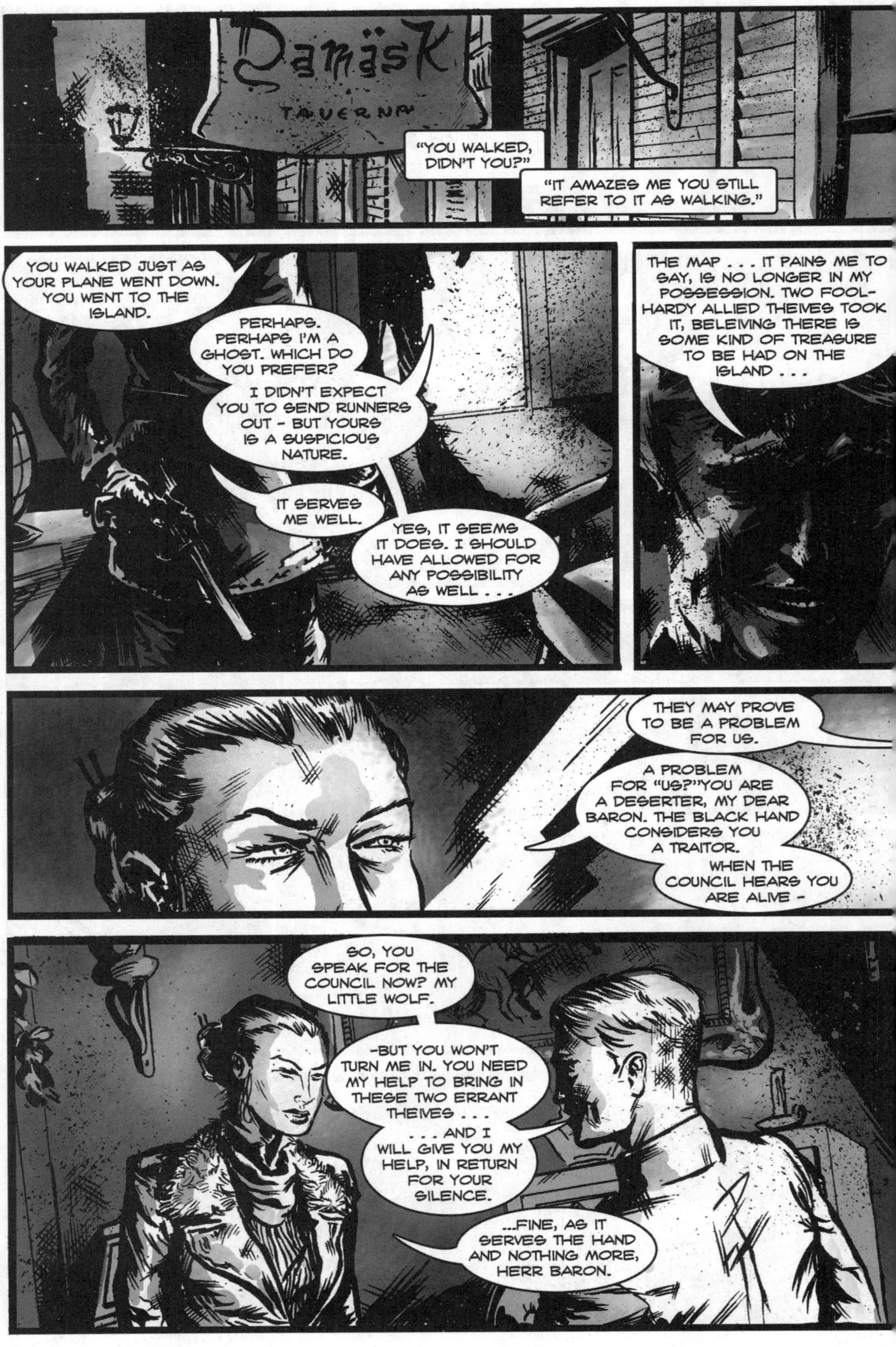

"YOU WALKED, DIDN'T YOU?"
"IT AMAZES ME YOU STILL REFER TO IT AS WALKING."
YOU WALKED JUST AS YOUR PLANE WENT DOWN. YOU WENT TO THE ISLAND.
PERHAPS. PERHAPS I'M A GHOST. WHICH DO YOU PREFER?
I DIDN'T EXPECT YOU TO SEND RUNNERS OUT - BUT YOURS IS A SUSPICIOUS NATURE.
IT SERVES ME WELL.
YES, IT SEEMS IT DOES. I SHOULD HAVE ALLOWED FOR ANY POSSIBILITY AS WELL . . .
THE MAP . . . IT PAINS ME TO SAY, IS NO LONGER IN MY POSSESSION. TWO FOOL-HARDY ALLIED THEIVES TOOK IT, BELEIVING THERE IS SOME KIND OF TREASURE TO BE HAD ON THE ISLAND . . .
THEY MAY PROVE TO BE A PROBLEM FOR US.
A PROBLEM FOR "US?"YOU ARE A DESERTER, MY DEAR BARON. THE BLACK HAND CONSIDERS YOU A TRAITOR.
WHEN THE COUNCIL HEARS YOU ARE ALIVE -
SO, YOU SPEAK FOR THE COUNCIL NOW? MY LITTLE WOLF.
-BUT YOU WON'T TURN ME IN. YOU NEED MY HELP TO BRING IN THESE TWO ERRANT THEIVES . . .
. . . AND I WILL GIVE YOU MY HELP, IN RETURN FOR YOUR SILENCE.
...FINE, AS IT SERVES THE HAND AND NOTHING MORE, HERR BARON.

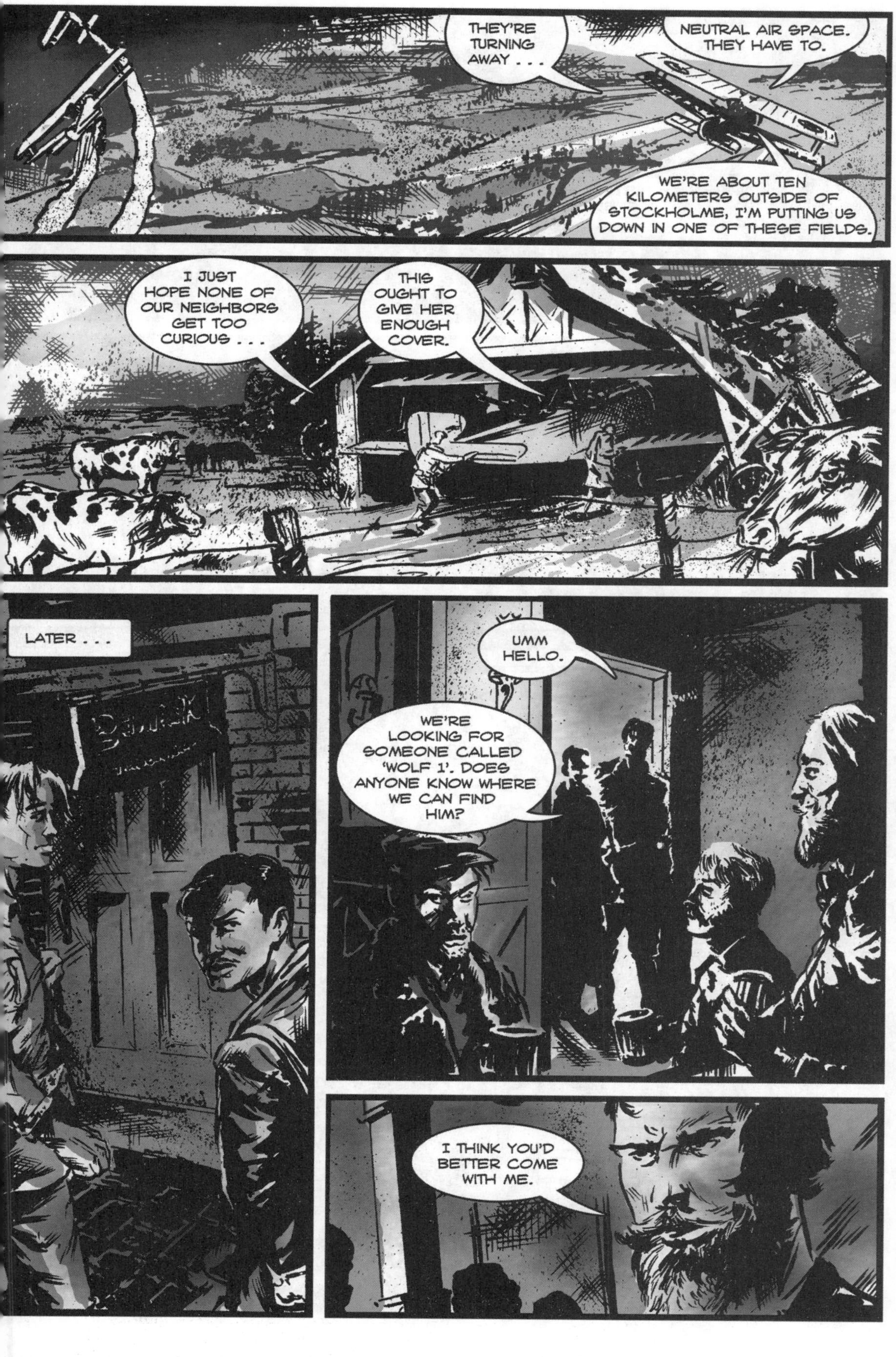
THEY'RE TURNING AWAY . . .
NEUTRAL AIR SPACE. THEY HAVE TO.
WE'RE ABOUT TEN KILOMETERS OUTSIDE OF STOCKHOLME, I'M PUTTING US DOWN IN ONE OF THESE FIELDS.
I JUST HOPE NONE OF OUR NEIGHBORS GET TOO CURIOUS . . .
THIS OUGHT TO GIVE HER ENOUGH COVER.
LATER . . .
UMM HELLO.
WE'RE LOOKING FOR SOMEONE CALLED 'WOLF 1'. DOES ANYONE KNOW WHERE WE CAN FIND HIM?
I THINK YOU'D BETTER COME WITH ME.

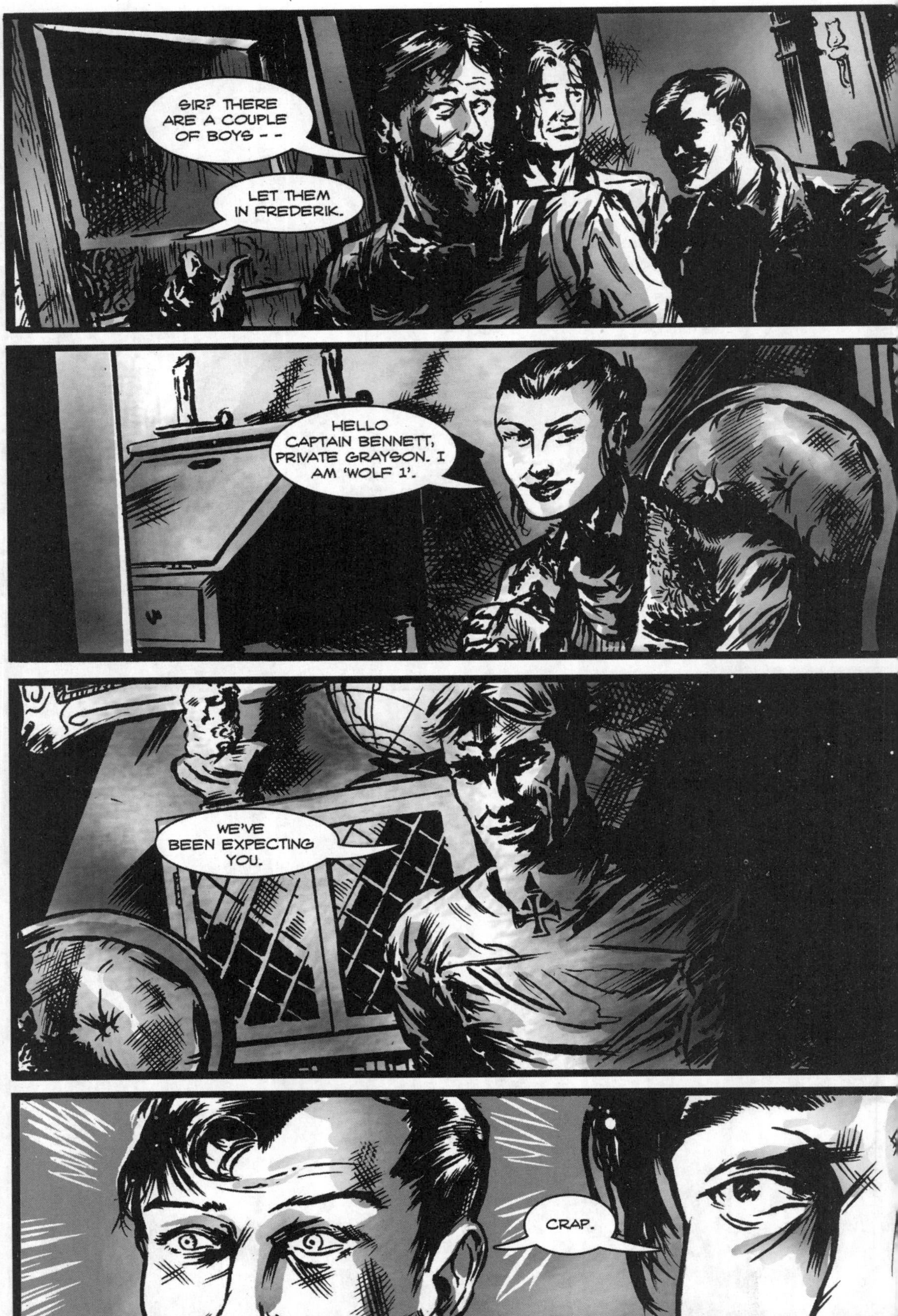
SIR? THERE ARE A COUPLE OF BOYS - -
LET THEM IN FREDERIK.
HELLO CAPTAIN BENNETT, PRIVATE GRAYSON. I AM 'WOLF 1'.
WE'VE BEEN EXPECTING YOU.
CRAP.

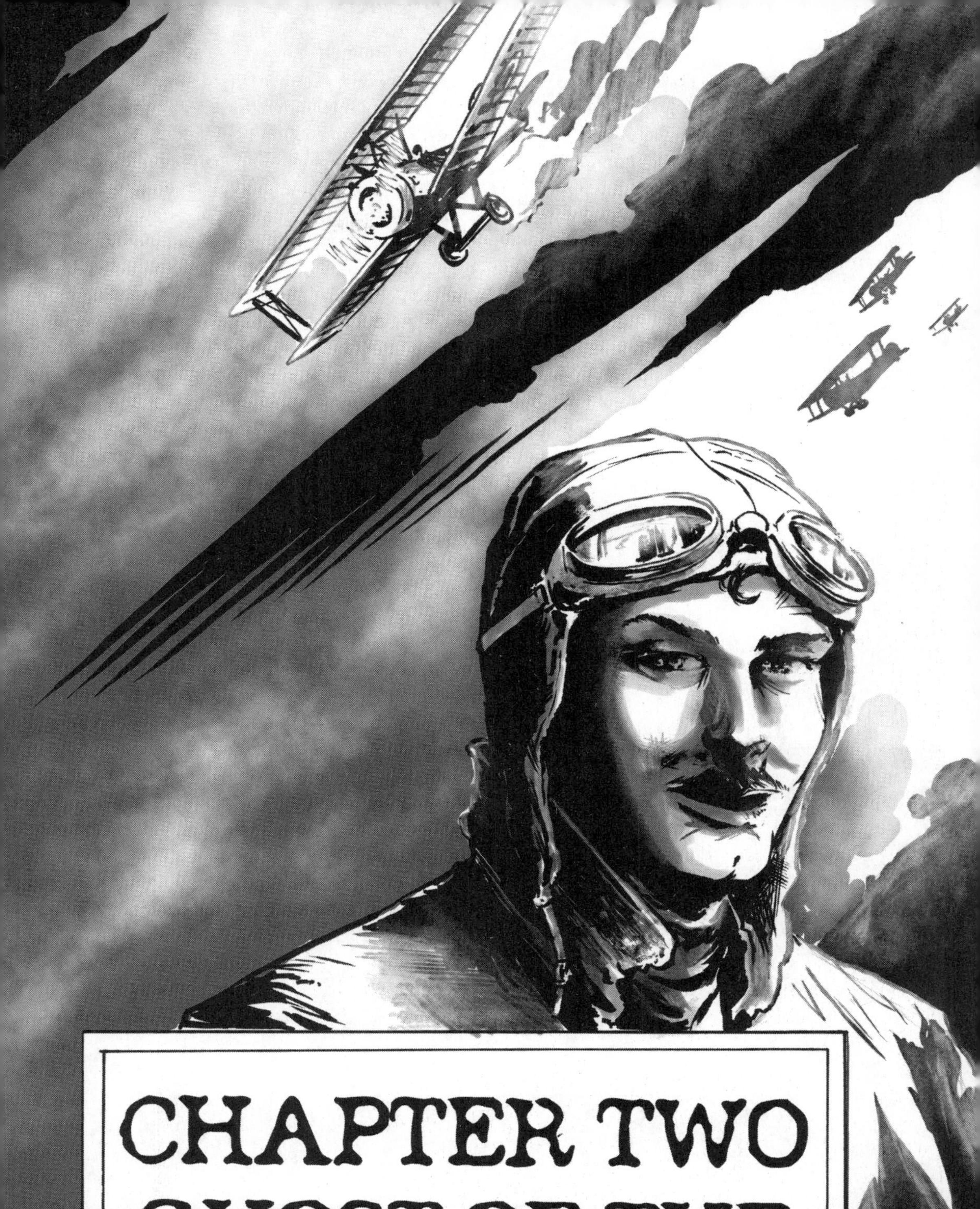

CHAPTER TWO
GHOST OF THE RED BARON

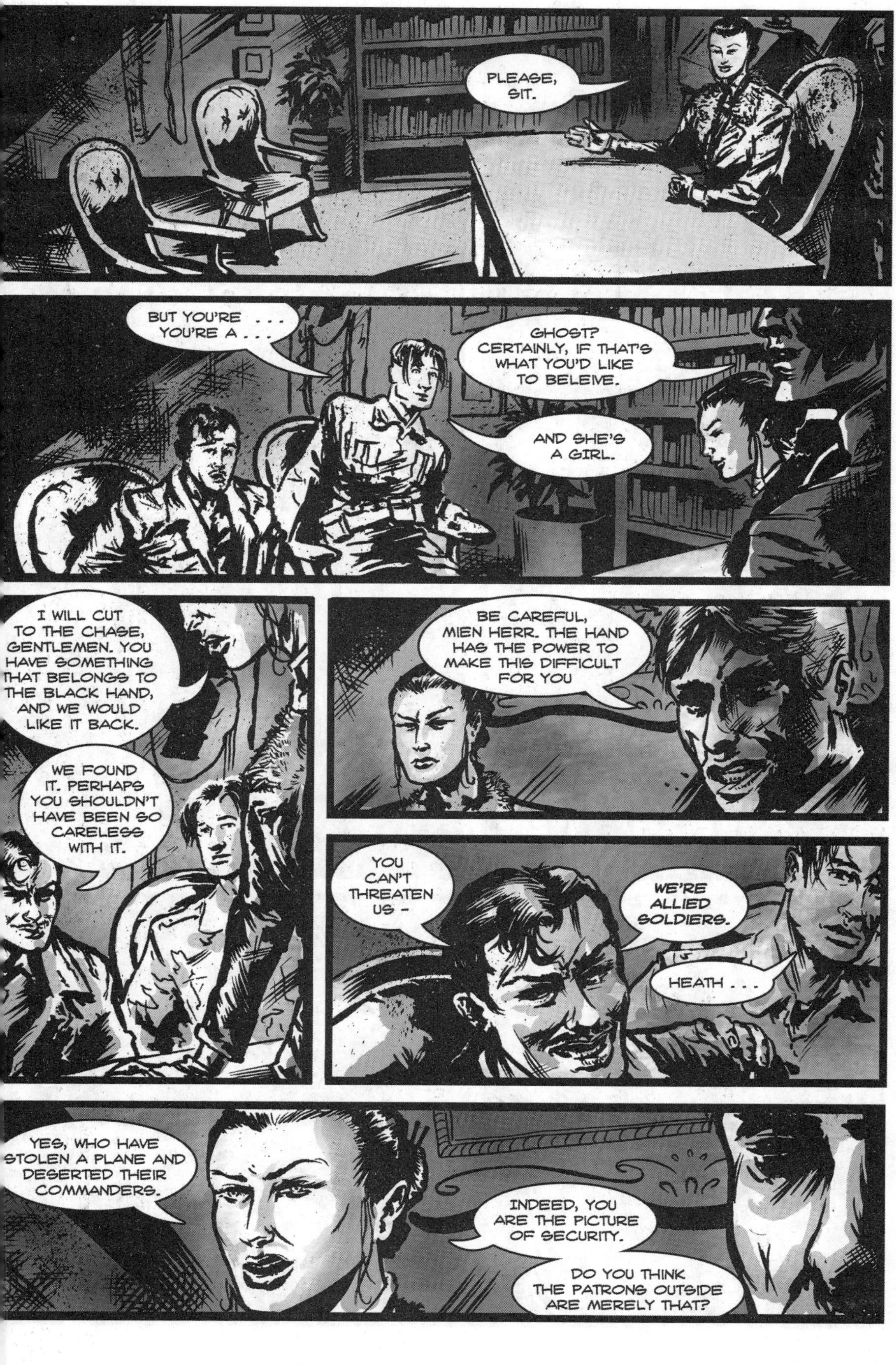
PLEASE, SIT.
BUT YOU'RE . . . YOU'RE A . . .
GHOST? CERTAINLY, IF THAT'S WHAT YOU'D LIKE TO BELEIVE.
AND SHE'S A GIRL.
I WILL CUT TO THE CHASE, GENTLEMEN. YOU HAVE SOMETHING THAT BELONGS TO THE BLACK HAND, AND WE WOULD LIKE IT BACK.
WE FOUND IT. PERHAPS YOU SHOULDN'T HAVE BEEN SO CARELESS WITH IT.
BE CAREFUL, MIEN HERR. THE HAND HAS THE POWER TO MAKE THIS DIFFICULT FOR YOU
YOU CAN'T THREATEN US -
WE'RE ALLIED SOLDIERS.
HEATH . . .
YES, WHO HAVE STOLEN A PLANE AND DESERTED THEIR COMMANDERS.
INDEED, YOU ARE THE PICTURE OF SECURITY.
DO YOU THINK THE PATRONS OUTSIDE ARE MERELY THAT?

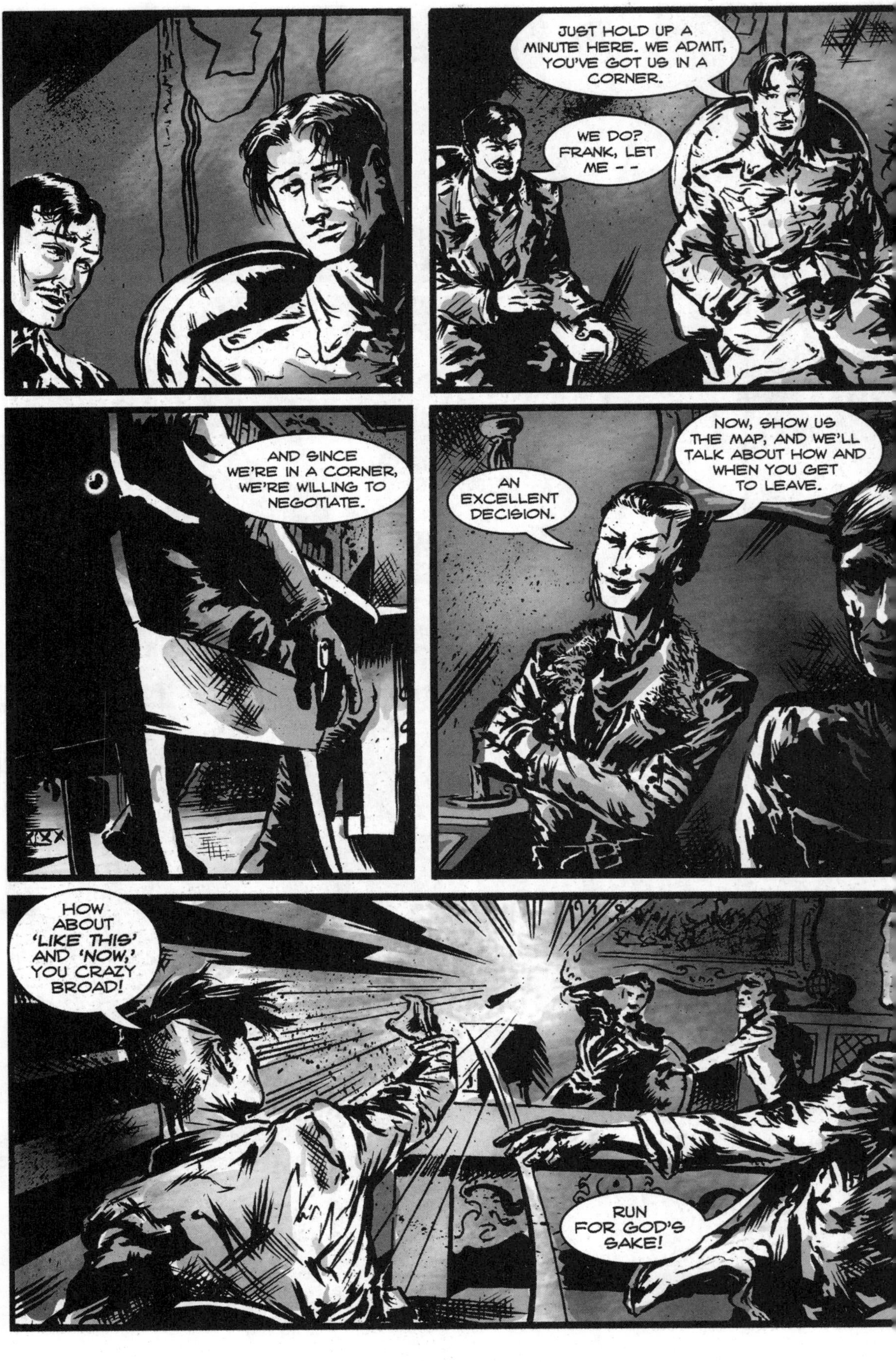
JUST HOLD UP A MINUTE HERE. WE ADMIT, YOU'VE GOT US IN A CORNER.
WE DO? FRANK, LET ME - -
AND SINCE WE'RE IN A CORNER, WE'RE WILLING TO NEGOTIATE.
AN EXCELLENT DECISION.
NOW, SHOW US THE MAP, AND WE'LL TALK ABOUT HOW AND WHEN YOU GET TO LEAVE.
HOW ABOUT 'LIKE THIS' AND 'NOW,' YOU CRAZY BROAD!
RUN FOR GOD'S SAKE!

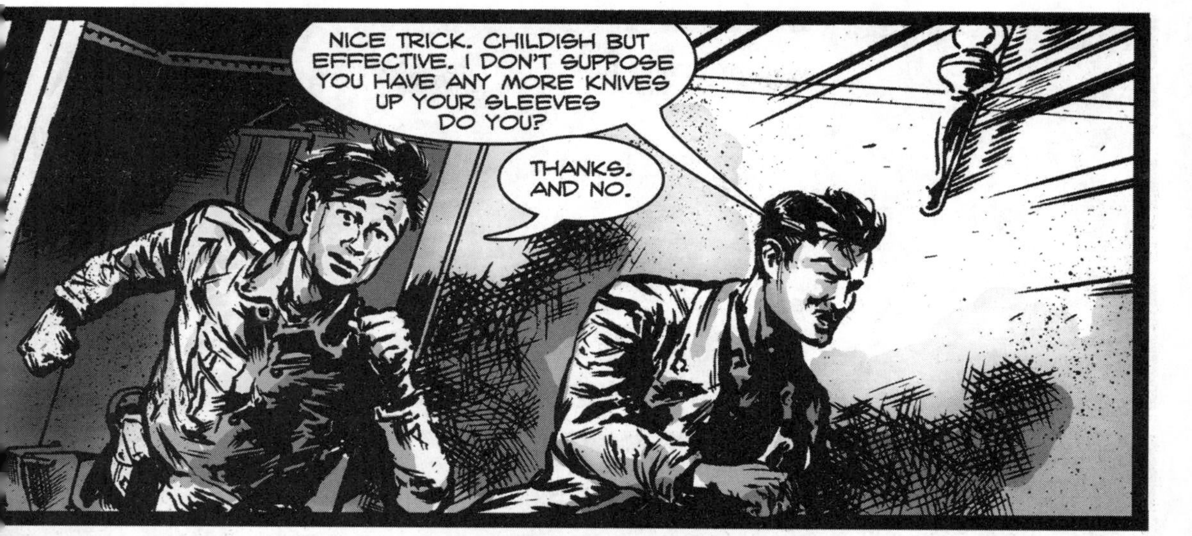
NICE TRICK. CHILDISH BUT EFFECTIVE. I DON'T SUPPOSE YOU HAVE ANY MORE KNIVES UP YOUR SLEEVES DO YOU?
THANKS. AND NO.

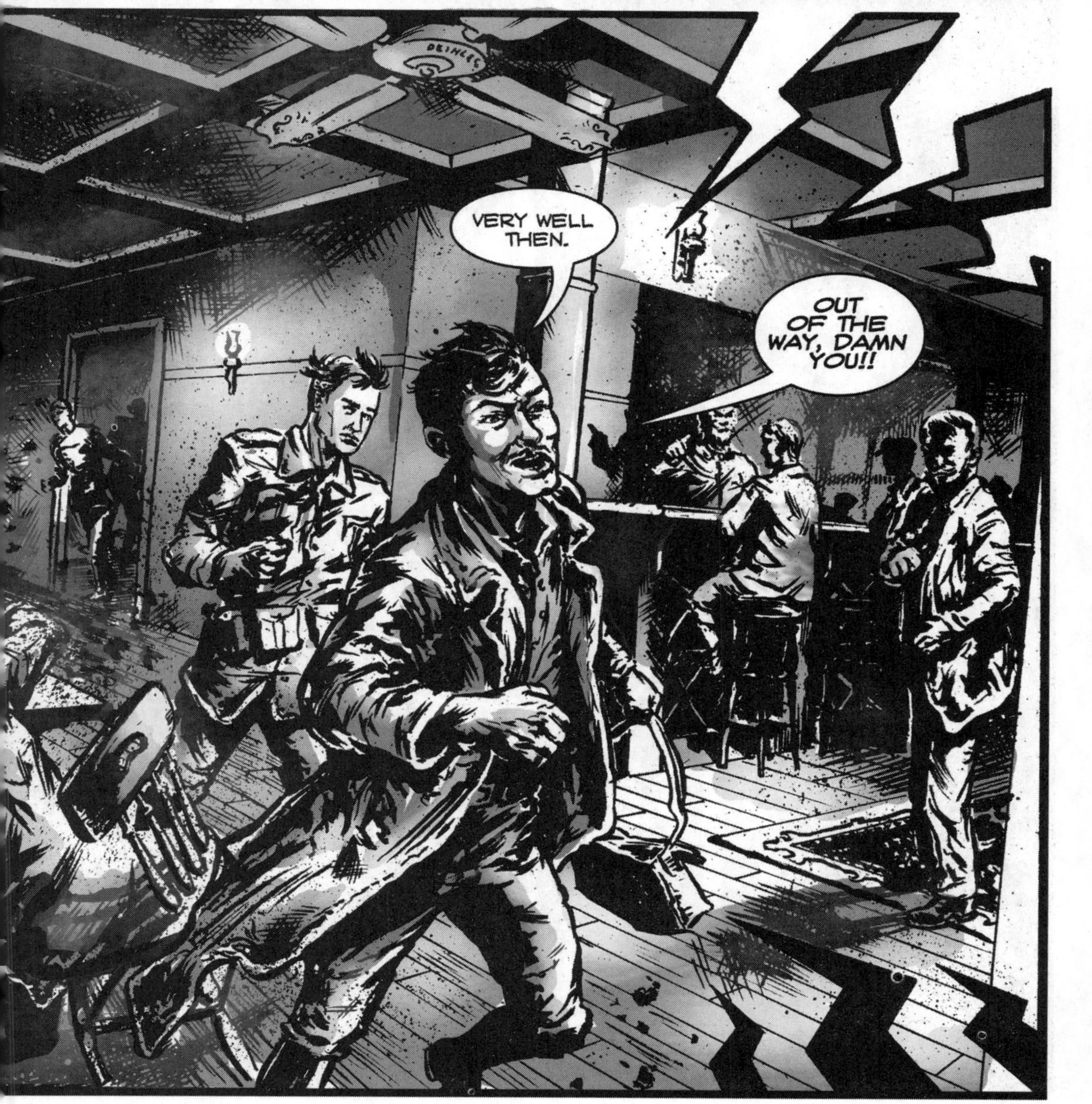
VERY WELL THEN.
OUT OF THE WAY, DAMN YOU!!

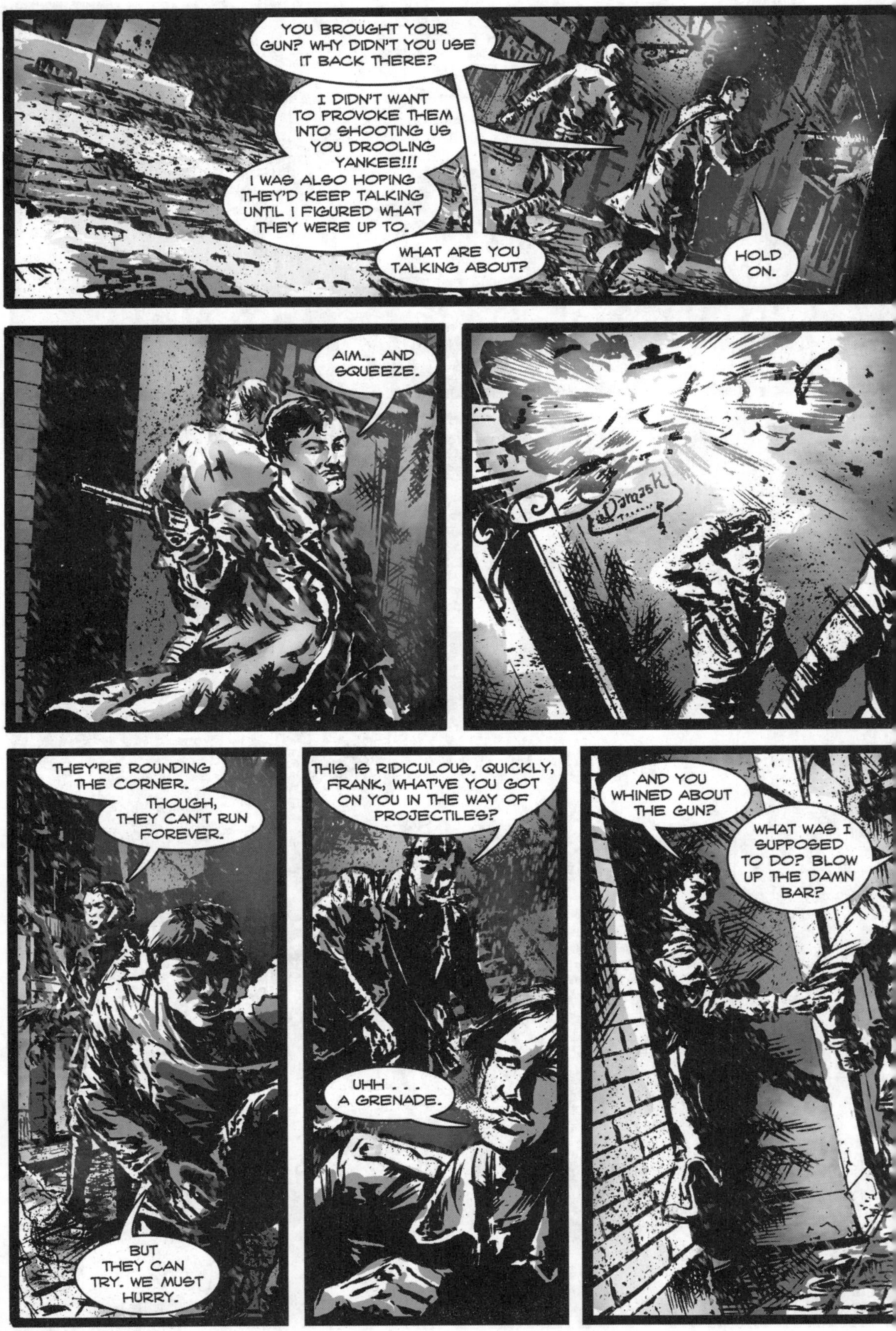
YOU BROUGHT YOUR GUN? WHY DIDN'T YOU USE IT BACK THERE?
I DIDN'T WANT TO PROVOKE THEM INTO SHOOTING US YOU DROOLING YANKEE!!!
I WAS ALSO HOPING THEY'D KEEP TALKING UNTIL I FIGURED WHAT THEY WERE UP TO.
WHAT ARE YOU TALKING ABOUT?
HOLD ON.
AIM... AND SQUEEZE.
Damask
THEY'RE ROUNDING THE CORNER.
THOUGH, THEY CAN'T RUN FOREVER.
BUT THEY CAN TRY. WE MUST HURRY.
THIS IS RIDICULOUS. QUICKLY, FRANK, WHAT'VE YOU GOT ON YOU IN THE WAY OF PROJECTILES?
UHH . . . A GRENADE.
AND YOU WHINED ABOUT THE GUN?
WHAT WAS I SUPPOSED TO DO? BLOW UP THE DAMN BAR?

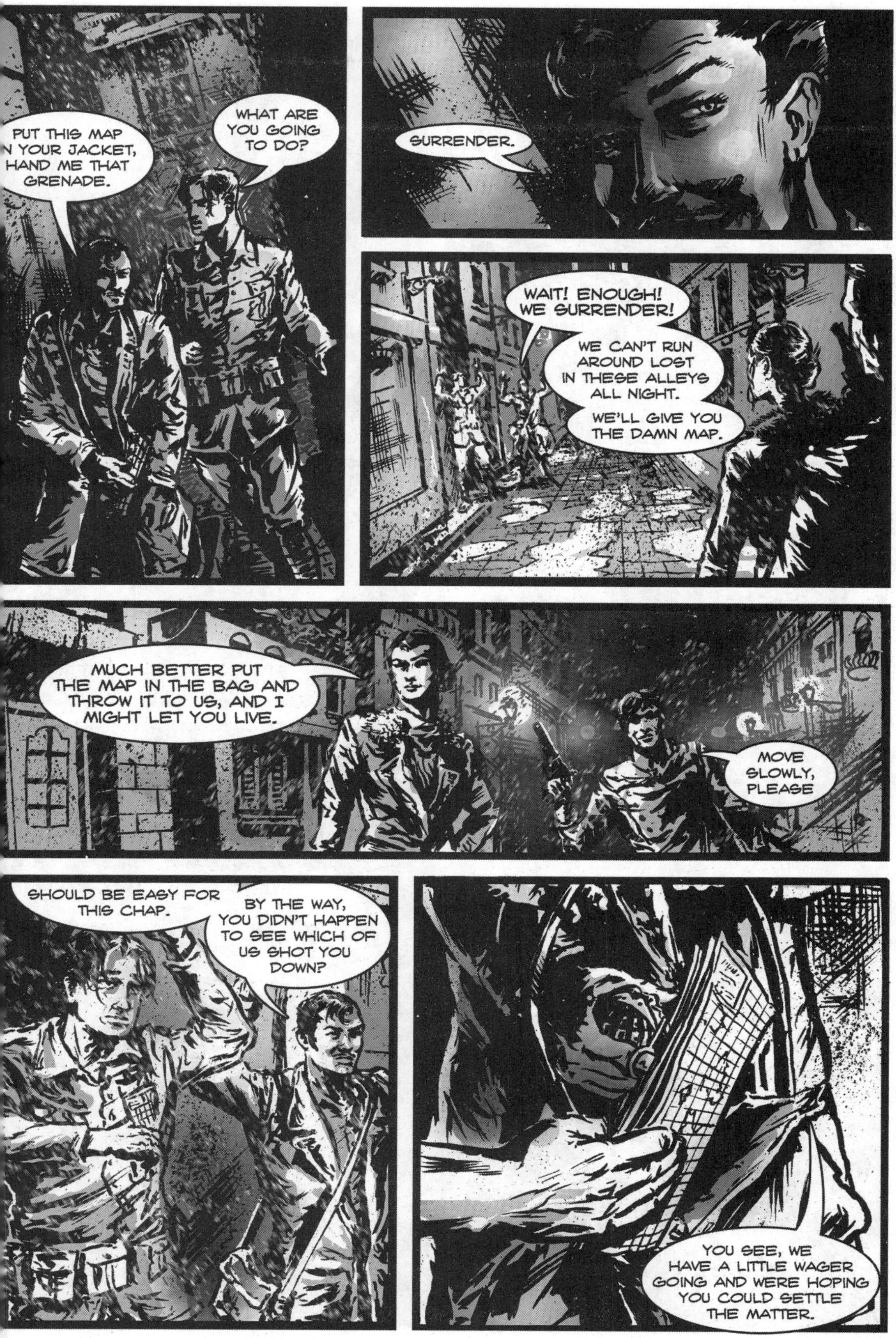
PUT THIS MAP
N YOUR JACKET,
HAND ME THAT
GRENADE.
WHAT ARE
YOU GOING
TO DO?
SURRENDER.
WAIT! ENOUGH!
WE SURRENDER!
WE CAN'T RUN
AROUND LOST
IN THESE ALLEYS
ALL NIGHT.
WE'LL GIVE YOU
THE DAMN MAP.
MUCH BETTER PUT
THE MAP IN THE BAG AND
THROW IT TO US, AND I
MIGHT LET YOU LIVE.
MOVE
SLOWLY,
PLEASE
SHOULD BE EASY FOR
THIS CHAP.
BY THE WAY,
YOU DIDN'T HAPPEN
TO SEE WHICH OF
US SHOT YOU
DOWN?
YOU SEE, WE
HAVE A LITTLE WAGER
GOING AND WERE HOPING
YOU COULD SETTLE
THE MATTER.

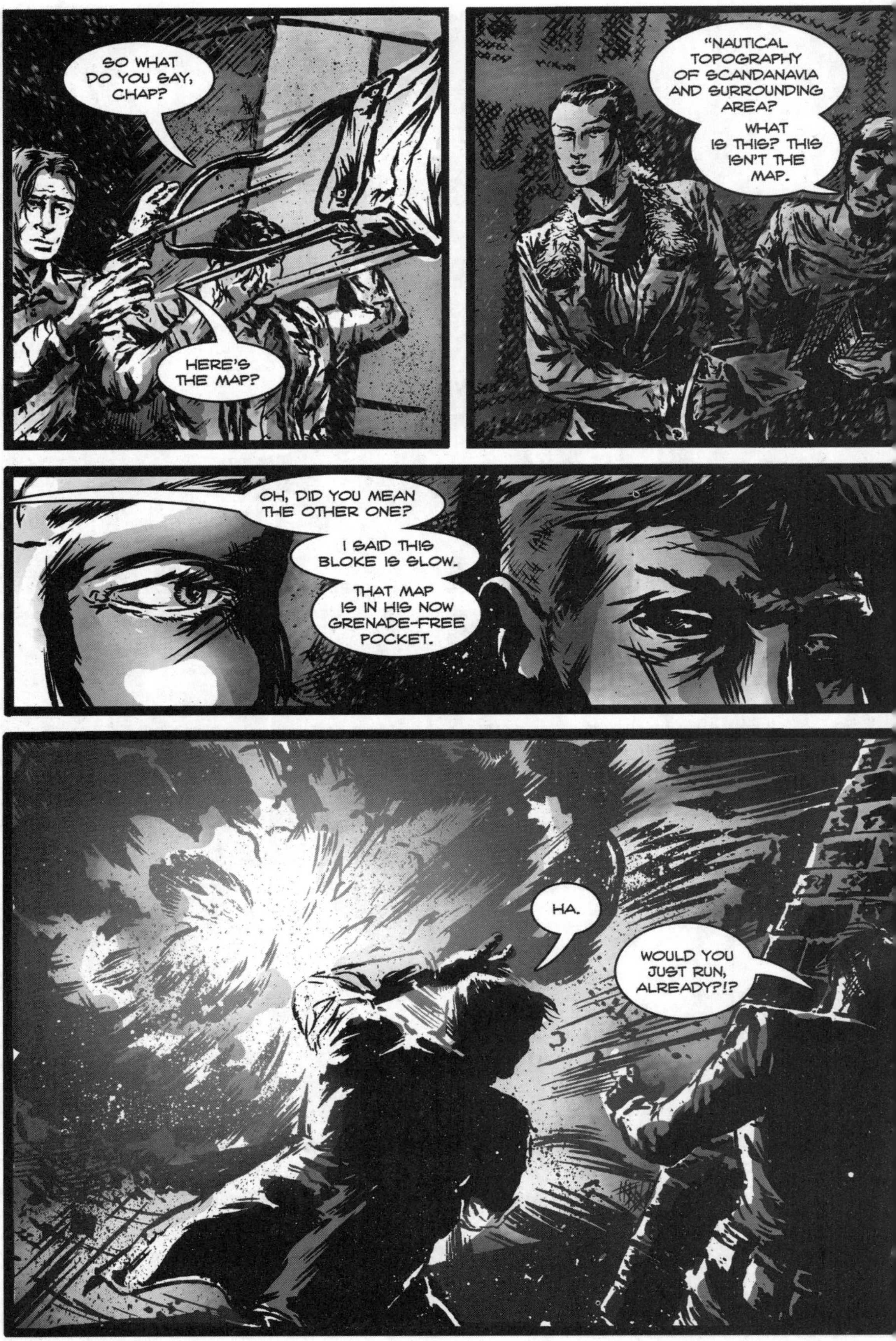
SO WHAT DO YOU SAY, CHAP?
HERE'S THE MAP?
"NAUTICAL TOPOGRAPHY OF SCANDANAVIA AND SURROUNDING AREA?
WHAT IS THIS? THIS ISN'T THE MAP.
OH, DID YOU MEAN THE OTHER ONE?
I SAID THIS BLOKE IS SLOW.
THAT MAP IS IN HIS NOW GRENADE-FREE POCKET.
HA.
WOULD YOU JUST RUN, ALREADY?!?

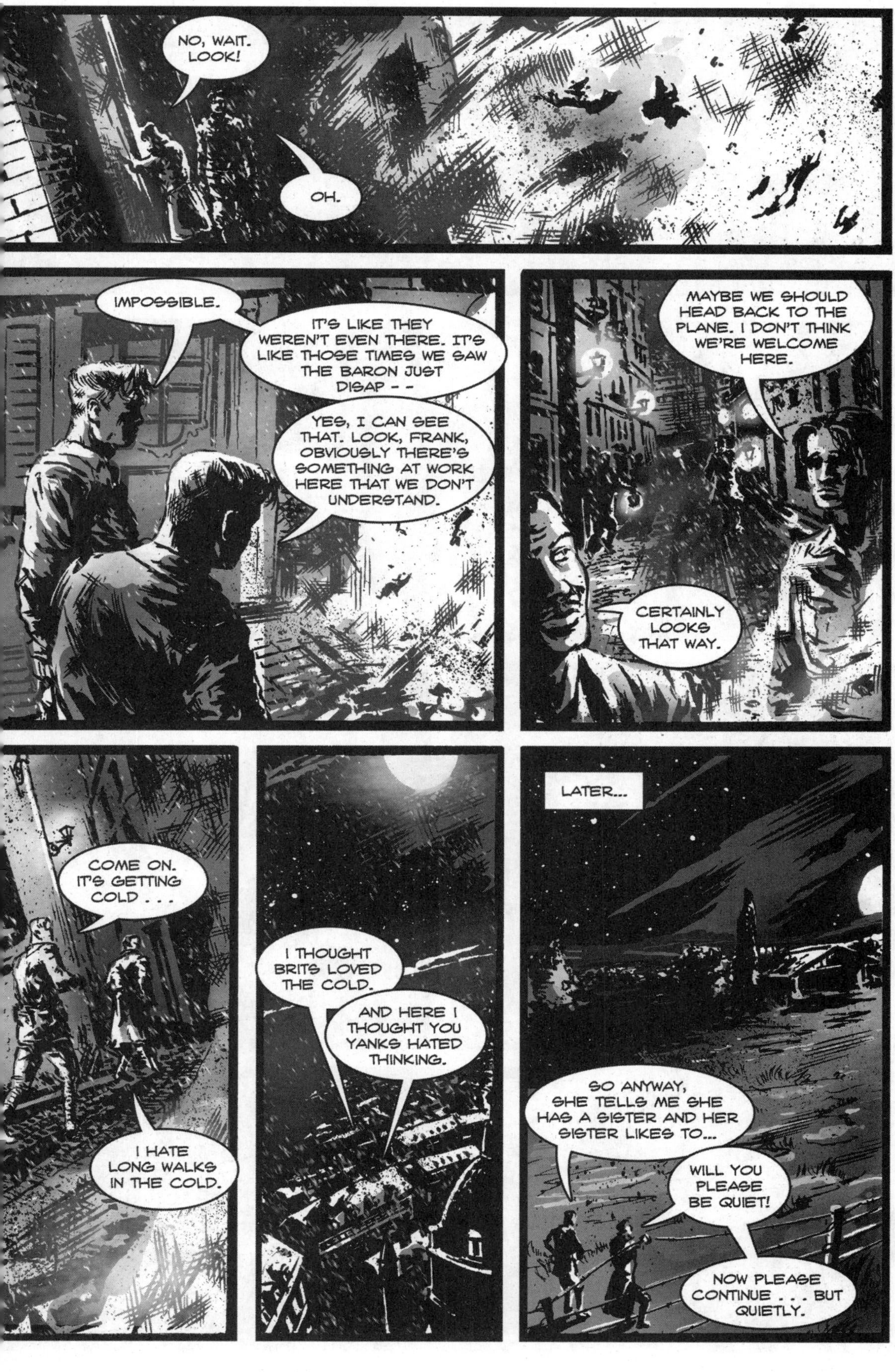
NO, WAIT. LOOK!
OH.
IMPOSSIBLE.
IT'S LIKE THEY WEREN'T EVEN THERE. IT'S LIKE THOSE TIMES WE SAW THE BARON JUST DISAP - -
YES, I CAN SEE THAT. LOOK, FRANK, OBVIOUSLY THERE'S SOMETHING AT WORK HERE THAT WE DON'T UNDERSTAND.
MAYBE WE SHOULD HEAD BACK TO THE PLANE. I DON'T THINK WE'RE WELCOME HERE.
CERTAINLY LOOKS THAT WAY.
COME ON. IT'S GETTING COLD . . .
I HATE LONG WALKS IN THE COLD.
I THOUGHT BRITS LOVED THE COLD.
AND HERE I THOUGHT YOU YANKS HATED THINKING.
LATER...
SO ANYWAY, SHE TELLS ME SHE HAS A SISTER AND HER SISTER LIKES TO...
WILL YOU PLEASE BE QUIET!
NOW PLEASE CONTINUE . . . BUT QUIETLY.

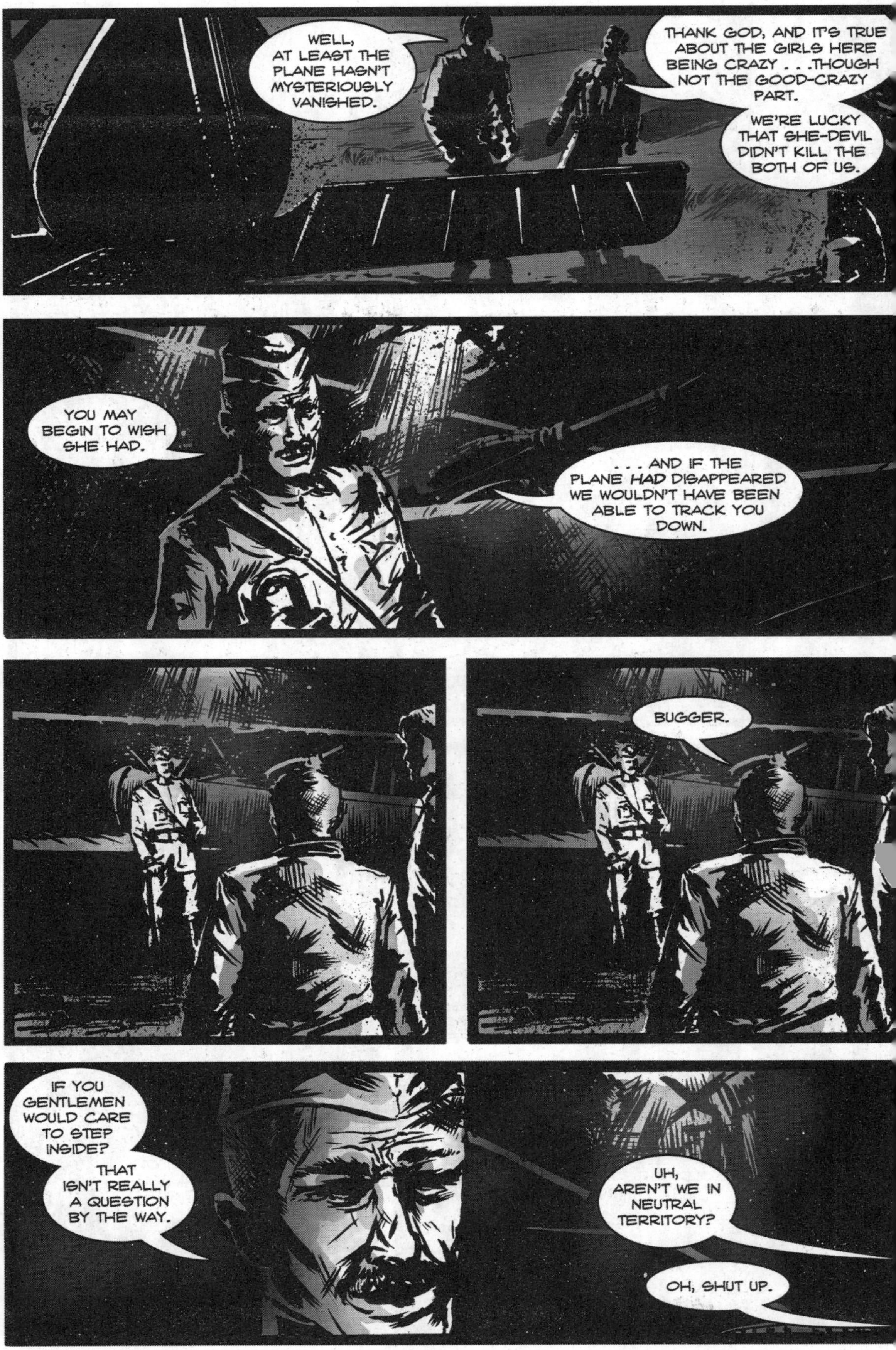
WELL, AT LEAST THE PLANE HASN'T MYSTERIOUSLY VANISHED.
THANK GOD, AND IT'S TRUE ABOUT THE GIRLS HERE BEING CRAZY . . .THOUGH NOT THE GOOD-CRAZY PART.
WE'RE LUCKY THAT SHE-DEVIL DIDN'T KILL THE BOTH OF US.
YOU MAY BEGIN TO WISH SHE HAD.
. . . AND IF THE PLANE *HAD* DISAPPEARED WE WOULDN'T HAVE BEEN ABLE TO TRACK YOU DOWN.
BUGGER.
IF YOU GENTLEMEN WOULD CARE TO STEP INSIDE?
THAT ISN'T REALLY A QUESTION BY THE WAY.
UH, AREN'T WE IN NEUTRAL TERRITORY?
OH, SHUT UP.

AND JUST WHAT MADE YOU THINK YOU COULD GET AWAY WITH THIS STUNT?

WELL WE... UH, I MEAN... HE SAID... SO... IT'S KINDA LIKE...

WE CAME ACROSS A PIECE OF INTELLIGENCE. WE FOLLOWED IT UP.

OH REALLY? MY, MY. I'M SURE YOUR TRIBUNAL WILL ENJOY HEARING THAT STORY.

TRIBUNAL? WHAT TRIBUNAL? WE'VE DONE NOTHING WRONG.

WE'VE NOT COMPRIMISED KING AND COUNTRY, WE JUST . . . BORROWED A PLANE.

NOW LOOK HERE, BENNETT. YOU STOLE A BRITISH PLANE. A BRITISH PLANE THAT SHOT AT OTHER BRITISH PLANES. QUITE POORLY I MIGHT ADD.

...CAUSING NO SMALL HEADACHE FOR HIS MAJESTY'S GOVERNMENT. AND NOW IT SEEMS YOU'VE BEEN WRECKING HAVOC ON NEUTRAL TERRITORY!

YOU ALSO INVOLVED AN AMERICAN SOLDIER IN THIS HAIRBRAINED SCHEME—

BUT—

WE HAVEN'T COME THIS FAR TO STOP! WHAT ARE YOU GONNA DO, THROW US IN THE CLINK BY YOURSELF? OOOOO, OR DID YOU HIDE YOUR MEN IN THE SHADOWS? HA!

PRECISELY! MEN, STEP FORWARD!

HELLO AGAIN, LADIES.

I THINK YOU'D BETTER COME ALONG WITH US.

AW, CRAP.

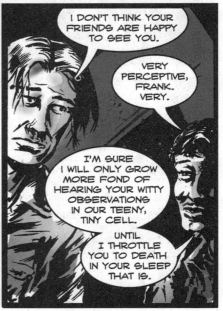

I DON'T THINK YOUR FRIENDS ARE HAPPY TO SEE YOU.

VERY PERCEPTIVE, FRANK. VERY.

I'M SURE I WILL ONLY GROW MORE FOND OF HEARING YOUR WITTY OBSERVATIONS IN OUR TEENY, TINY CELL.

UNTIL I THROTTLE YOU TO DEATH IN YOUR SLEEP THAT IS.

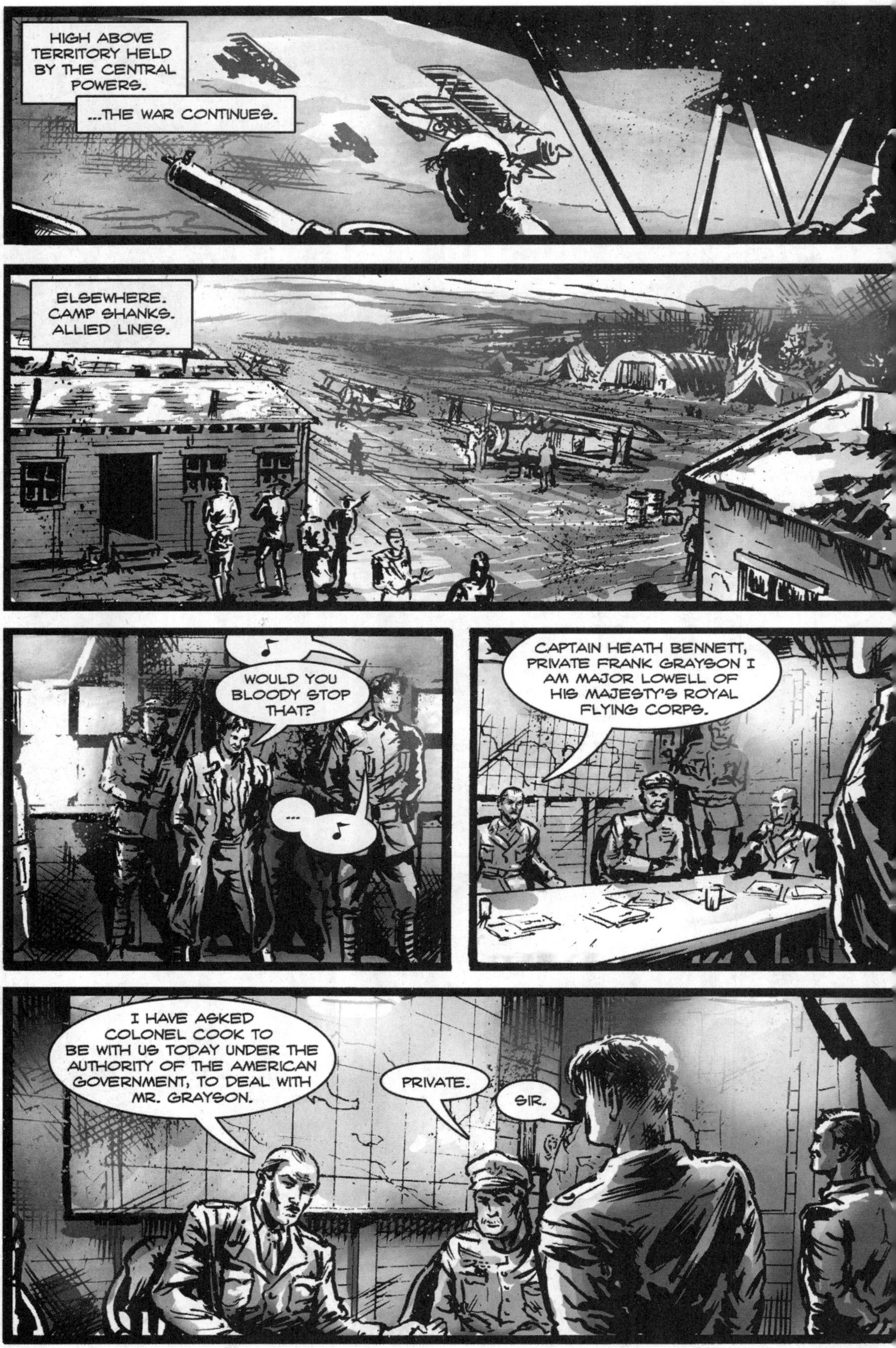
HIGH ABOVE TERRITORY HELD BY THE CENTRAL POWERS.
...THE WAR CONTINUES.
ELSEWHERE. CAMP SHANKS. ALLIED LINES.
♪
WOULD YOU BLOODY STOP THAT?
...
♪
CAPTAIN HEATH BENNETT, PRIVATE FRANK GRAYSON I AM MAJOR LOWELL OF HIS MAJESTY'S ROYAL FLYING CORPS.
I HAVE ASKED COLONEL COOK TO BE WITH US TODAY UNDER THE AUTHORITY OF THE AMERICAN GOVERNMENT, TO DEAL WITH MR. GRAYSON.
PRIVATE.
SIR.

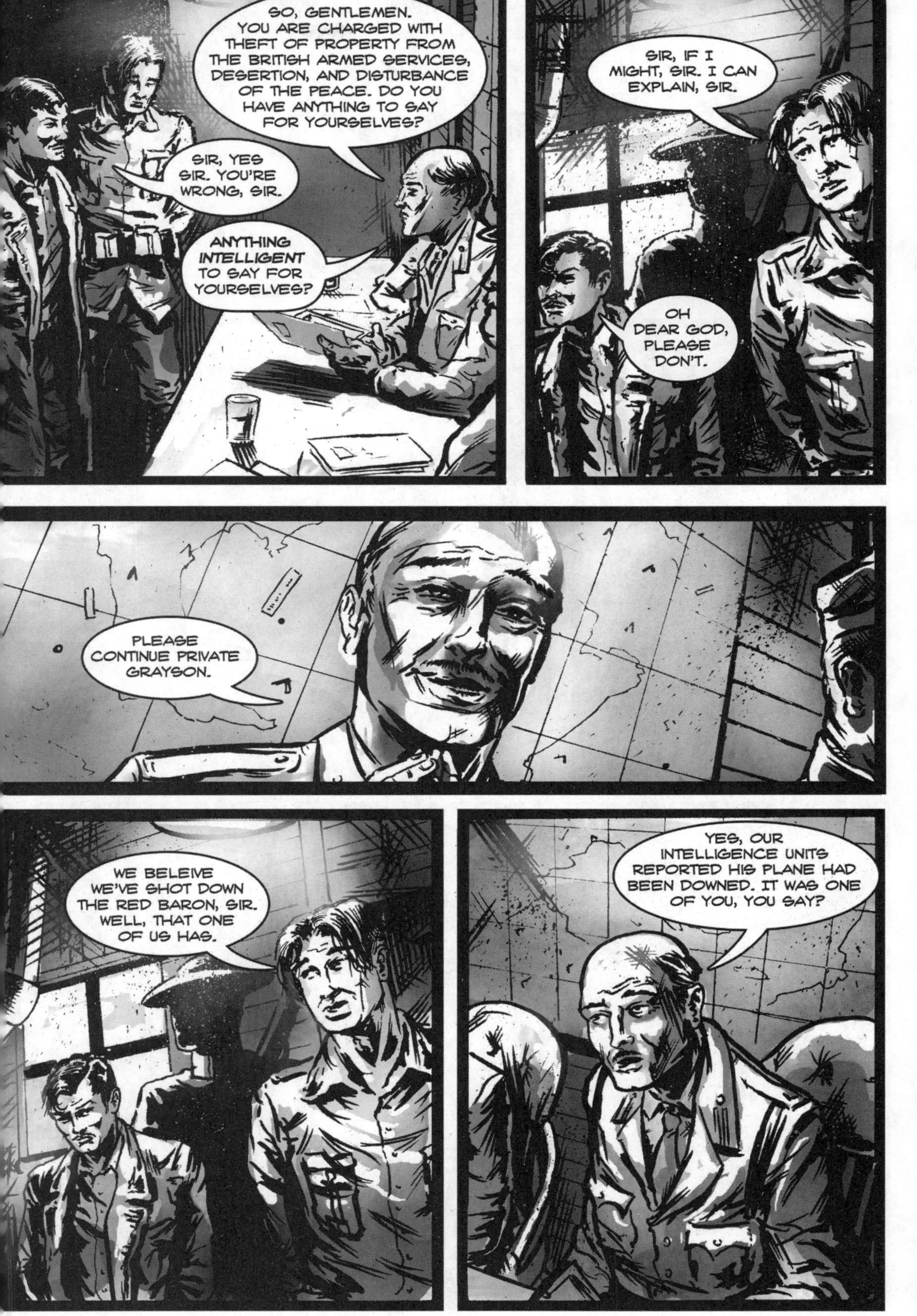
SO, GENTLEMEN. YOU ARE CHARGED WITH THEFT OF PROPERTY FROM THE BRITISH ARMED SERVICES, DESERTION, AND DISTURBANCE OF THE PEACE. DO YOU HAVE ANYTHING TO SAY FOR YOURSELVES?
SIR, YES SIR. YOU'RE WRONG, SIR.
ANYTHING *INTELLIGENT* TO SAY FOR YOURSELVES?
SIR, IF I MIGHT, SIR. I CAN EXPLAIN, SIR.
OH DEAR GOD, PLEASE DON'T.
PLEASE CONTINUE PRIVATE GRAYSON.
WE BELEIVE WE'VE SHOT DOWN THE RED BARON, SIR. WELL, THAT ONE OF US HAS.
YES, OUR INTELLIGENCE UNITS REPORTED HIS PLANE HAD BEEN DOWNED. IT WAS ONE OF YOU, YOU SAY?

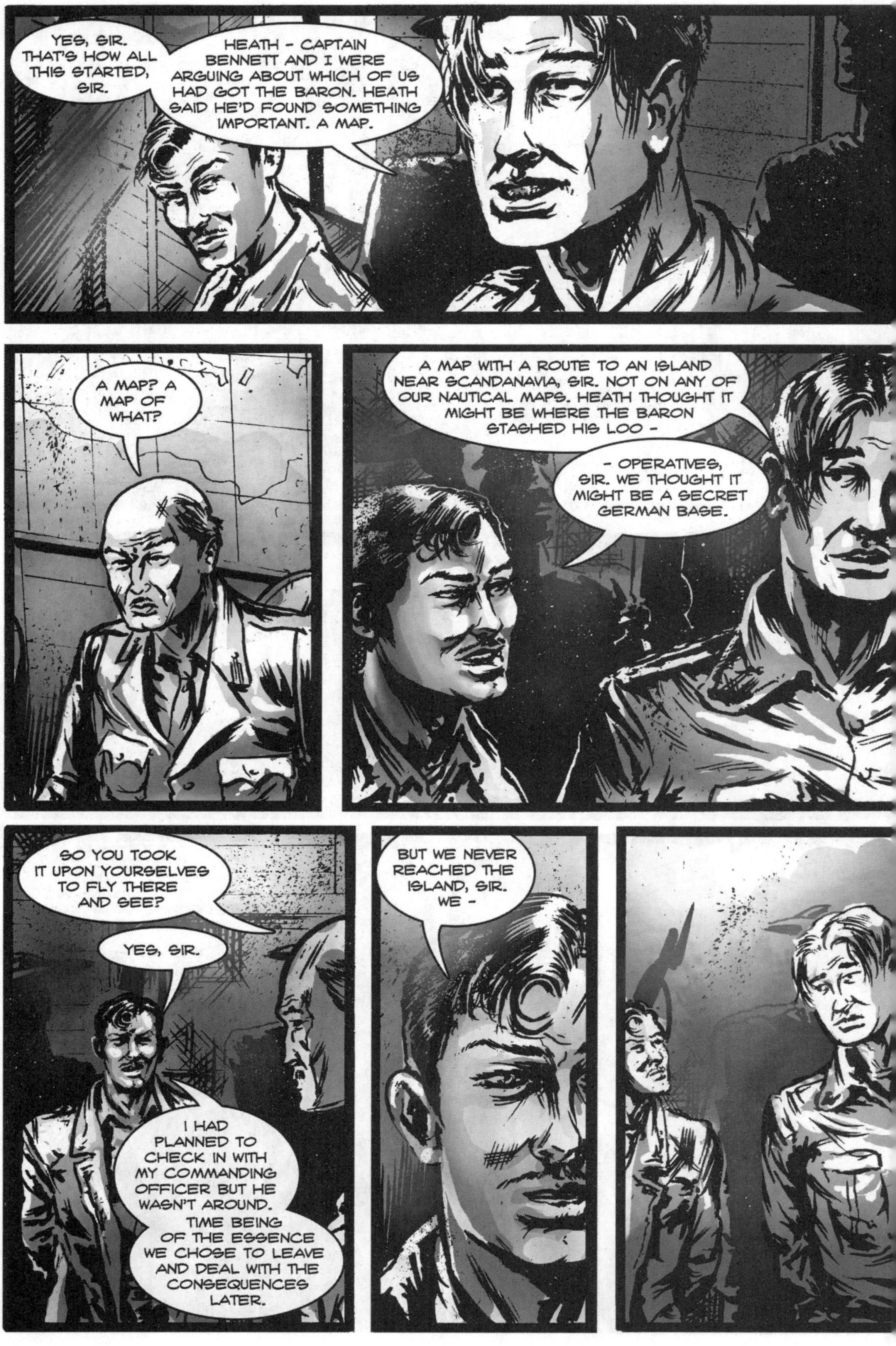
YES, SIR. THAT'S HOW ALL THIS STARTED, SIR.
HEATH - CAPTAIN BENNETT AND I WERE ARGUING ABOUT WHICH OF US HAD GOT THE BARON. HEATH SAID HE'D FOUND SOMETHING IMPORTANT. A MAP.
A MAP? A MAP OF WHAT?
A MAP WITH A ROUTE TO AN ISLAND NEAR SCANDANAVIA, SIR. NOT ON ANY OF OUR NAUTICAL MAPS. HEATH THOUGHT IT MIGHT BE WHERE THE BARON STASHED HIS LOO -
- OPERATIVES, SIR. WE THOUGHT IT MIGHT BE A SECRET GERMAN BASE.
SO YOU TOOK IT UPON YOURSELVES TO FLY THERE AND SEE?
YES, SIR.
I HAD PLANNED TO CHECK IN WITH MY COMMANDING OFFICER BUT HE WASN'T AROUND.
TIME BEING OF THE ESSENCE WE CHOSE TO LEAVE AND DEAL WITH THE CONSEQUENCES LATER.
BUT WE NEVER REACHED THE ISLAND, SIR. WE -

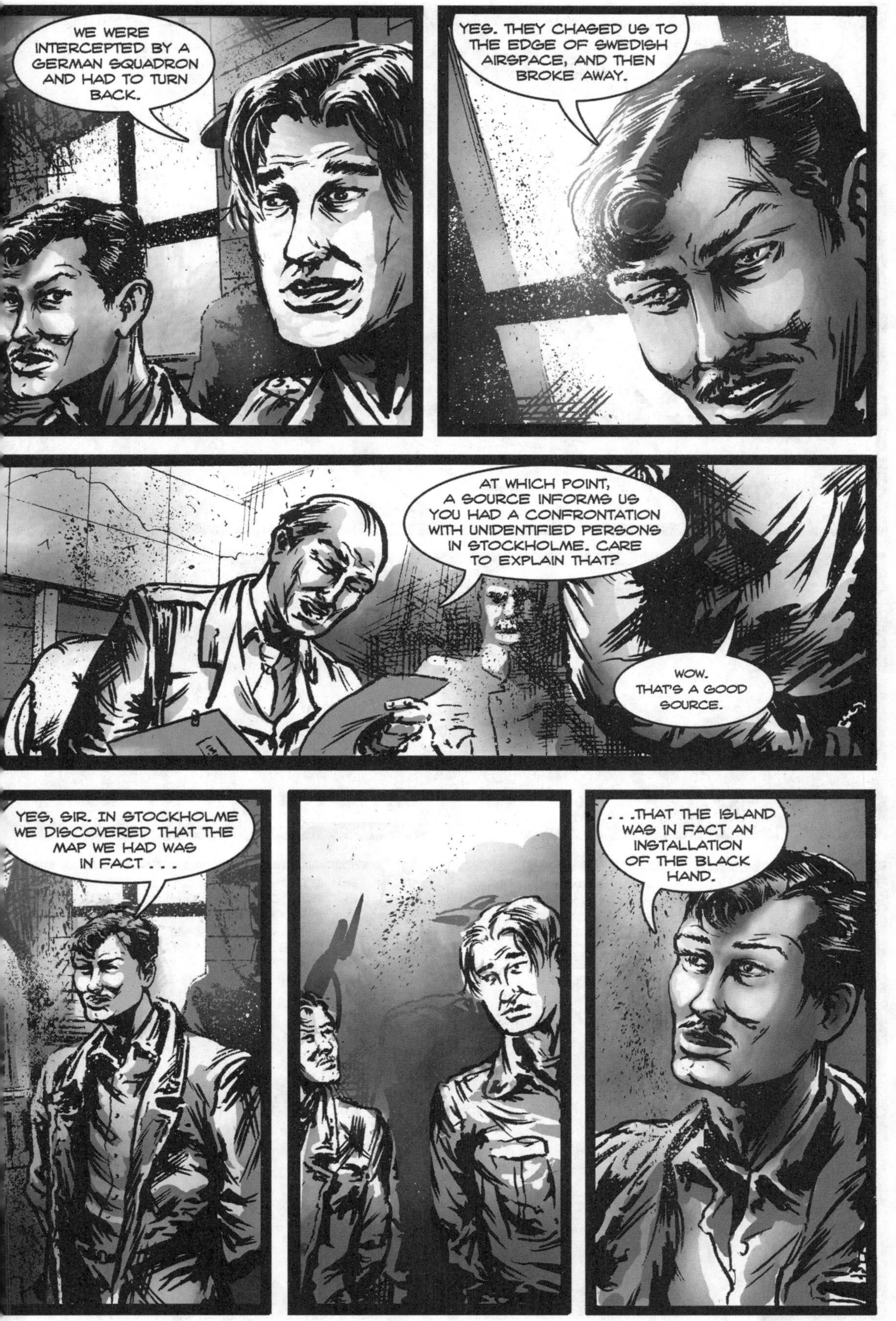
WE WERE INTERCEPTED BY A GERMAN SQUADRON AND HAD TO TURN BACK.
YES. THEY CHASED US TO THE EDGE OF SWEDISH AIRSPACE, AND THEN BROKE AWAY.
AT WHICH POINT, A SOURCE INFORMS US YOU HAD A CONFRONTATION WITH UNIDENTIFIED PERSONS IN STOCKHOLME. CARE TO EXPLAIN THAT?
WOW. THAT'S A GOOD SOURCE.
YES, SIR. IN STOCKHOLME WE DISCOVERED THAT THE MAP WE HAD WAS IN FACT . . .
. . .THAT THE ISLAND WAS IN FACT AN INSTALLATION OF THE BLACK HAND.

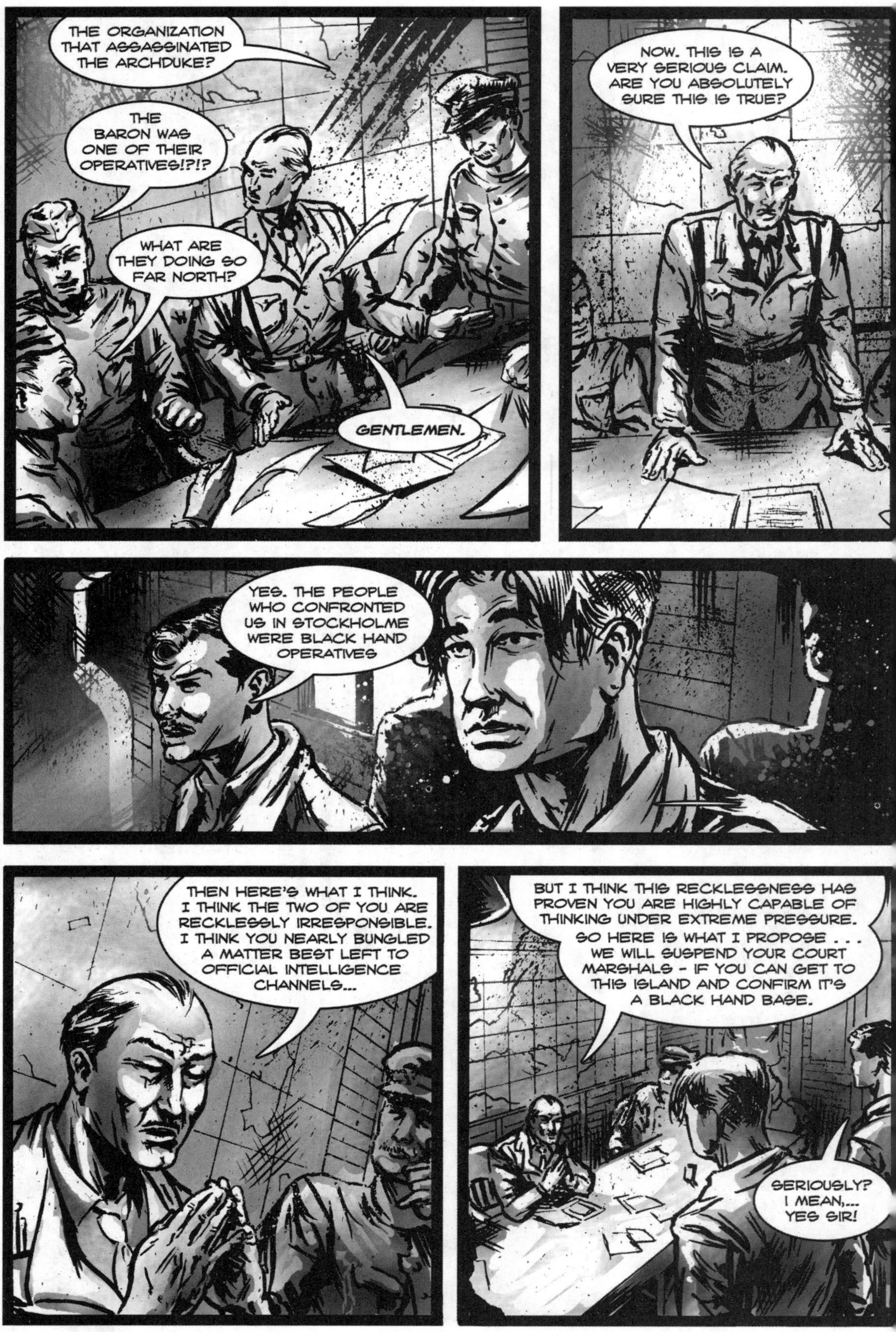
THE ORGANIZATION THAT ASSASSINATED THE ARCHDUKE?
THE BARON WAS ONE OF THEIR OPERATIVES!?!?
WHAT ARE THEY DOING SO FAR NORTH?
GENTLEMEN.
NOW. THIS IS A VERY SERIOUS CLAIM. ARE YOU ABSOLUTELY SURE THIS IS TRUE?
YES. THE PEOPLE WHO CONFRONTED US IN STOCKHOLME WERE BLACK HAND OPERATIVES
THEN HERE'S WHAT I THINK. I THINK THE TWO OF YOU ARE RECKLESSLY IRRESPONSIBLE. I THINK YOU NEARLY BUNGLED A MATTER BEST LEFT TO OFFICIAL INTELLIGENCE CHANNELS...
BUT I THINK THIS RECKLESSNESS HAS PROVEN YOU ARE HIGHLY CAPABLE OF THINKING UNDER EXTREME PRESSURE.
SO HERE IS WHAT I PROPOSE . . . WE WILL SUSPEND YOUR COURT MARSHALS - IF YOU CAN GET TO THIS ISLAND AND CONFIRM IT'S A BLACK HAND BASE.
SERIOUSLY? I MEAN,... YES SIR!

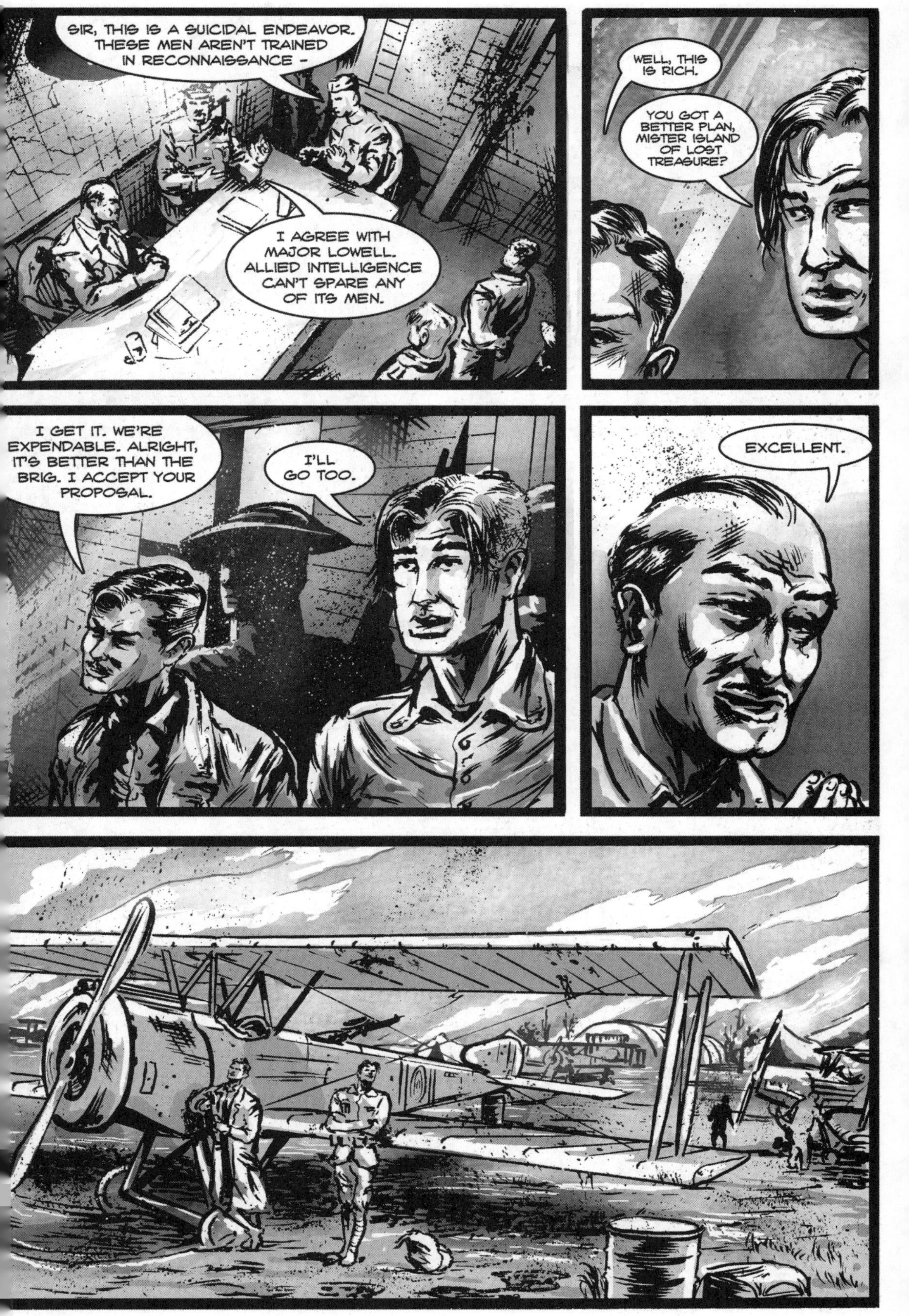
SIR, THIS IS A SUICIDAL ENDEAVOR. THESE MEN AREN'T TRAINED IN RECONNAISSANCE -
I AGREE WITH MAJOR LOWELL. ALLIED INTELLIGENCE CAN'T SPARE ANY OF ITS MEN.
WELL, THIS IS RICH.
YOU GOT A BETTER PLAN, MISTER ISLAND OF LOST TREASURE?
I GET IT. WE'RE EXPENDABLE. ALRIGHT, IT'S BETTER THAN THE BRIG. I ACCEPT YOUR PROPOSAL.
I'LL GO TOO.
EXCELLENT.

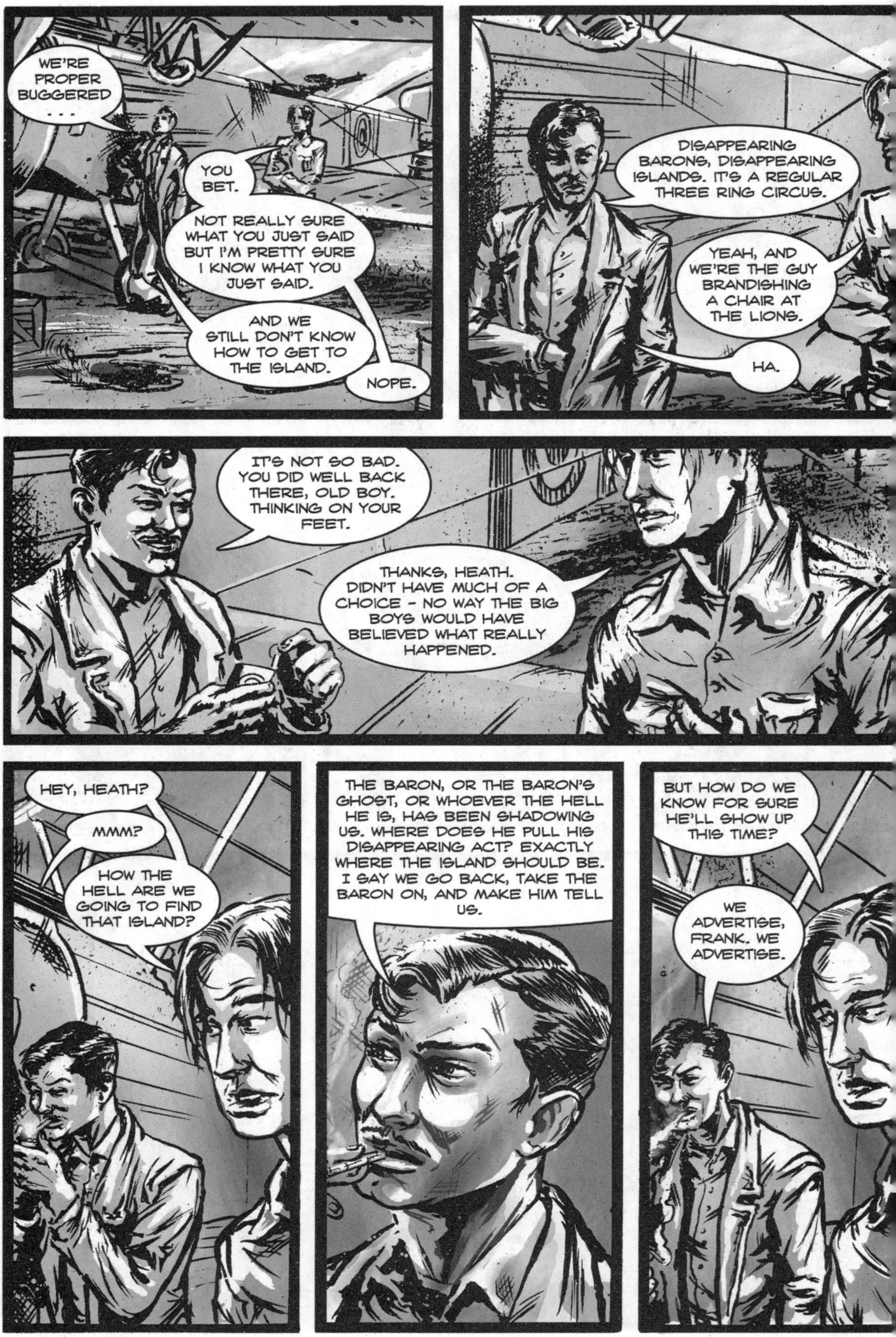
WE'RE PROPER BUGGERED . . .
YOU BET.
NOT REALLY SURE WHAT YOU JUST SAID BUT I'M PRETTY SURE I KNOW WHAT YOU JUST SAID.
AND WE STILL DON'T KNOW HOW TO GET TO THE ISLAND.
NOPE.
DISAPPEARING BARONS, DISAPPEARING ISLANDS. IT'S A REGULAR THREE RING CIRCUS.
YEAH, AND WE'RE THE GUY BRANDISHING A CHAIR AT THE LIONS.
HA.
IT'S NOT SO BAD. YOU DID WELL BACK THERE, OLD BOY. THINKING ON YOUR FEET.
THANKS, HEATH. DIDN'T HAVE MUCH OF A CHOICE - NO WAY THE BIG BOYS WOULD HAVE BELIEVED WHAT REALLY HAPPENED.
HEY, HEATH?
MMM?
HOW THE HELL ARE WE GOING TO FIND THAT ISLAND?
THE BARON, OR THE BARON'S GHOST, OR WHOEVER THE HELL HE IS, HAS BEEN SHADOWING US. WHERE DOES HE PULL HIS DISAPPEARING ACT? EXACTLY WHERE THE ISLAND SHOULD BE. I SAY WE GO BACK, TAKE THE BARON ON, AND MAKE HIM TELL US.
BUT HOW DO WE KNOW FOR SURE HE'LL SHOW UP THIS TIME?
WE ADVERTISE, FRANK. WE ADVERTISE.

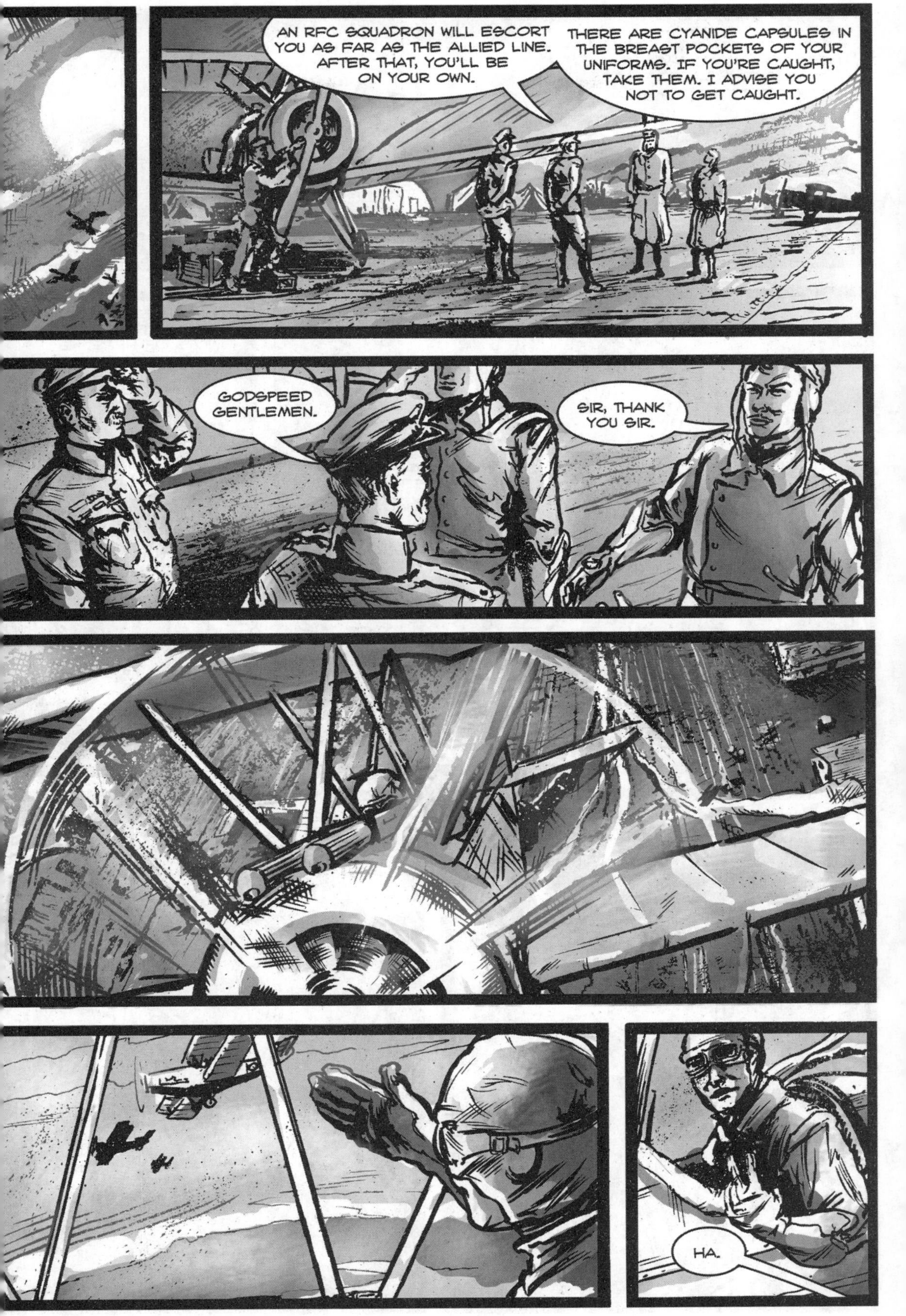
AN RFC SQUADRON WILL ESCORT YOU AS FAR AS THE ALLIED LINE. AFTER THAT, YOU'LL BE ON YOUR OWN.
THERE ARE CYANIDE CAPSULES IN THE BREAST POCKETS OF YOUR UNIFORMS. IF YOU'RE CAUGHT, TAKE THEM. I ADVISE YOU NOT TO GET CAUGHT.
GODSPEED GENTLEMEN.
SIR, THANK YOU SIR.
HA.

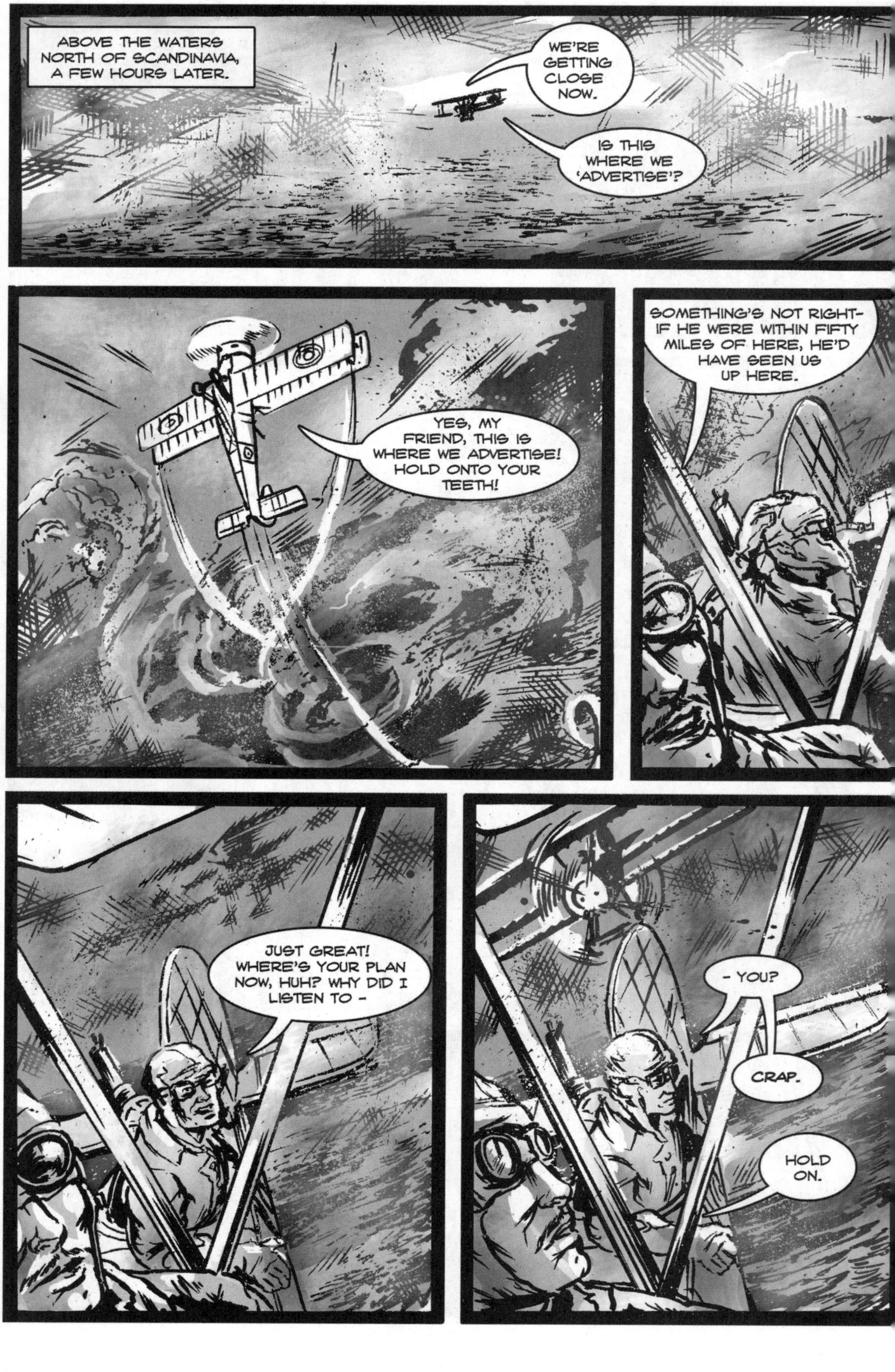
ABOVE THE WATERS NORTH OF SCANDINAVIA, A FEW HOURS LATER.
WE'RE GETTING CLOSE NOW.
IS THIS WHERE WE 'ADVERTISE'?
YES, MY FRIEND, THIS IS WHERE WE ADVERTISE! HOLD ONTO YOUR TEETH!
SOMETHING'S NOT RIGHT- IF HE WERE WITHIN FIFTY MILES OF HERE, HE'D HAVE SEEN US UP HERE.
JUST GREAT! WHERE'S YOUR PLAN NOW, HUH? WHY DID I LISTEN TO -
- YOU?
CRAP.
HOLD ON.

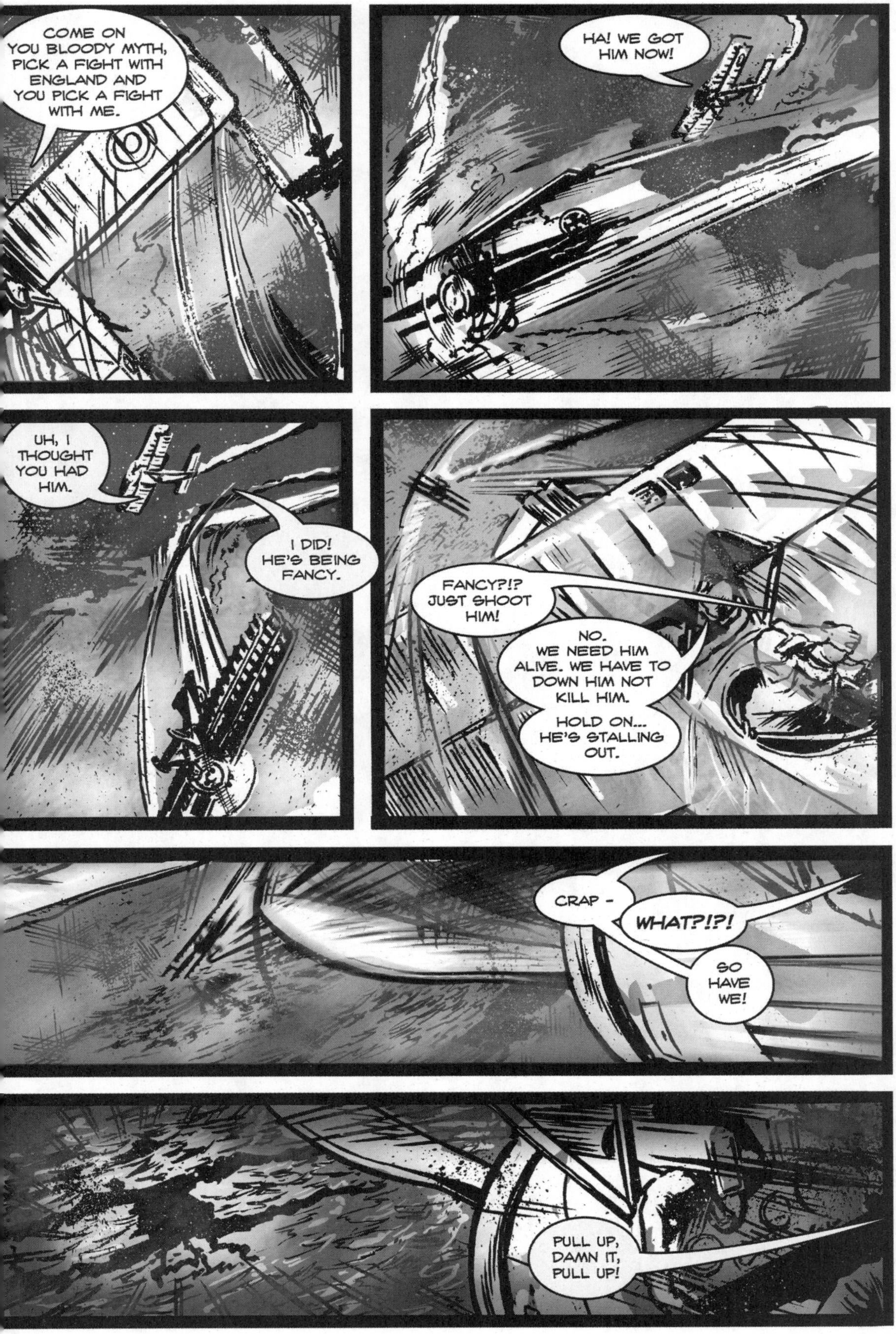
COME ON YOU BLOODY MYTH, PICK A FIGHT WITH ENGLAND AND YOU PICK A FIGHT WITH ME.
HA! WE GOT HIM NOW!
UH, I THOUGHT YOU HAD HIM.
I DID! HE'S BEING FANCY.
FANCY?!? JUST SHOOT HIM!
NO. WE NEED HIM ALIVE. WE HAVE TO DOWN HIM NOT KILL HIM.
HOLD ON... HE'S STALLING OUT.
CRAP -
WHAT?!?!
SO HAVE WE!
PULL UP, DAMN IT, PULL UP!

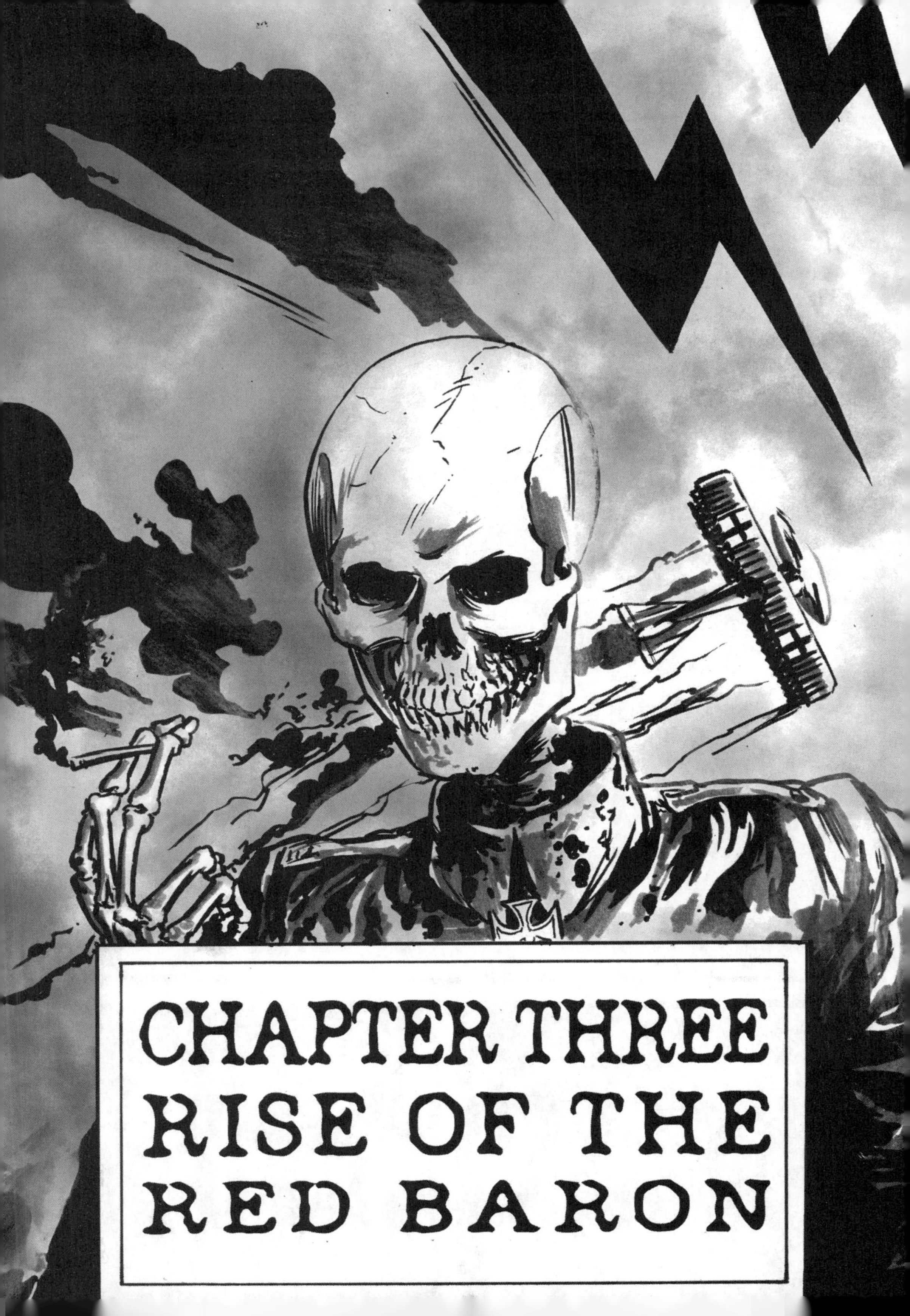
CHAPTER THREE
RISE OF THE
RED BARON

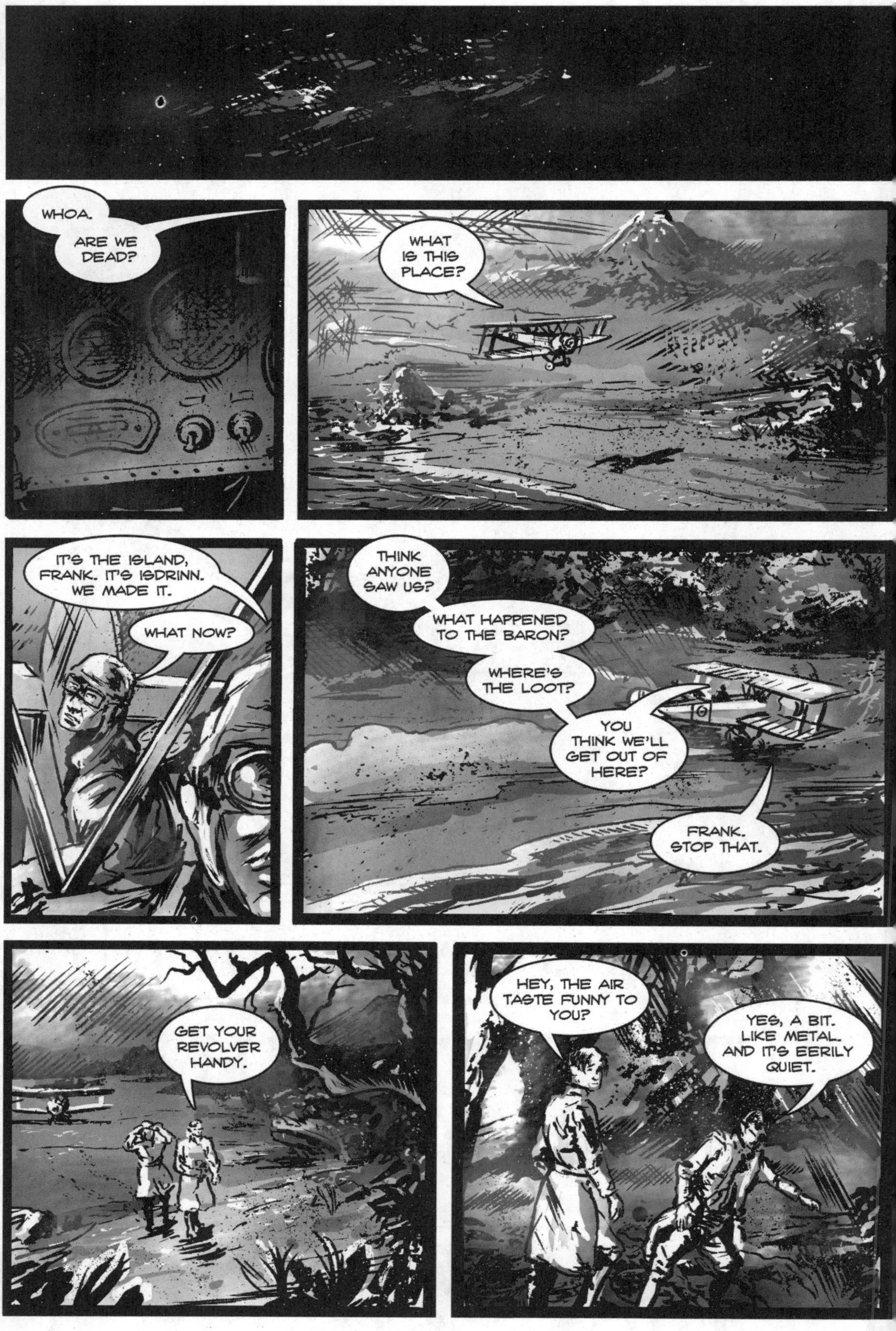
WHOA.
ARE WE DEAD?
WHAT IS THIS PLACE?
IT'S THE ISLAND, FRANK. IT'S ISDRINN. WE MADE IT.
WHAT NOW?
THINK ANYONE SAW US?
WHAT HAPPENED TO THE BARON?
WHERE'S THE LOOT?
YOU THINK WE'LL GET OUT OF HERE?
FRANK. STOP THAT.
GET YOUR REVOLVER HANDY.
HEY, THE AIR TASTE FUNNY TO YOU?
YES, A BIT. LIKE METAL. AND IT'S EERILY QUIET.

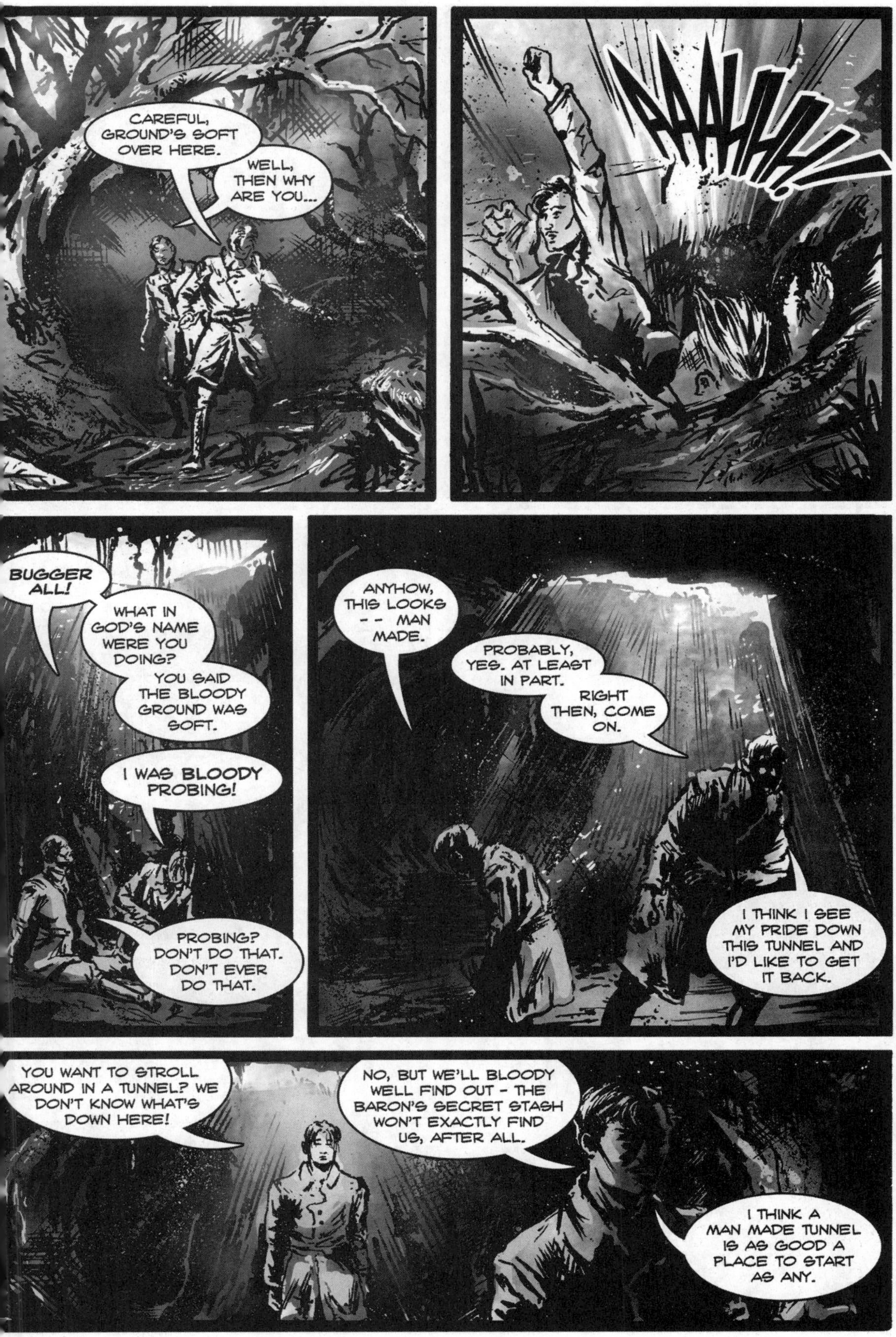
CAREFUL, GROUND'S SOFT OVER HERE.
WELL, THEN WHY ARE YOU...
AAAHHH!
BUGGER ALL!
WHAT IN GOD'S NAME WERE YOU DOING?
YOU SAID THE BLOODY GROUND WAS SOFT.
I WAS BLOODY PROBING!
PROBING? DON'T DO THAT. DON'T EVER DO THAT.
ANYHOW, THIS LOOKS - - MAN MADE.
PROBABLY, YES. AT LEAST IN PART.
RIGHT THEN, COME ON.
I THINK I SEE MY PRIDE DOWN THIS TUNNEL AND I'D LIKE TO GET IT BACK.
YOU WANT TO STROLL AROUND IN A TUNNEL? WE DON'T KNOW WHAT'S DOWN HERE!
NO, BUT WE'LL BLOODY WELL FIND OUT - THE BARON'S SECRET STASH WON'T EXACTLY FIND US, AFTER ALL.
I THINK A MAN MADE TUNNEL IS AS GOOD A PLACE TO START AS ANY.

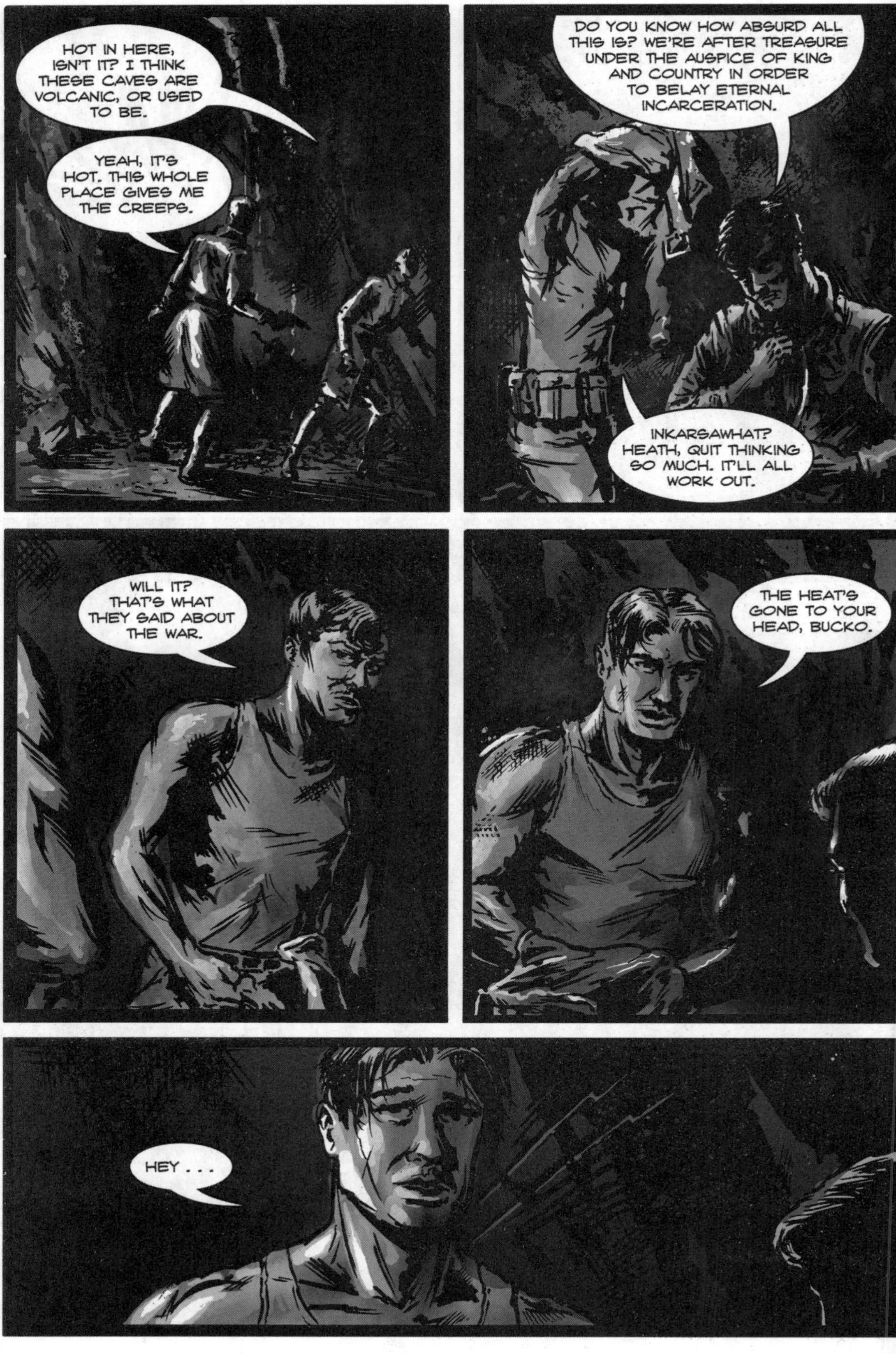
HOT IN HERE, ISN'T IT? I THINK THESE CAVES ARE VOLCANIC, OR USED TO BE.
YEAH, IT'S HOT. THIS WHOLE PLACE GIVES ME THE CREEPS.
DO YOU KNOW HOW ABSURD ALL THIS IS? WE'RE AFTER TREASURE UNDER THE AUSPICE OF KING AND COUNTRY IN ORDER TO BELAY ETERNAL INCARCERATION.
INKARSAWHAT? HEATH, QUIT THINKING SO MUCH. IT'LL ALL WORK OUT.
WILL IT? THAT'S WHAT THEY SAID ABOUT THE WAR.
THE HEAT'S GONE TO YOUR HEAD, BUCKO.
HEY . . .

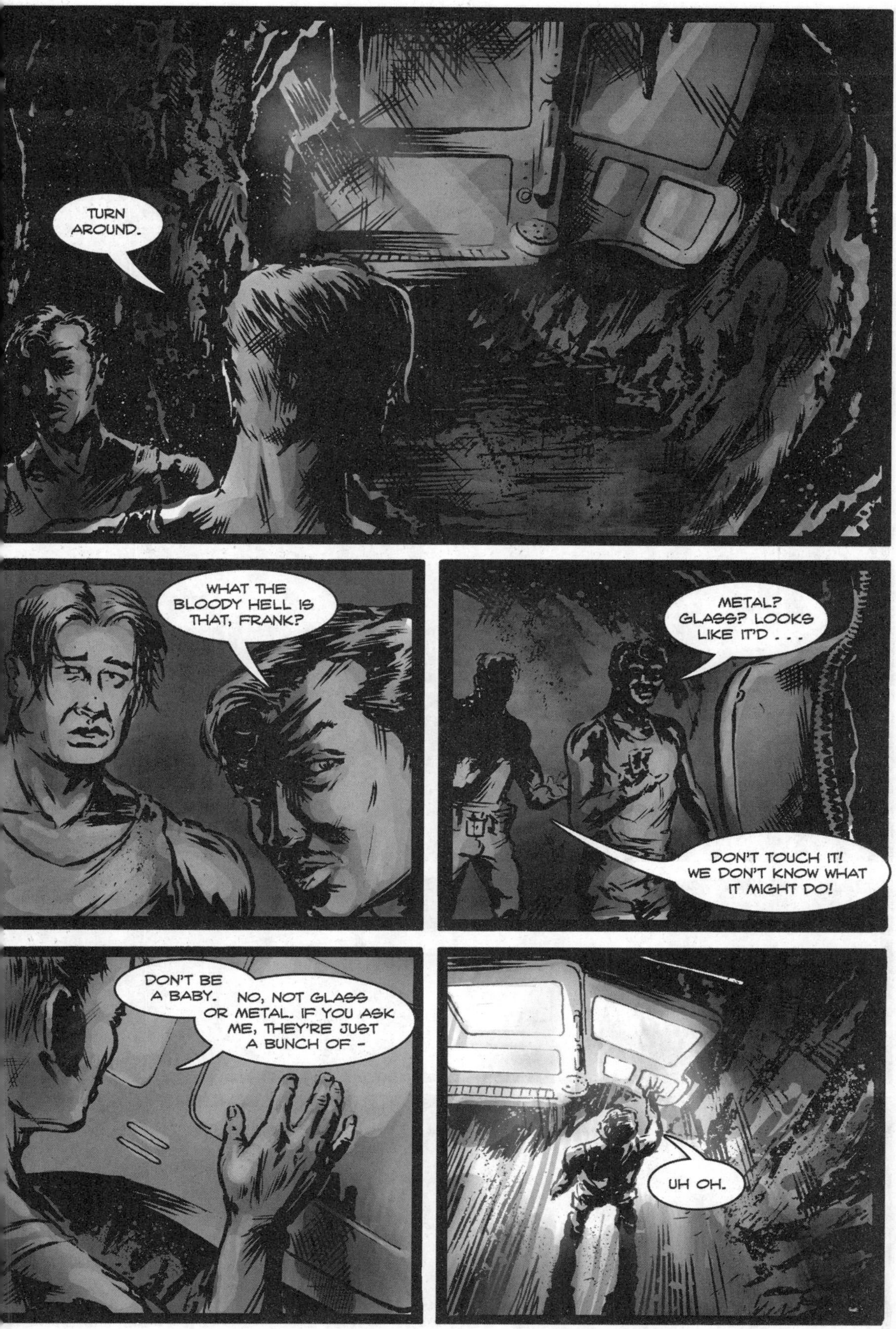
TURN AROUND.
WHAT THE BLOODY HELL IS THAT, FRANK?
METAL? GLASS? LOOKS LIKE IT'D . . .
DON'T TOUCH IT! WE DON'T KNOW WHAT IT MIGHT DO!
DON'T BE A BABY.
NO, NOT GLASS OR METAL. IF YOU ASK ME, THEY'RE JUST A BUNCH OF -
UH OH.

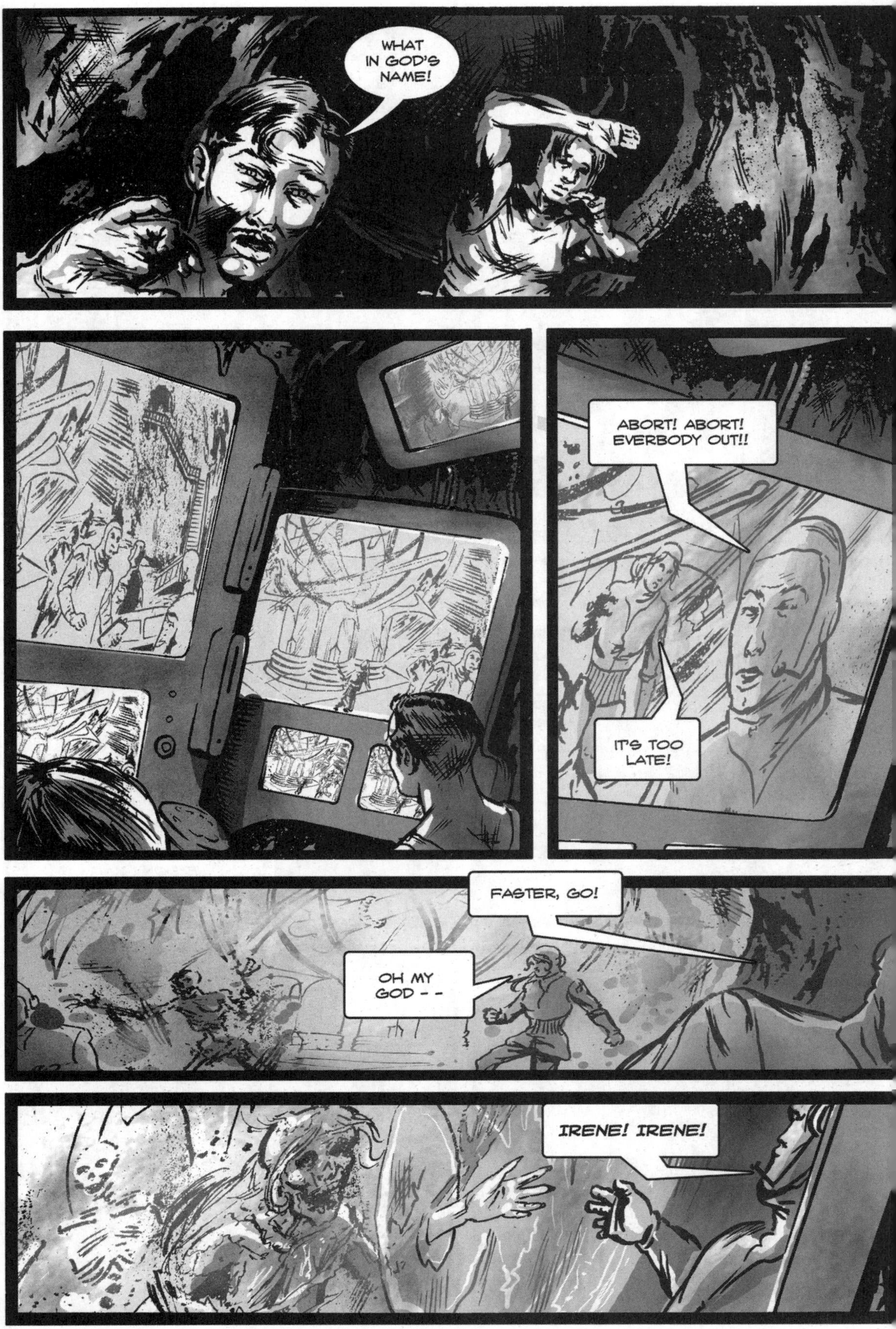
WHAT IN GOD'S NAME!
ABORT! ABORT! EVERBODY OUT!!
IT'S TOO LATE!
FASTER, GO!
OH MY GOD - -
IRENE! IRENE!

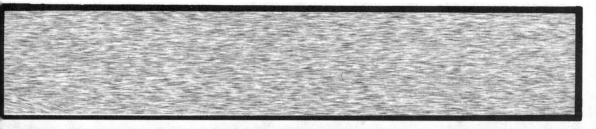

HAIL MARY, FULL OF GRACE.

THAT CAVERN IN THE MOTION-PICTURE . . . IT'S DOWN HERE, IT HAS TO BE.

LOOKED . . . LOOKED THAT WAY DIDN'T IT?

LET'S GO.

HEY!

LET'S NOT DO ANYTHING CRAZY, ALL RIGHT?

WE'RE HERE TO FIND HARD CURRENCY REMEMBER?

QUIET. LOOK.

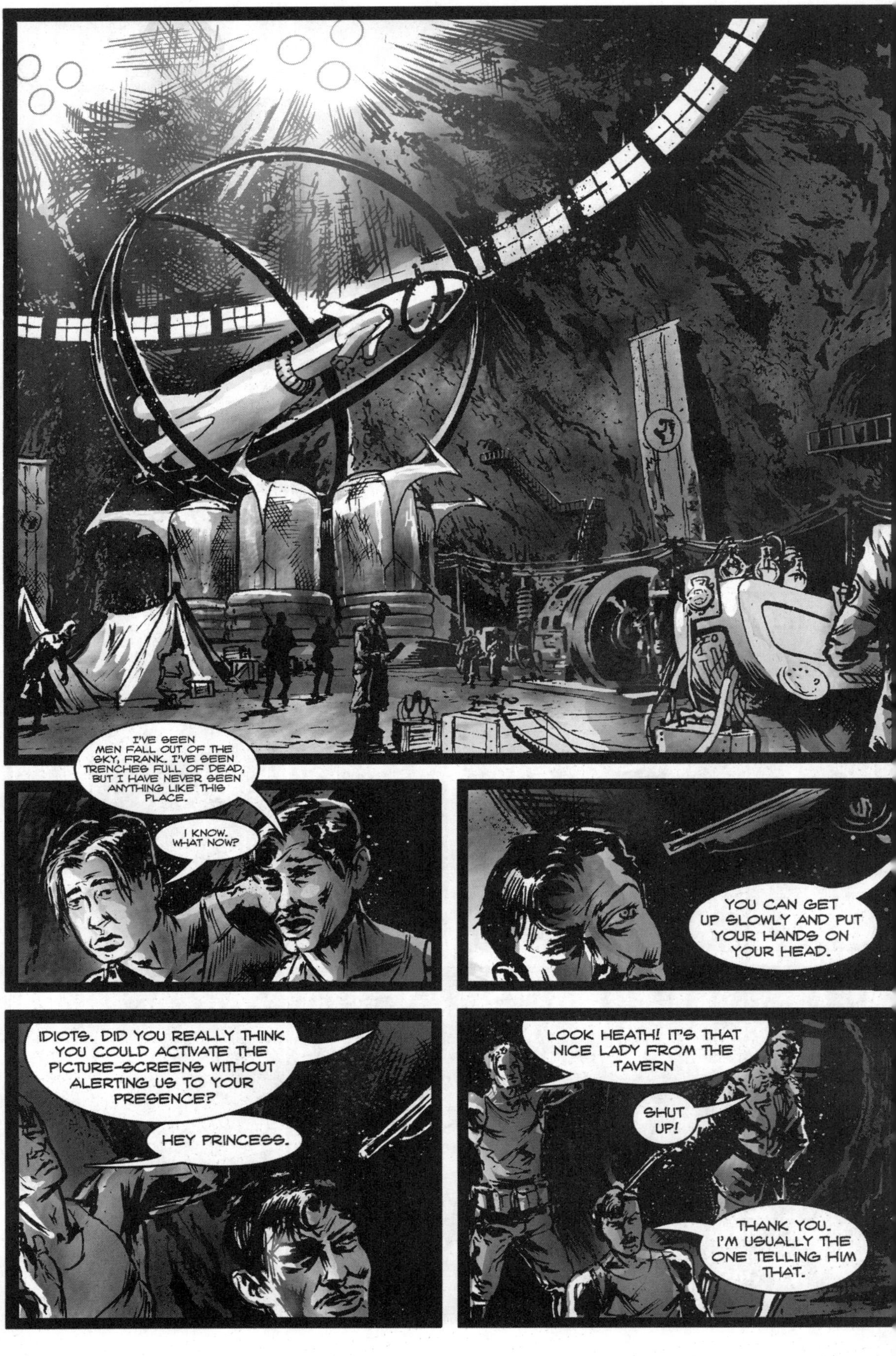

I'VE SEEN MEN FALL OUT OF THE SKY, FRANK. I'VE SEEN TRENCHES FULL OF DEAD, BUT I HAVE NEVER SEEN ANYTHING LIKE THIS PLACE.
I KNOW. WHAT NOW?
YOU CAN GET UP SLOWLY AND PUT YOUR HANDS ON YOUR HEAD.
IDIOTS. DID YOU REALLY THINK YOU COULD ACTIVATE THE PICTURE-SCREENS WITHOUT ALERTING US TO YOUR PRESENCE?
HEY PRINCESS.
LOOK HEATH! IT'S THAT NICE LADY FROM THE TAVERN
SHUT UP!
THANK YOU. I'M USUALLY THE ONE TELLING HIM THAT.

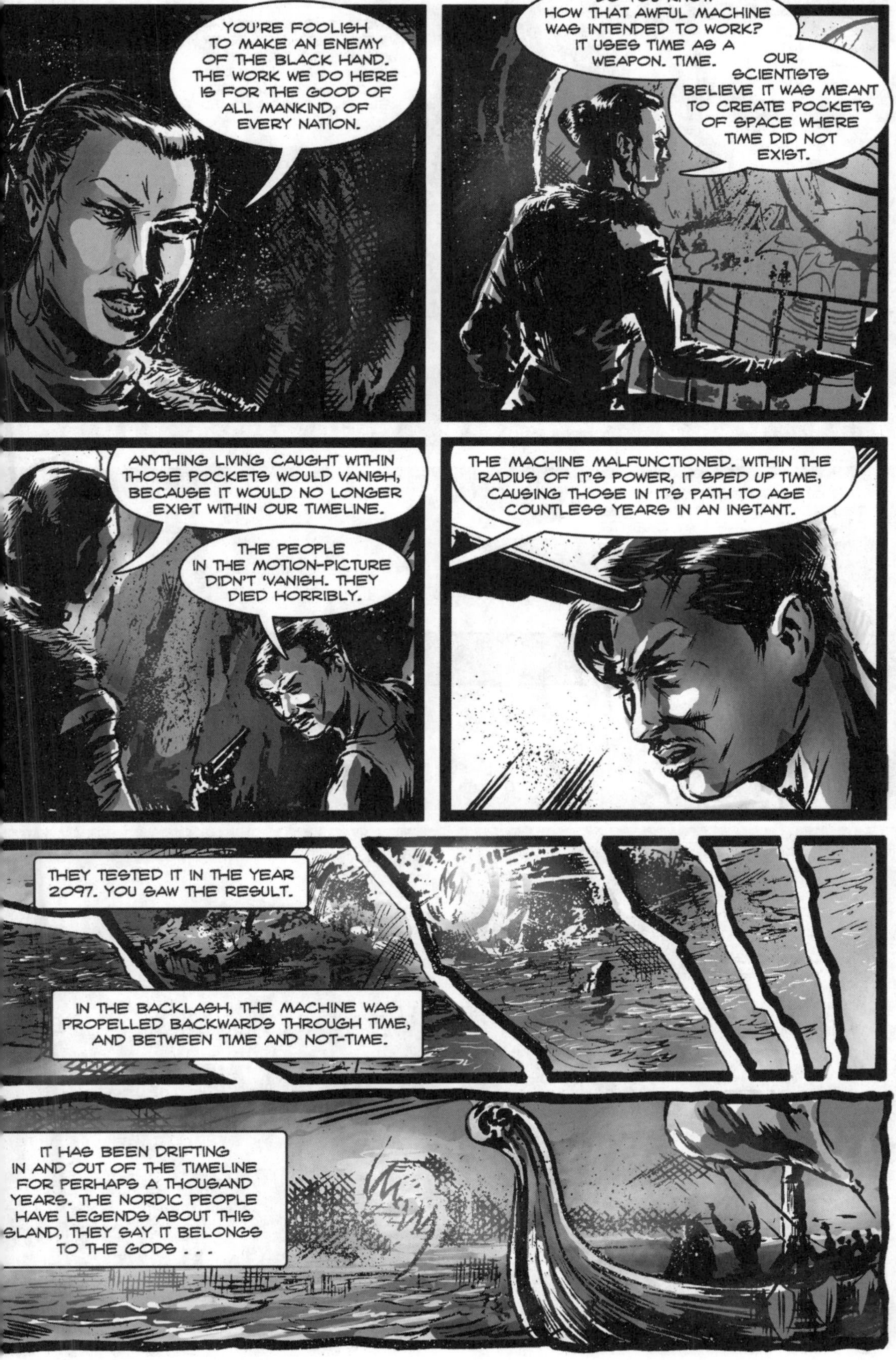
YOU'RE FOOLISH TO MAKE AN ENEMY OF THE BLACK HAND. THE WORK WE DO HERE IS FOR THE GOOD OF ALL MANKIND, OF EVERY NATION.
DO YOU KNOW HOW THAT AWFUL MACHINE WAS INTENDED TO WORK? IT USES TIME AS A WEAPON. TIME.
OUR SCIENTISTS BELIEVE IT WAS MEANT TO CREATE POCKETS OF SPACE WHERE TIME DID NOT EXIST.
ANYTHING LIVING CAUGHT WITHIN THOSE POCKETS WOULD VANISH, BECAUSE IT WOULD NO LONGER EXIST WITHIN OUR TIMELINE.
THE PEOPLE IN THE MOTION-PICTURE DIDN'T 'VANISH. THEY DIED HORRIBLY.
THE MACHINE MALFUNCTIONED. WITHIN THE RADIUS OF IT'S POWER, IT SPED UP TIME, CAUSING THOSE IN IT'S PATH TO AGE COUNTLESS YEARS IN AN INSTANT.
THEY TESTED IT IN THE YEAR 2097. YOU SAW THE RESULT.
IN THE BACKLASH, THE MACHINE WAS PROPELLED BACKWARDS THROUGH TIME, AND BETWEEN TIME AND NOT-TIME.
IT HAS BEEN DRIFTING IN AND OUT OF THE TIMELINE FOR PERHAPS A THOUSAND YEARS. THE NORDIC PEOPLE HAVE LEGENDS ABOUT THIS SLAND, THEY SAY IT BELONGS TO THE GODS . . .

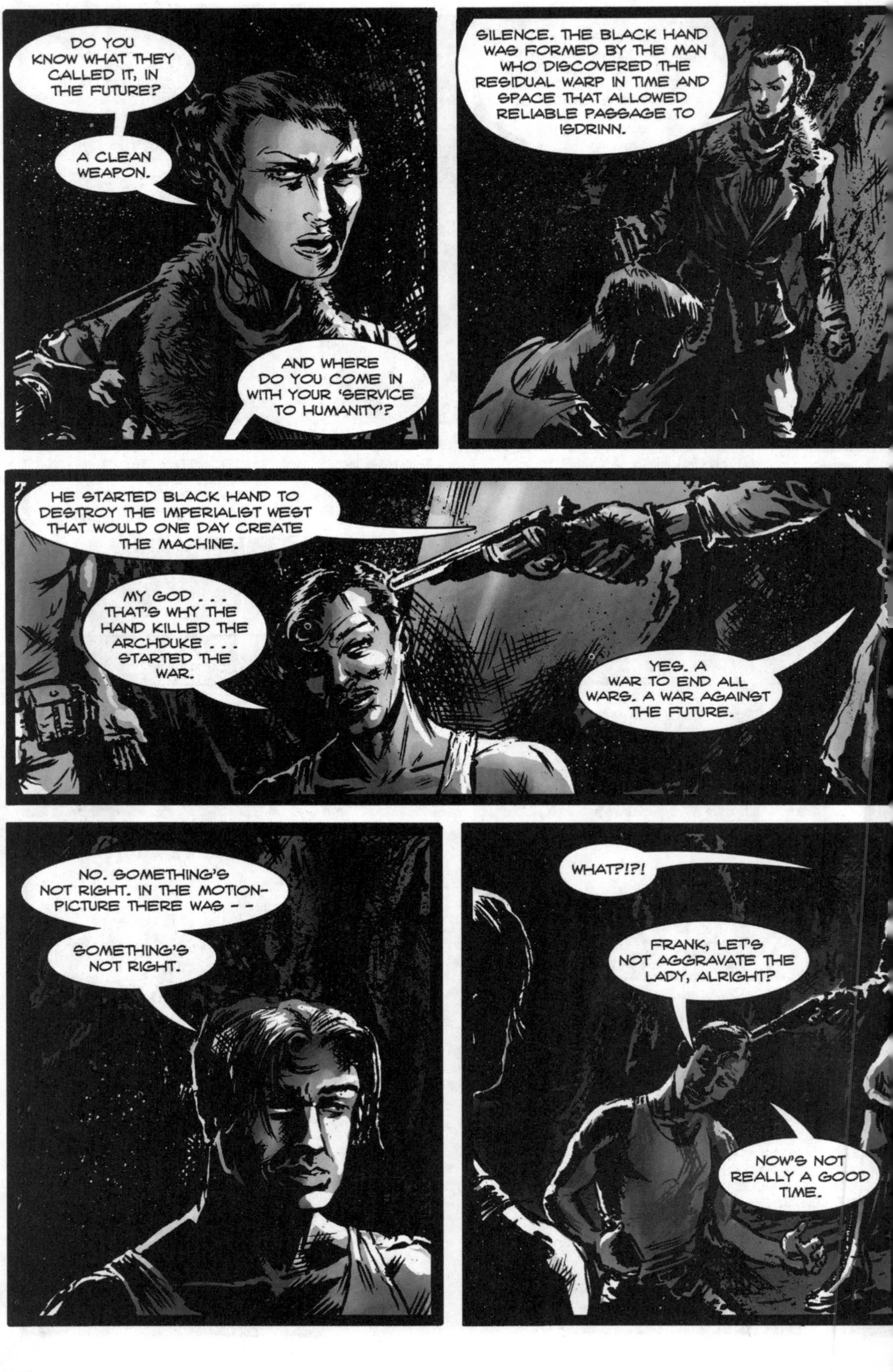
DO YOU KNOW WHAT THEY CALLED IT, IN THE FUTURE?
A CLEAN WEAPON.
AND WHERE DO YOU COME IN WITH YOUR 'SERVICE TO HUMANITY'?
SILENCE. THE BLACK HAND WAS FORMED BY THE MAN WHO DISCOVERED THE RESIDUAL WARP IN TIME AND SPACE THAT ALLOWED RELIABLE PASSAGE TO ISDRINN.
HE STARTED BLACK HAND TO DESTROY THE IMPERIALIST WEST THAT WOULD ONE DAY CREATE THE MACHINE.
MY GOD . . . THAT'S WHY THE HAND KILLED THE ARCHDUKE . . . STARTED THE WAR.
YES. A WAR TO END ALL WARS. A WAR AGAINST THE FUTURE.
NO. SOMETHING'S NOT RIGHT. IN THE MOTION-PICTURE THERE WAS - -
SOMETHING'S NOT RIGHT.
WHAT?!?!
FRANK, LET'S NOT AGGRAVATE THE LADY, ALRIGHT?
NOW'S NOT REALLY A GOOD TIME.

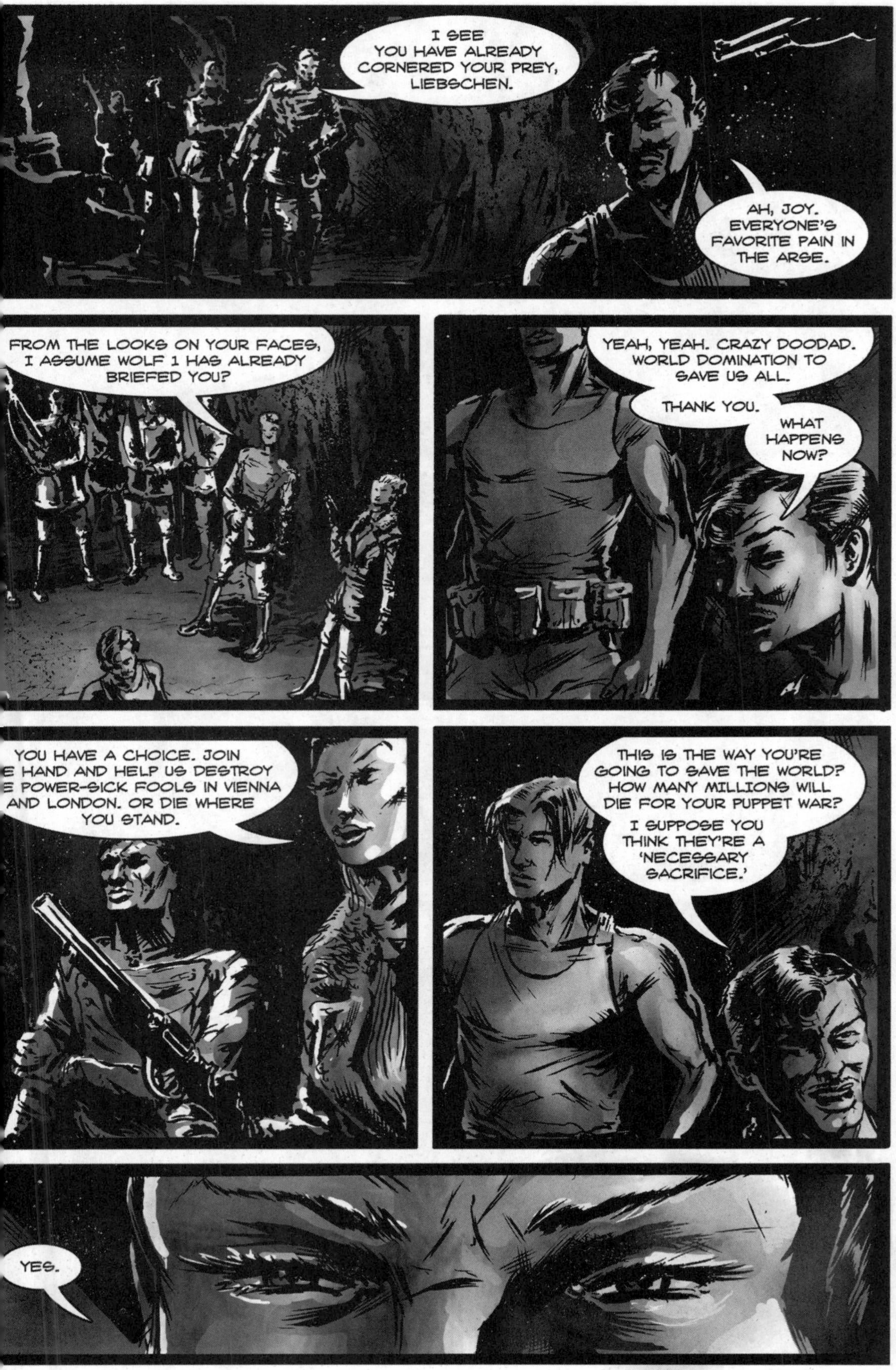
I SEE YOU HAVE ALREADY CORNERED YOUR PREY, LIEBSCHEN.
AH, JOY. EVERYONE'S FAVORITE PAIN IN THE ARSE.
FROM THE LOOKS ON YOUR FACES, I ASSUME WOLF 1 HAS ALREADY BRIEFED YOU?
YEAH, YEAH. CRAZY DOODAD. WORLD DOMINATION TO SAVE US ALL.
THANK YOU.
WHAT HAPPENS NOW?
YOU HAVE A CHOICE. JOIN E HAND AND HELP US DESTROY E POWER-SICK FOOLS IN VIENNA AND LONDON. OR DIE WHERE YOU STAND.
THIS IS THE WAY YOU'RE GOING TO SAVE THE WORLD? HOW MANY MILLIONS WILL DIE FOR YOUR PUPPET WAR?
I SUPPOSE YOU THINK THEY'RE A 'NECESSARY SACRIFICE.'
YES.

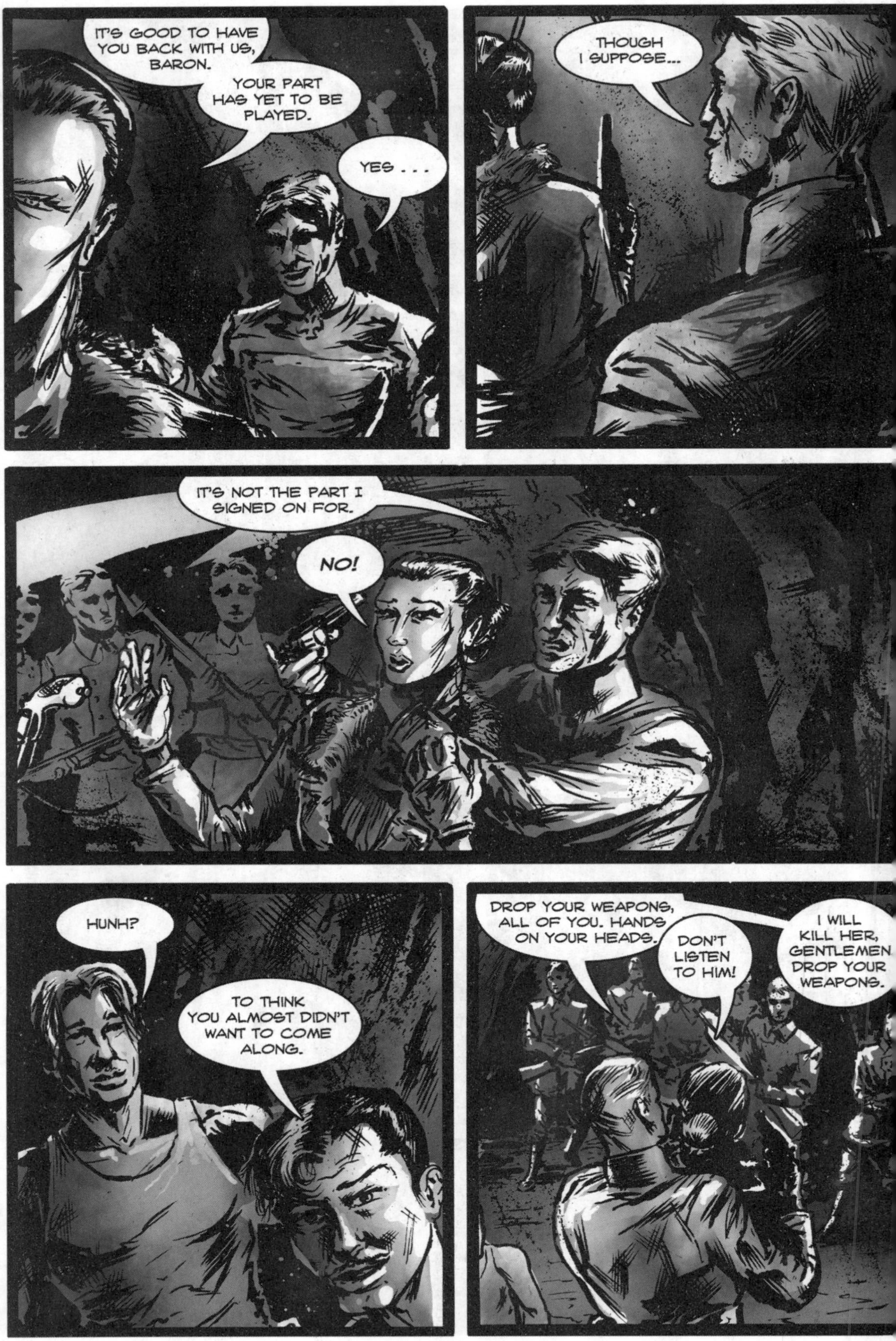
IT'S GOOD TO HAVE YOU BACK WITH US, BARON.
YOUR PART HAS YET TO BE PLAYED.
YES . . .
THOUGH I SUPPOSE...
IT'S NOT THE PART I SIGNED ON FOR.
NO!
HUNH?
TO THINK YOU ALMOST DIDN'T WANT TO COME ALONG.
DROP YOUR WEAPONS, ALL OF YOU. HANDS ON YOUR HEADS.
DON'T LISTEN TO HIM!
I WILL KILL HER, GENTLEMEN DROP YOUR WEAPONS.

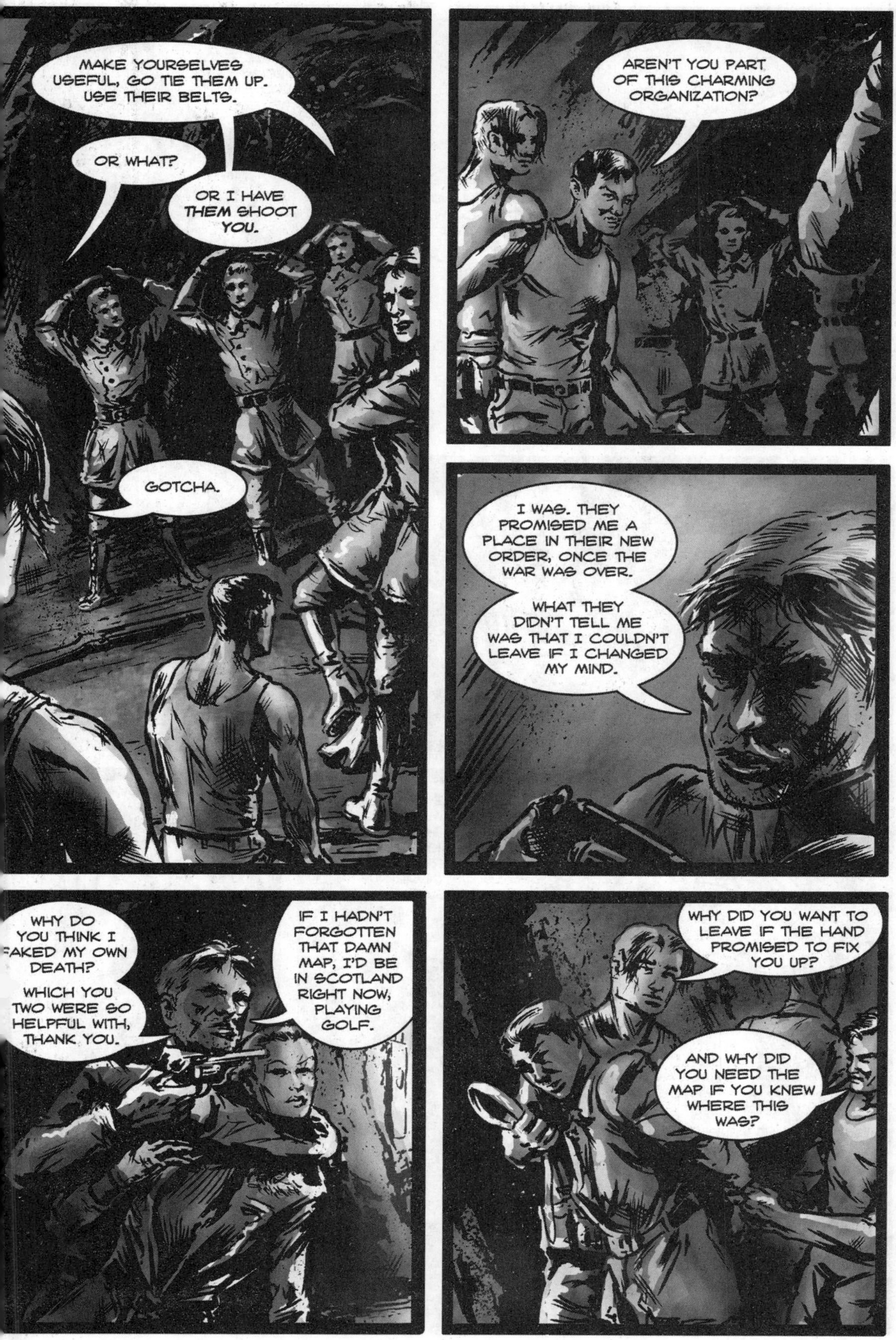
MAKE YOURSELVES USEFUL, GO TIE THEM UP. USE THEIR BELTS.
OR WHAT?
OR I HAVE THEM SHOOT YOU.
GOTCHA.
AREN'T YOU PART OF THIS CHARMING ORGANIZATION?
I WAS. THEY PROMISED ME A PLACE IN THEIR NEW ORDER, ONCE THE WAR WAS OVER.
WHAT THEY DIDN'T TELL ME WAS THAT I COULDN'T LEAVE IF I CHANGED MY MIND.
WHY DO YOU THINK I FAKED MY OWN DEATH?
WHICH YOU TWO WERE SO HELPFUL WITH, THANK YOU.
IF I HADN'T FORGOTTEN THAT DAMN MAP, I'D BE IN SCOTLAND RIGHT NOW, PLAYING GOLF.
WHY DID YOU WANT TO LEAVE IF THE HAND PROMISED TO FIX YOU UP?
AND WHY DID YOU NEED THE MAP IF YOU KNEW WHERE THIS WAS?

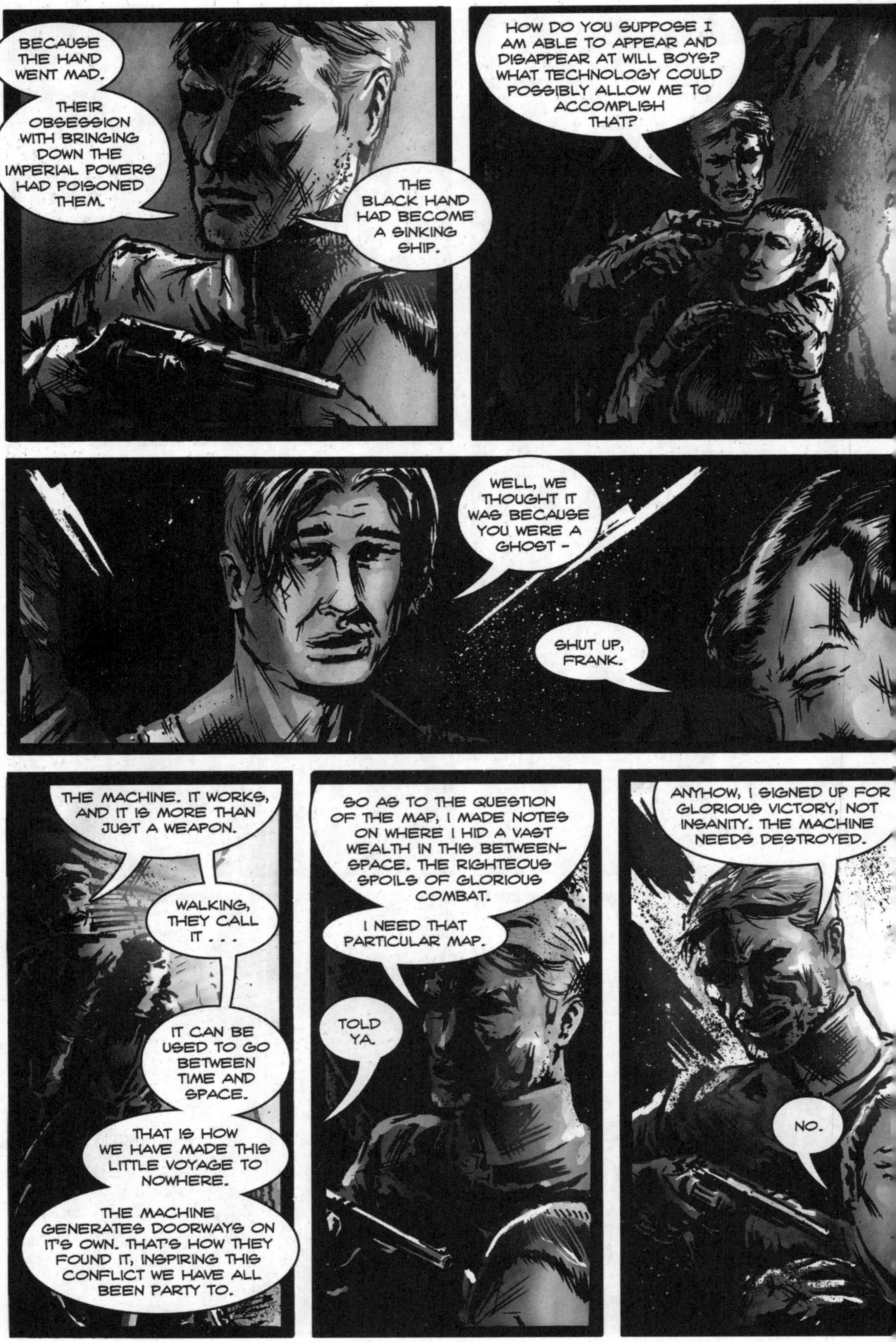
BECAUSE THE HAND WENT MAD.
THEIR OBSESSION WITH BRINGING DOWN THE IMPERIAL POWERS HAD POISONED THEM.
THE BLACK HAND HAD BECOME A SINKING SHIP.
HOW DO YOU SUPPOSE I AM ABLE TO APPEAR AND DISAPPEAR AT WILL BOYS? WHAT TECHNOLOGY COULD POSSIBLY ALLOW ME TO ACCOMPLISH THAT?
WELL, WE THOUGHT IT WAS BECAUSE YOU WERE A GHOST -
SHUT UP, FRANK.
THE MACHINE. IT WORKS, AND IT IS MORE THAN JUST A WEAPON.
WALKING, THEY CALL IT . . .
IT CAN BE USED TO GO BETWEEN TIME AND SPACE.
THAT IS HOW WE HAVE MADE THIS LITTLE VOYAGE TO NOWHERE.
THE MACHINE GENERATES DOORWAYS ON IT'S OWN. THAT'S HOW THEY FOUND IT, INSPIRING THIS CONFLICT WE HAVE ALL BEEN PARTY TO.
SO AS TO THE QUESTION OF THE MAP, I MADE NOTES ON WHERE I HID A VAST WEALTH IN THIS BETWEEN-SPACE. THE RIGHTEOUS SPOILS OF GLORIOUS COMBAT.
I NEED THAT PARTICULAR MAP.
TOLD YA.
ANYHOW, I SIGNED UP FOR GLORIOUS VICTORY, NOT INSANITY. THE MACHINE NEEDS DESTROYED.
NO.

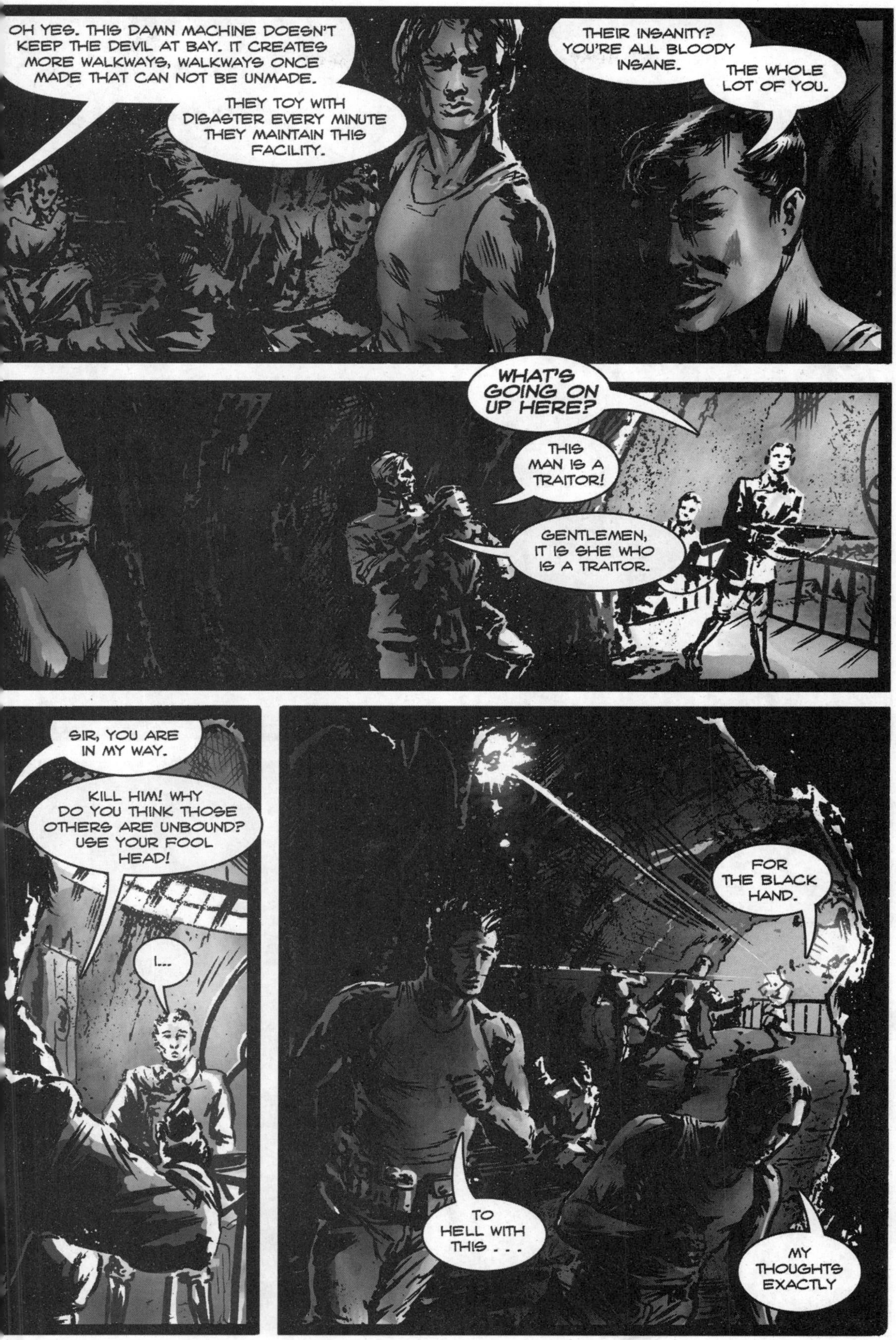
OH YES. THIS DAMN MACHINE DOESN'T KEEP THE DEVIL AT BAY. IT CREATES MORE WALKWAYS, WALKWAYS ONCE MADE THAT CAN NOT BE UNMADE.
THEY TOY WITH DISASTER EVERY MINUTE THEY MAINTAIN THIS FACILITY.
THEIR INSANITY? YOU'RE ALL BLOODY INSANE.
THE WHOLE LOT OF YOU.
WHAT'S GOING ON UP HERE?
THIS MAN IS A TRAITOR!
GENTLEMEN, IT IS SHE WHO IS A TRAITOR.
SIR, YOU ARE IN MY WAY.
KILL HIM! WHY DO YOU THINK THOSE OTHERS ARE UNBOUND? USE YOUR FOOL HEAD!
I...
FOR THE BLACK HAND.
TO HELL WITH THIS . . .
MY THOUGHTS EXACTLY

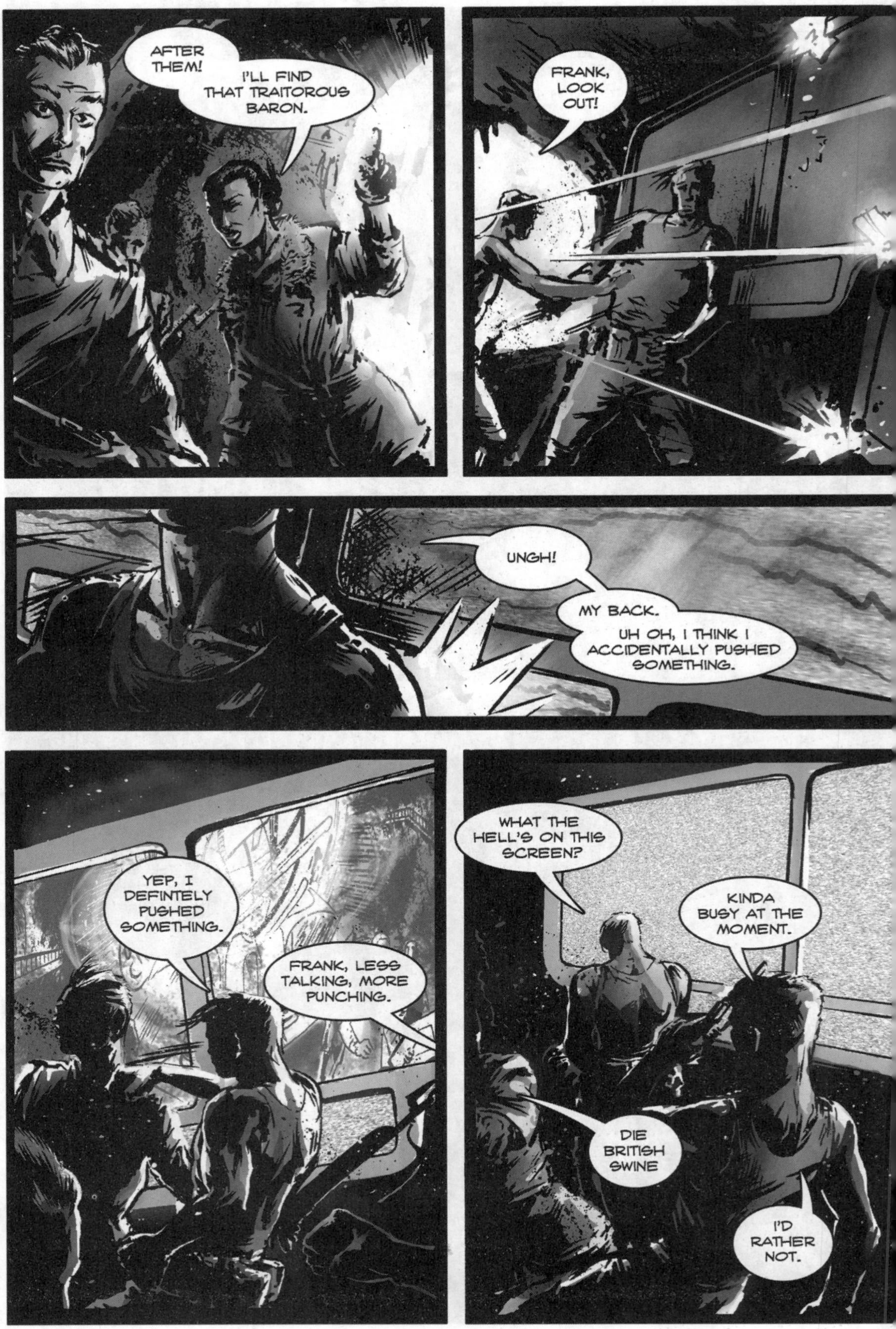
AFTER THEM!
I'LL FIND THAT TRAITOROUS BARON.
FRANK, LOOK OUT!
UNGH!
MY BACK.
UH OH, I THINK I ACCIDENTALLY PUSHED SOMETHING.
YEP, I DEFINTELY PUSHED SOMETHING.
FRANK, LESS TALKING, MORE PUNCHING.
WHAT THE HELL'S ON THIS SCREEN?
KINDA BUSY AT THE MOMENT.
DIE BRITISH SWINE
I'D RATHER NOT.

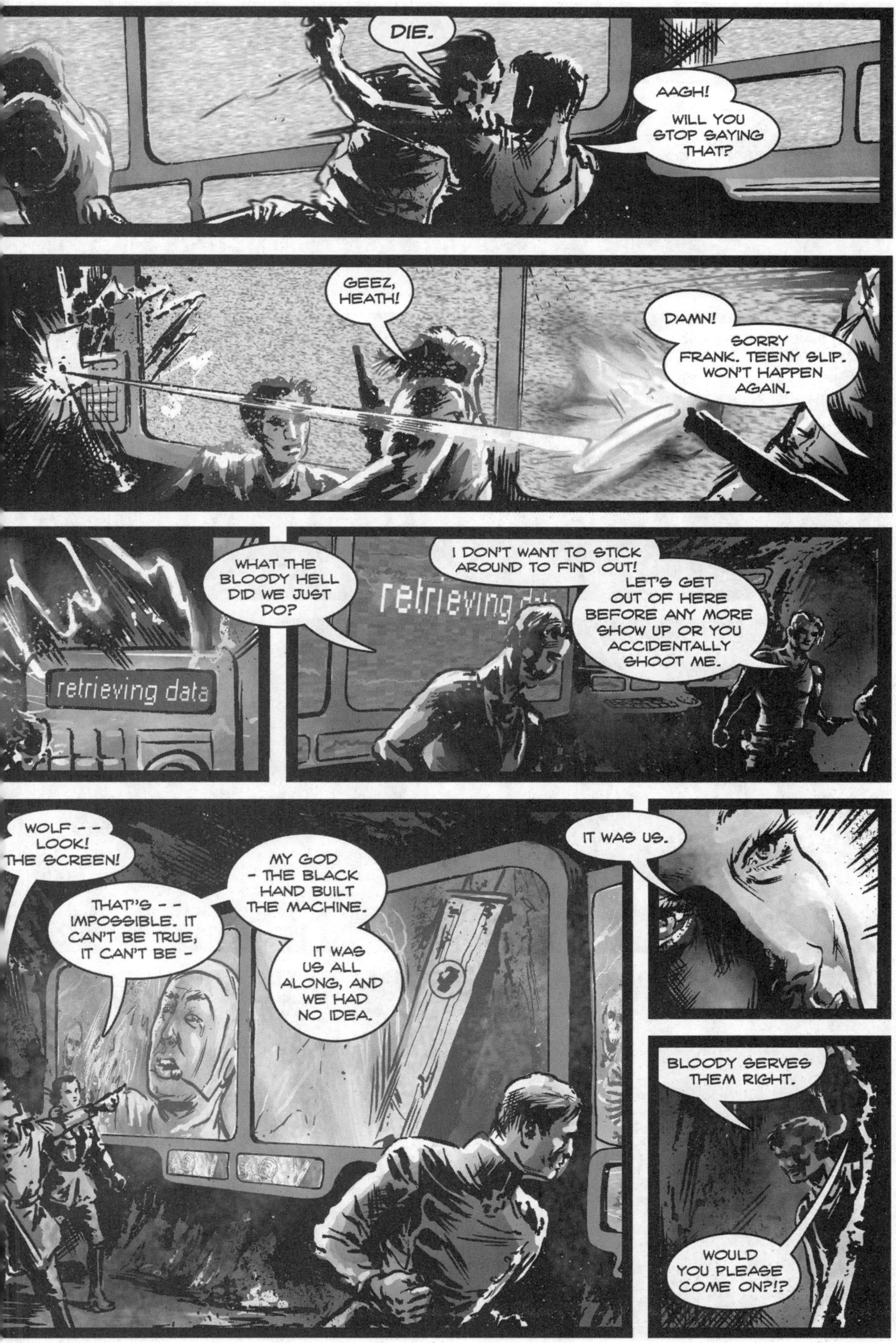
DIE.
AAGH!
WILL YOU STOP SAYING THAT?
GEEZ, HEATH!
DAMN!
SORRY FRANK. TEENY SLIP. WON'T HAPPEN AGAIN.
retrieving data
WHAT THE BLOODY HELL DID WE JUST DO?
retrieving d
I DON'T WANT TO STICK AROUND TO FIND OUT!
LET'S GET OUT OF HERE BEFORE ANY MORE SHOW UP OR YOU ACCIDENTALLY SHOOT ME.
WOLF - - LOOK! THE SCREEN!
THAT'S - - IMPOSSIBLE. IT CAN'T BE TRUE, IT CAN'T BE -
MY GOD - THE BLACK HAND BUILT THE MACHINE.
IT WAS US ALL ALONG, AND WE HAD NO IDEA.
IT WAS US.
BLOODY SERVES THEM RIGHT.
WOULD YOU PLEASE COME ON?!?

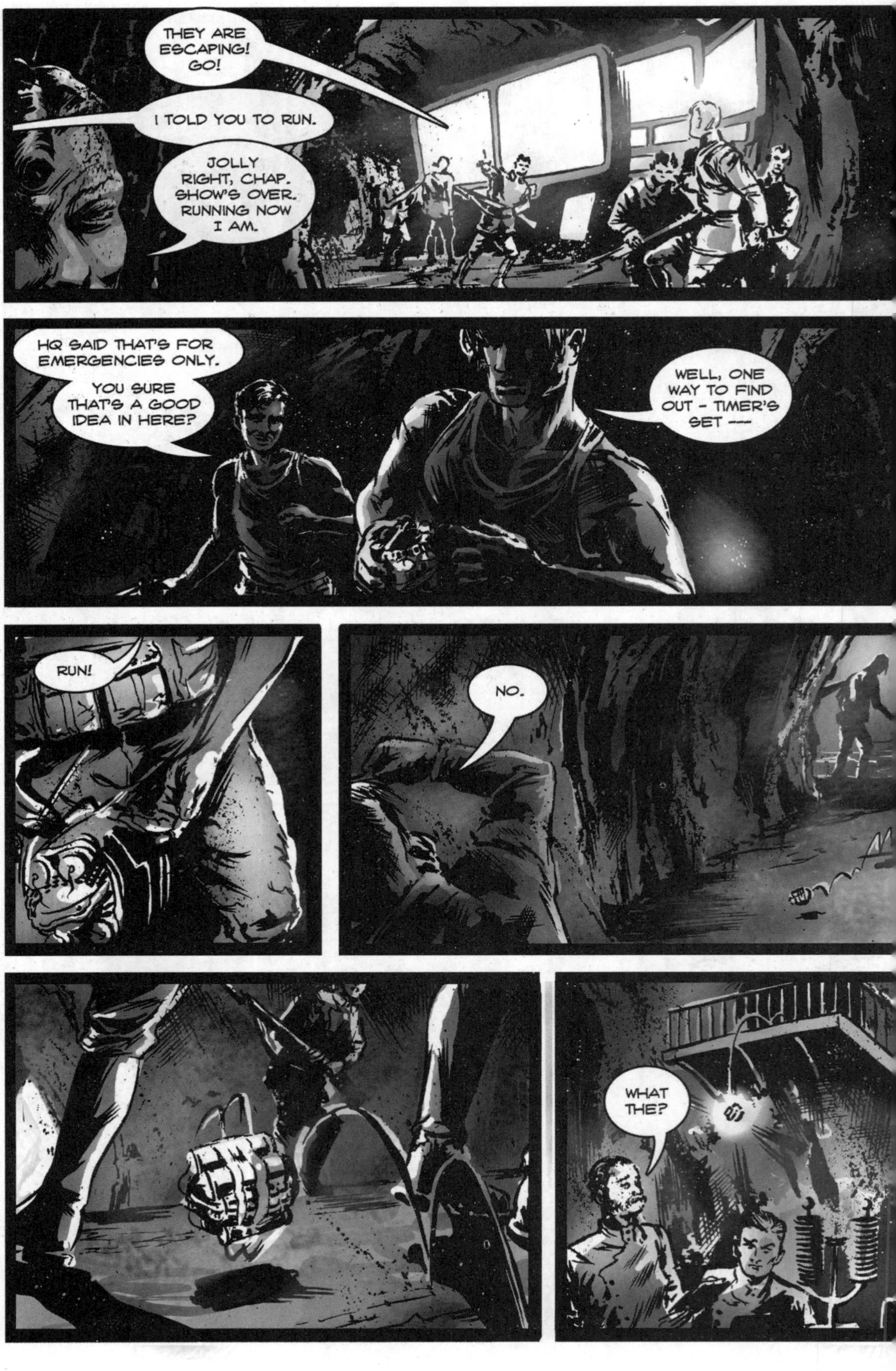
THEY ARE ESCAPING! GO!
I TOLD YOU TO RUN.
JOLLY RIGHT, CHAP. SHOW'S OVER. RUNNING NOW I AM.
HQ SAID THAT'S FOR EMERGENCIES ONLY.
YOU SURE THAT'S A GOOD IDEA IN HERE?
WELL, ONE WAY TO FIND OUT - TIMER'S SET ---
RUN!
NO.
WHAT THE?

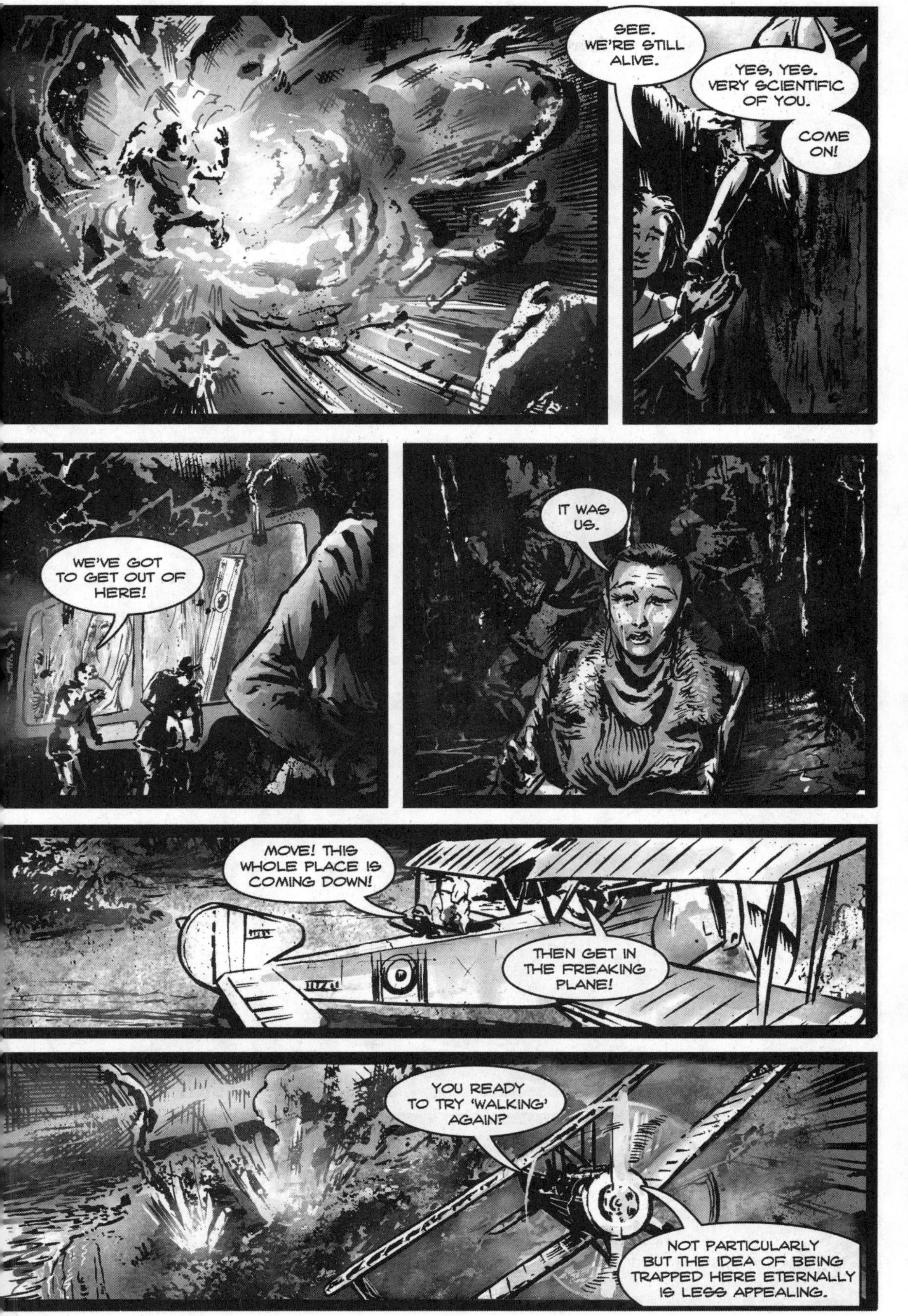
SEE. WE'RE STILL ALIVE.
YES, YES. VERY SCIENTIFIC OF YOU.
COME ON!
WE'VE GOT TO GET OUT OF HERE!
IT WAS US.
MOVE! THIS WHOLE PLACE IS COMING DOWN!
THEN GET IN THE FREAKING PLANE!
YOU READY TO TRY 'WALKING' AGAIN?
NOT PARTICULARLY BUT THE IDEA OF BEING TRAPPED HERE ETERNALLY IS LESS APPEALING.

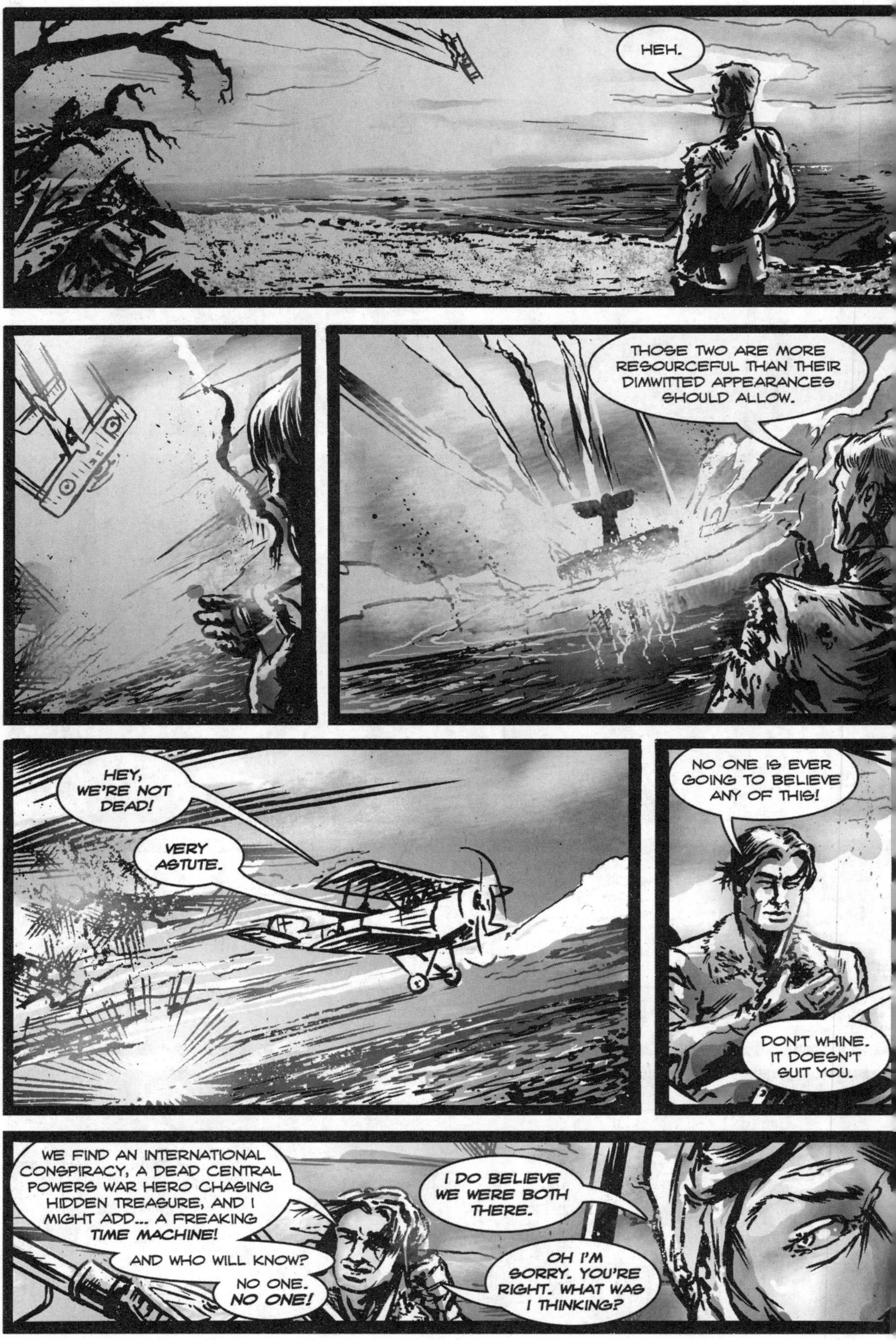
HEH.
THOSE TWO ARE MORE RESOURCEFUL THAN THEIR DIMWITTED APPEARANCES SHOULD ALLOW.
HEY, WE'RE NOT DEAD!
VERY ASTUTE.
NO ONE IS EVER GOING TO BELIEVE ANY OF THIS!
DON'T WHINE. IT DOESN'T SUIT YOU.
WE FIND AN INTERNATIONAL CONSPIRACY, A DEAD CENTRAL POWERS WAR HERO CHASING HIDDEN TREASURE, AND I MIGHT ADD... A FREAKING TIME MACHINE!
I DO BELIEVE WE WERE BOTH THERE.
AND WHO WILL KNOW?
NO ONE. NO ONE!
OH I'M SORRY. YOU'RE RIGHT. WHAT WAS I THINKING?

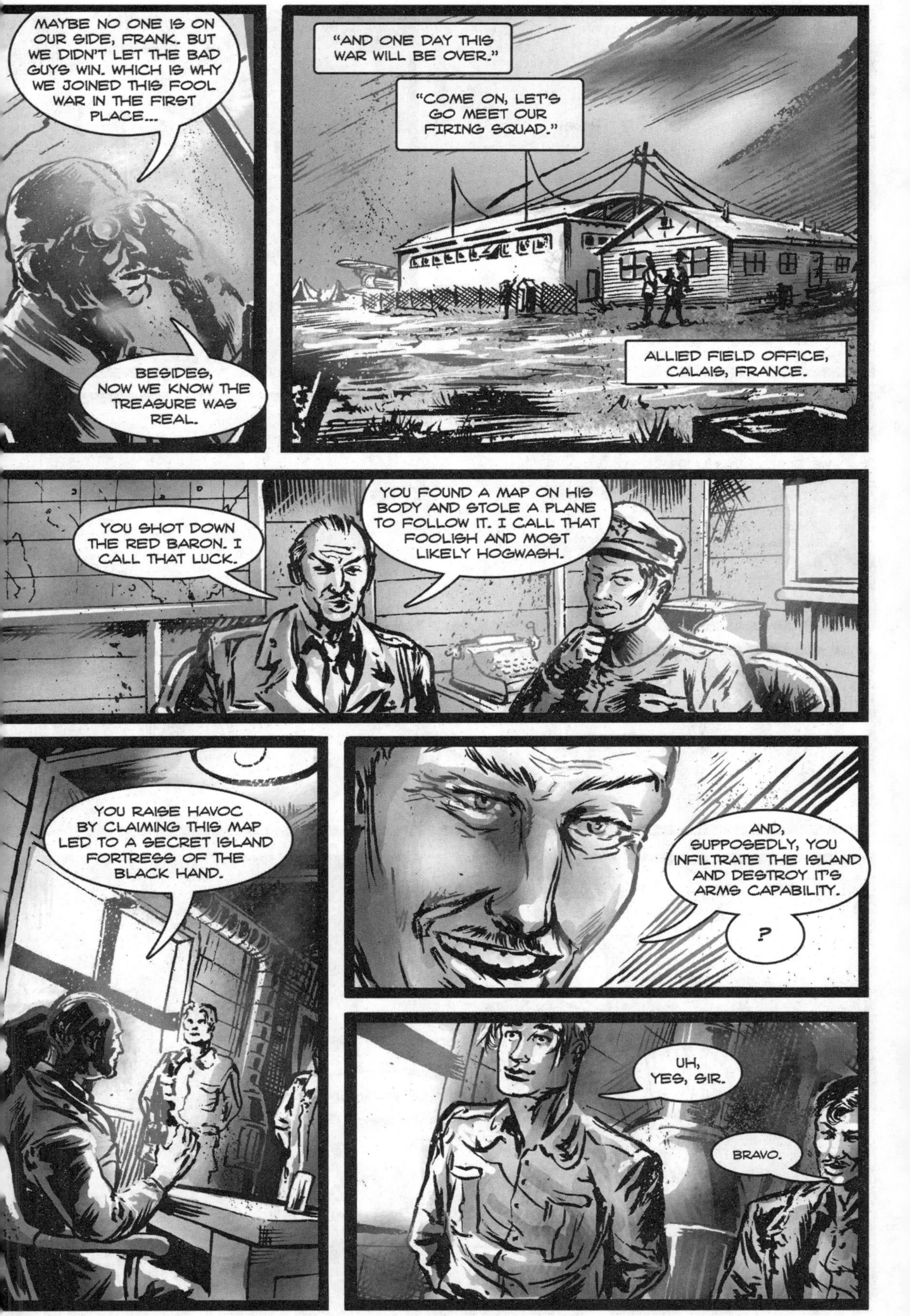
MAYBE NO ONE IS ON OUR SIDE, FRANK. BUT WE DIDN'T LET THE BAD GUYS WIN. WHICH IS WHY WE JOINED THIS FOOL WAR IN THE FIRST PLACE...
BESIDES, NOW WE KNOW THE TREASURE WAS REAL.
"AND ONE DAY THIS WAR WILL BE OVER."
"COME ON, LET'S GO MEET OUR FIRING SQUAD."
ALLIED FIELD OFFICE, CALAIS, FRANCE.
YOU SHOT DOWN THE RED BARON. I CALL THAT LUCK.
YOU FOUND A MAP ON HIS BODY AND STOLE A PLANE TO FOLLOW IT. I CALL THAT FOOLISH AND MOST LIKELY HOGWASH.
YOU RAISE HAVOC BY CLAIMING THIS MAP LED TO A SECRET ISLAND FORTRESS OF THE BLACK HAND.
AND, SUPPOSEDLY, YOU INFILTRATE THE ISLAND AND DESTROY IT'S ARMS CAPABILITY.
?
UH, YES, SIR.
BRAVO.

SO, THE MAJOR AND I ARE INVESTING YOU AS OFFICERS OF THE ALLIED INTELLIGENCE FORCE.

SIR, THANK YOU, SIR!

WHAT?!?!

I FORGOT - YOU'RE LUCKY WE DISCOVERED THE RED BARON WAS STILL ALIVE, AND THAT YOU CONVINCED HIM TO SEEK ASYLUM WITH THE ALLIES. THAT WAS A BRILLIANT PIECE OF WORK!

BECAUSE, IF HE HADN'T CORROBORATED EVERYTHING IN YOUR REPORT I'D CALL YOU DAMN FOOL LIARS.

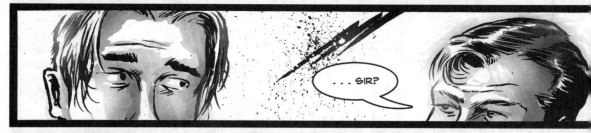

...SIR?

AH, HERE HE IS NOW. BARON VON RICHTHOVEN?

I'VE COME TO DISCUSS THE TERMS OF MY ASYLUM, MAJOR.

VERY GOOD.

GENTLEMEN.

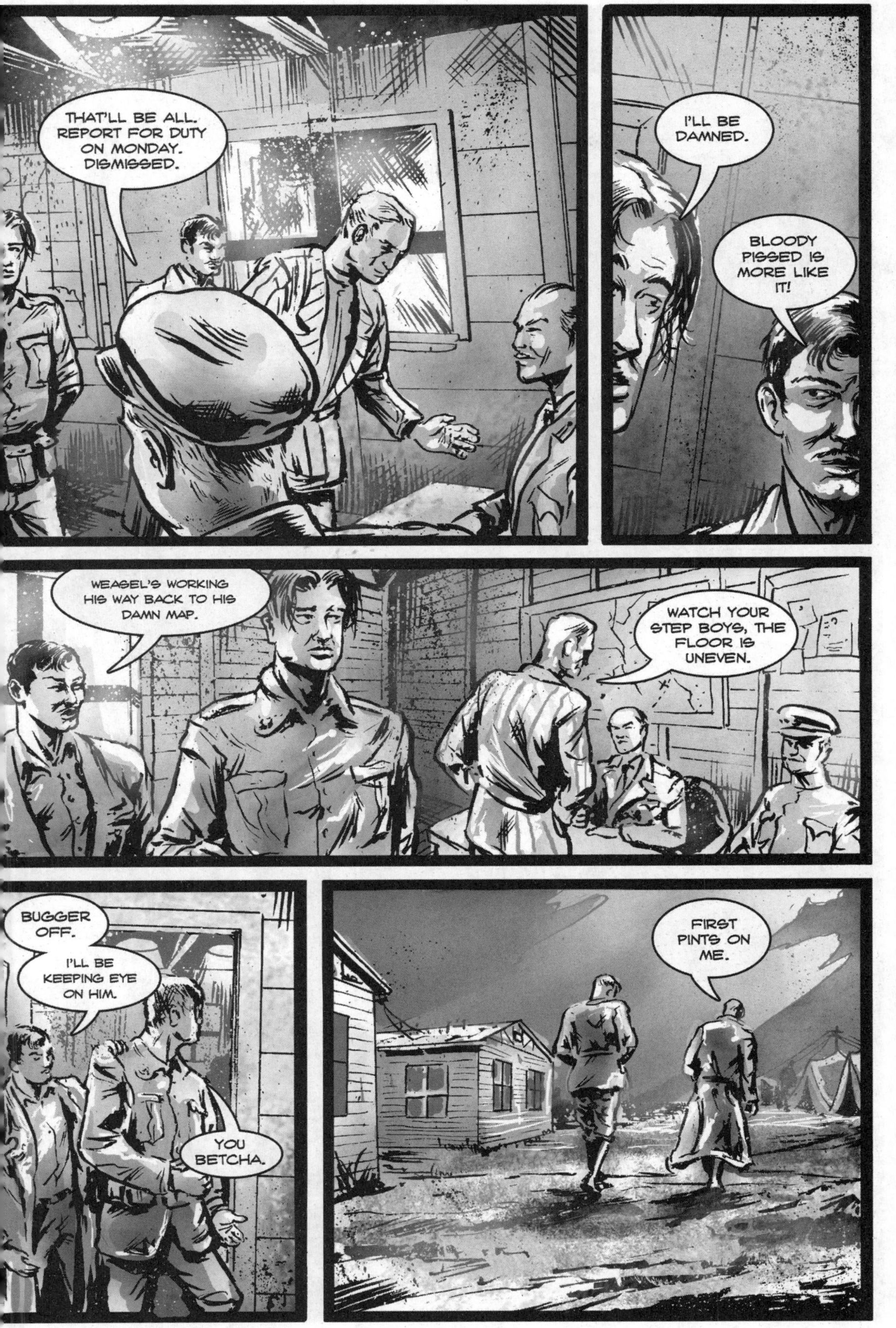
THAT'LL BE ALL. REPORT FOR DUTY ON MONDAY. DISMISSED.
I'LL BE DAMNED.
BLOODY PISSED IS MORE LIKE IT!
WEASEL'S WORKING HIS WAY BACK TO HIS DAMN MAP.
WATCH YOUR STEP BOYS, THE FLOOR IS UNEVEN.
BUGGER OFF.
I'LL BE KEEPING EYE ON HIM.
YOU BETCHA.
FIRST PINTS ON ME.

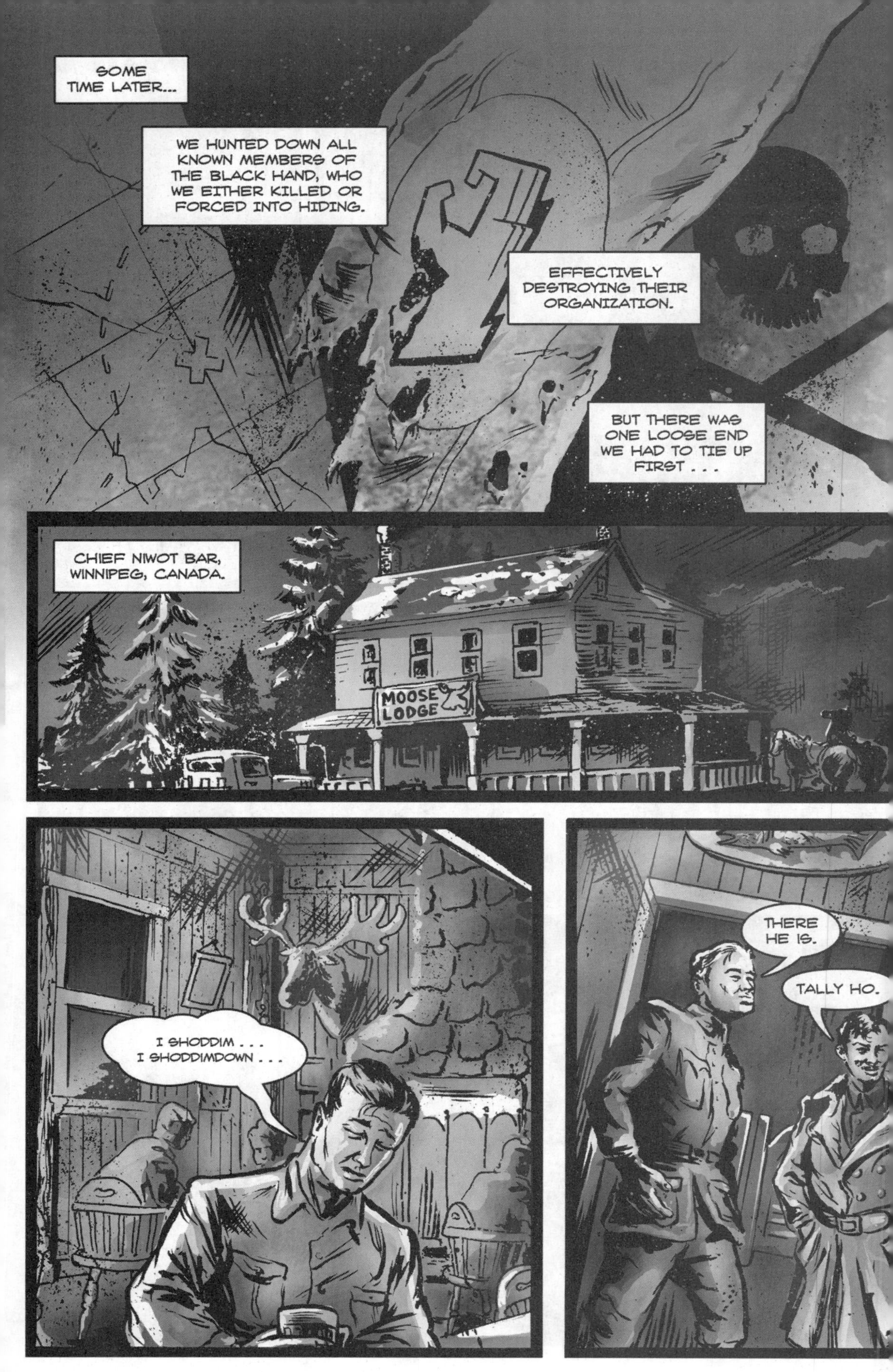

SOME TIME LATER...
WE HUNTED DOWN ALL KNOWN MEMBERS OF THE BLACK HAND, WHO WE EITHER KILLED OR FORCED INTO HIDING.
EFFECTIVELY DESTROYING THEIR ORGANIZATION.
BUT THERE WAS ONE LOOSE END WE HAD TO TIE UP FIRST . . .
CHIEF NIWOT BAR, WINNIPEG, CANADA.
MOOSE LODGE
I SHODDIM . . . I SHODDIMDOWN . . .
THERE HE IS.
TALLY HO.

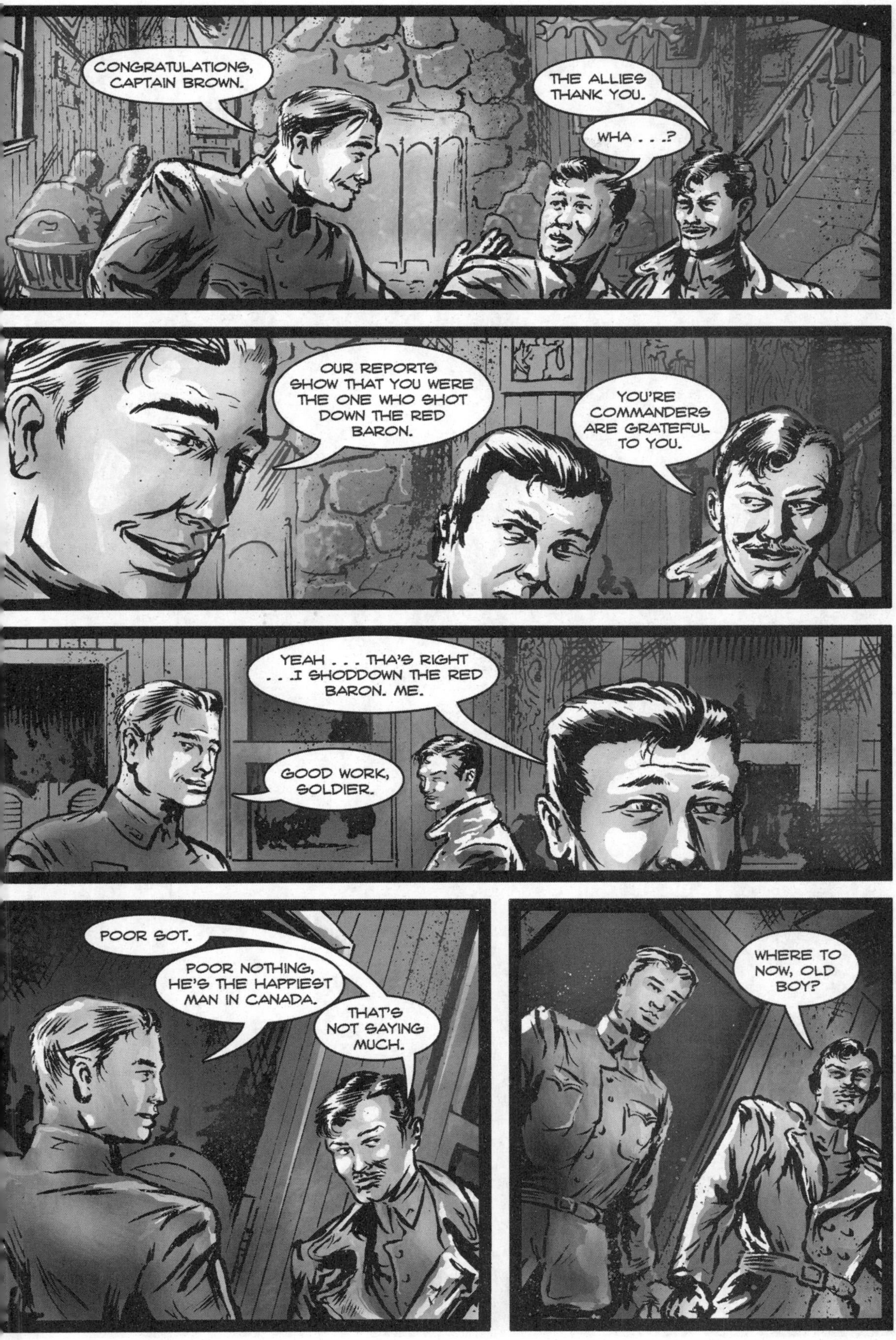
CONGRATULATIONS, CAPTAIN BROWN.
THE ALLIES THANK YOU.
WHA . . .?
OUR REPORTS SHOW THAT YOU WERE THE ONE WHO SHOT DOWN THE RED BARON.
YOU'RE COMMANDERS ARE GRATEFUL TO YOU.
YEAH . . . THA'S RIGHT . . .I SHODDOWN THE RED BARON. ME.
GOOD WORK, SOLDIER.
POOR SOT.
POOR NOTHING, HE'S THE HAPPIEST MAN IN CANADA.
THAT'S NOT SAYING MUCH.
WHERE TO NOW, OLD BOY?

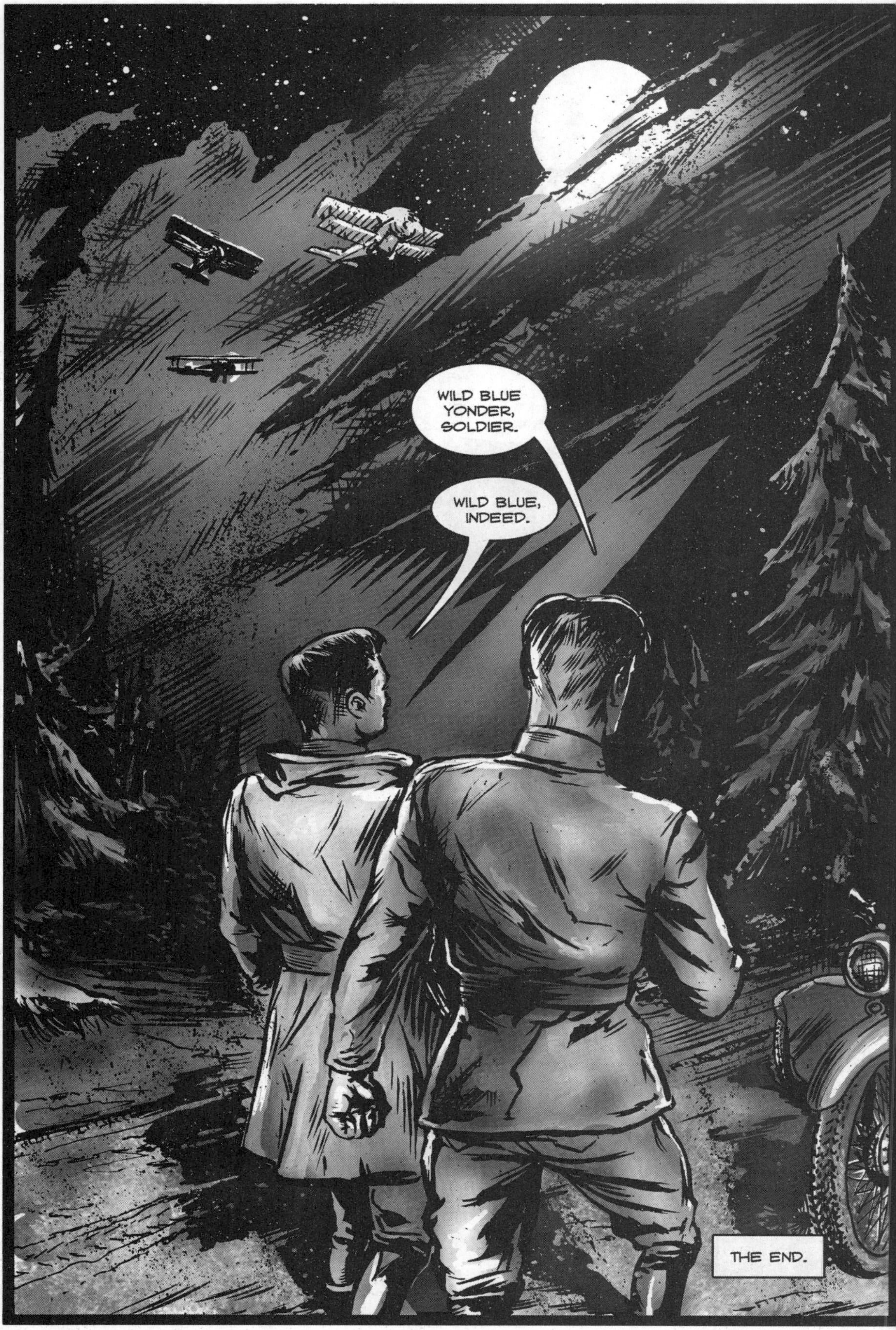
WILD BLUE YONDER, SOLDIER.
WILD BLUE, INDEED.
THE END.

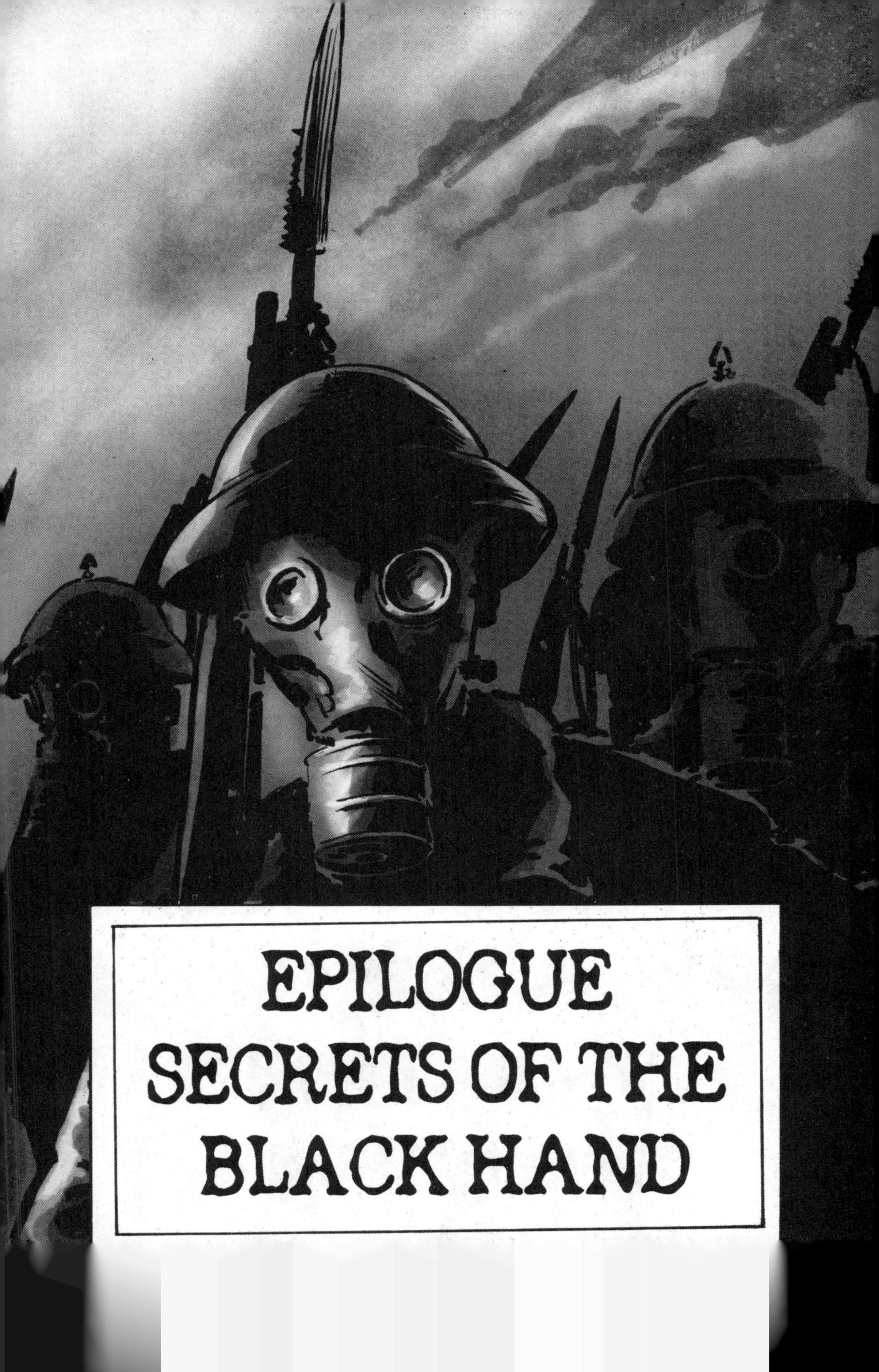
EPILOGUE
SECRETS OF THE
BLACK HAND

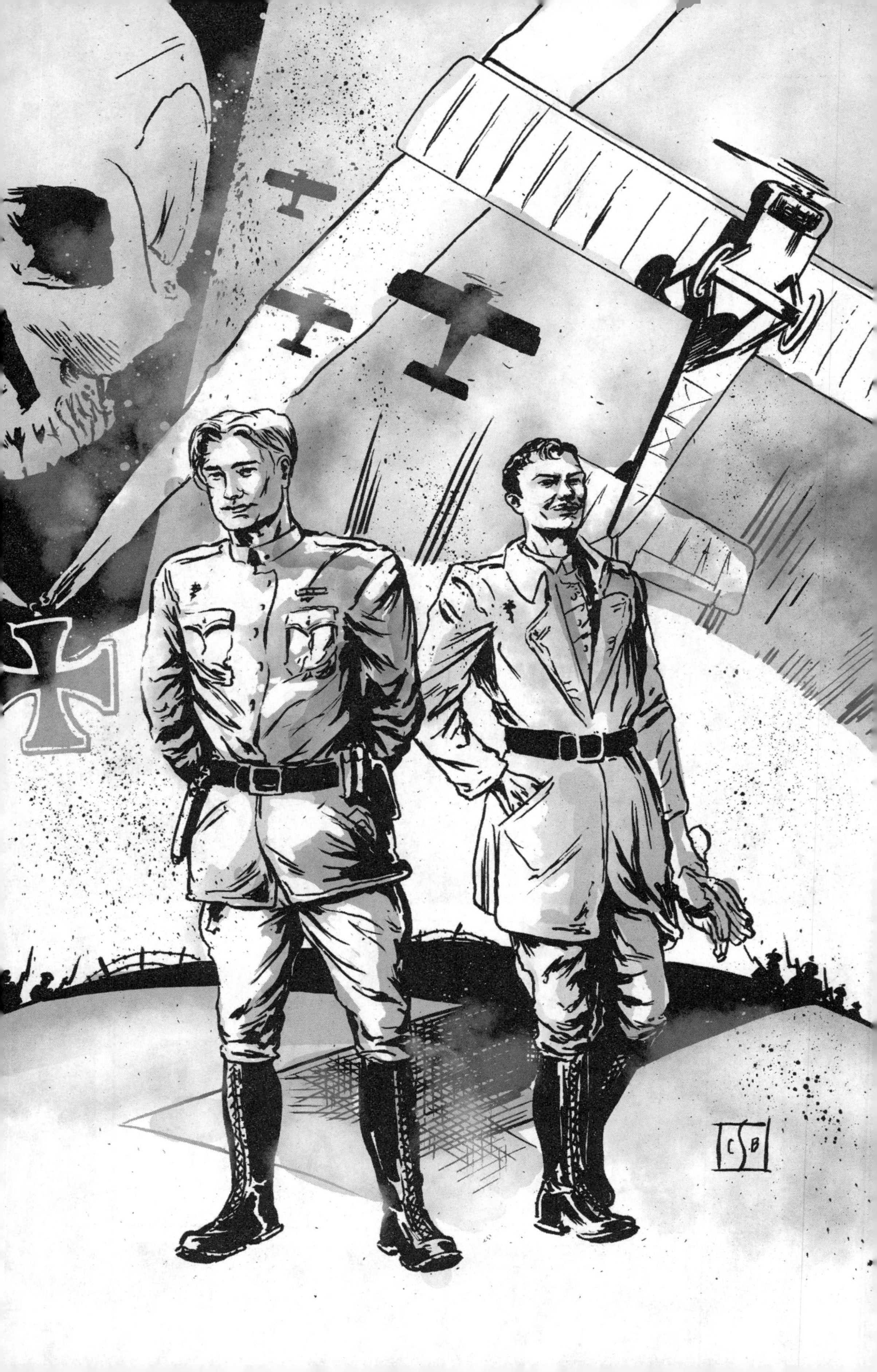

Captain Heath Bennett

Served in her majesty's Royal Air Force before being appointed to the newly formed Allied Intelligence department. Considered by commanding officers to be a capable man in the field as well as an outstanding pilot. Records indicate he may have a certain disregard for the chain of command which may interfere with his execution of orders in the future. This was however taken into consideration by his commanding officers as a possible asset in the field of intelligence gathering.

Along with Private Frank Grayson, was responsible for the major breakthrough uncovering the secret plot of the 'Black Hand'. See attached files 1-37B.2 , 2-37B.2

Private Frank Grayson

Appointed to the Allied Intelligence Department from the rank of private in the US infantry with no prior advancements in rank. Considered a dependable gunner with multiple deployments to the front by his commanding officers. Executes orders given and commands respect from fellow soldiers but lacks leadership skills. Reports filed for using unusual explosive devices in the feild against regulations, but feild journals indicate successful detonations with positive results. See attached files

US.FJ-27.1916-22.23

Along with Captain Heath Bennett, was responsible for the major intelligence breatkthrough uncovering the secret plot of the 'Black Hand'. See attached files 1-38B.1 , 2-38B.1

codename 'Red Baron' apprehended and in custody. interrogation transcripts attached. See files 227.A66

codename 'Wolf 1' Whereabouts unknown. Files referenced in archives cannot be found. Search of EF archives authorized. Awaiting results. Reference file UN-35E.77

The following moving picture reel was produced by the joint Allied Intelligence Department
This information is considered classified.
Do not disseminate.

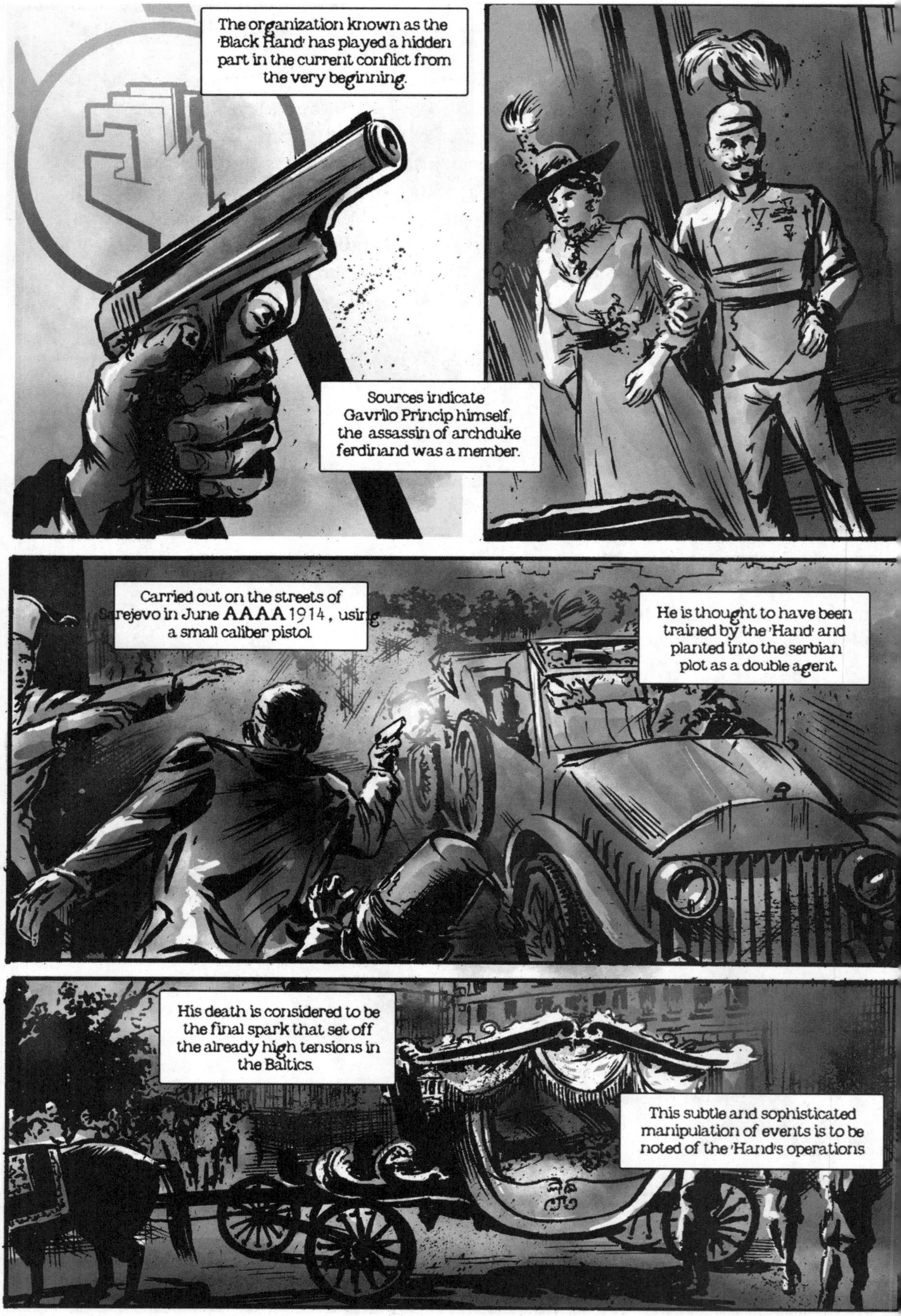
The organization known as the 'Black Hand' has played a hidden part in the current conflict from the very beginning.
Sources indicate Gavrilo Princip himself, the assassin of archduke ferdinand was a member.
Carried out on the streets of Sarejevo in June AAAA 1914, using a small caliber pistol.
He is thought to have been trained by the 'Hand' and planted into the serbian plot as a double agent.
His death is considered to be the final spark that set off the already high tensions in the Baltics.
This subtle and sophisticated manipulation of events is to be noted of the 'Hand's operations

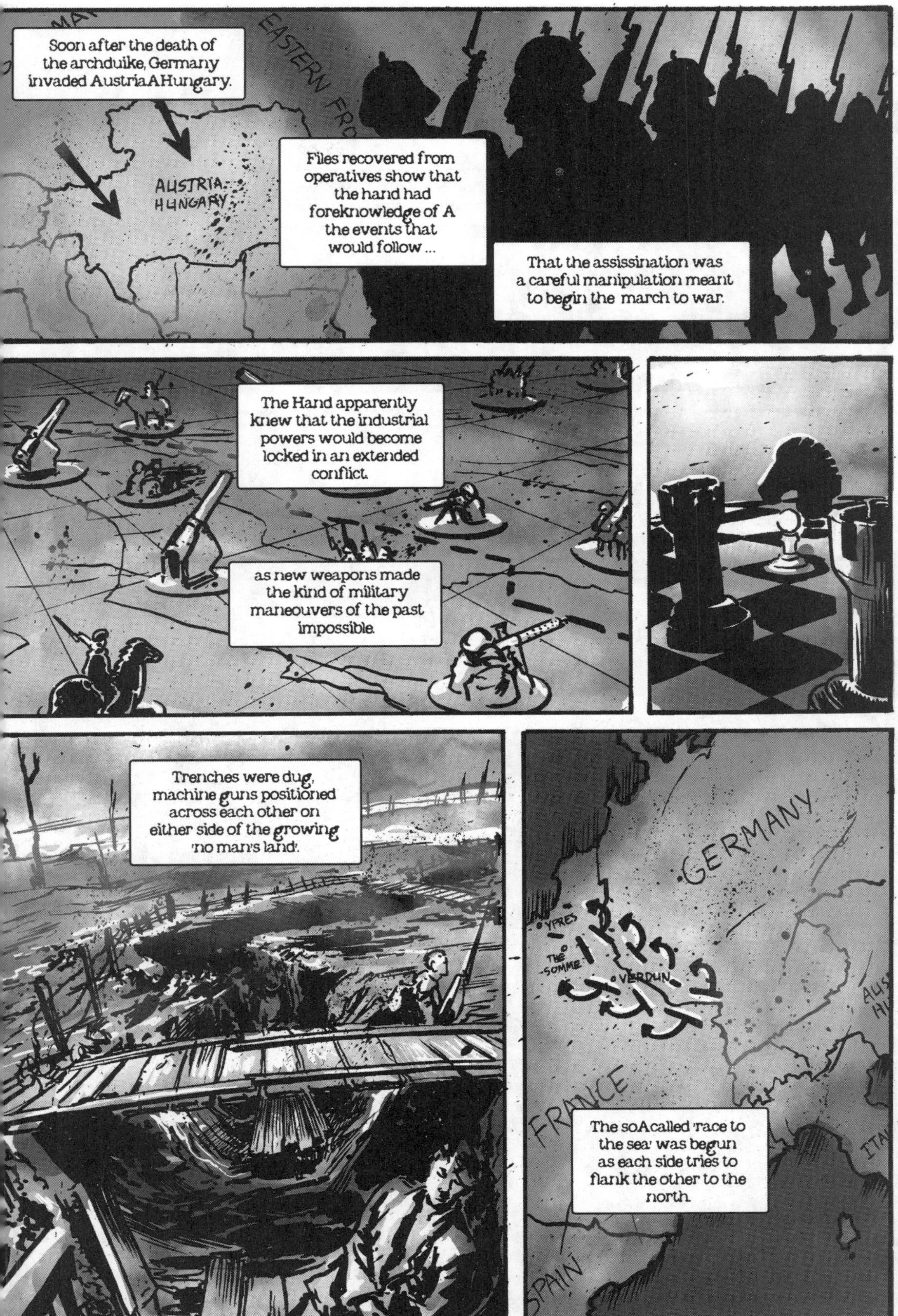
Soon after the death of the archduike, Germany invaded AustriaAHungary.
AUSTRIA HUNGARY
Files recovered from operatives show that the hand had foreknowledge of A the events that would follow ...
That the assissination was a careful manipulation meant to begin the march to war.
The Hand apparently knew that the industrial powers would become locked in an extended conflict.
as new weapons made the kind of military maneouvers of the past impossible.
Trenches were dug, machine guns positioned across each other on either side of the growing 'no man's land'.
GERMANY
YPRES
THE SOMME
VERDUN
FRANCE
SPAIN
The soAcalled 'race to the sea' was begun as each side tries to flank the other to the north.

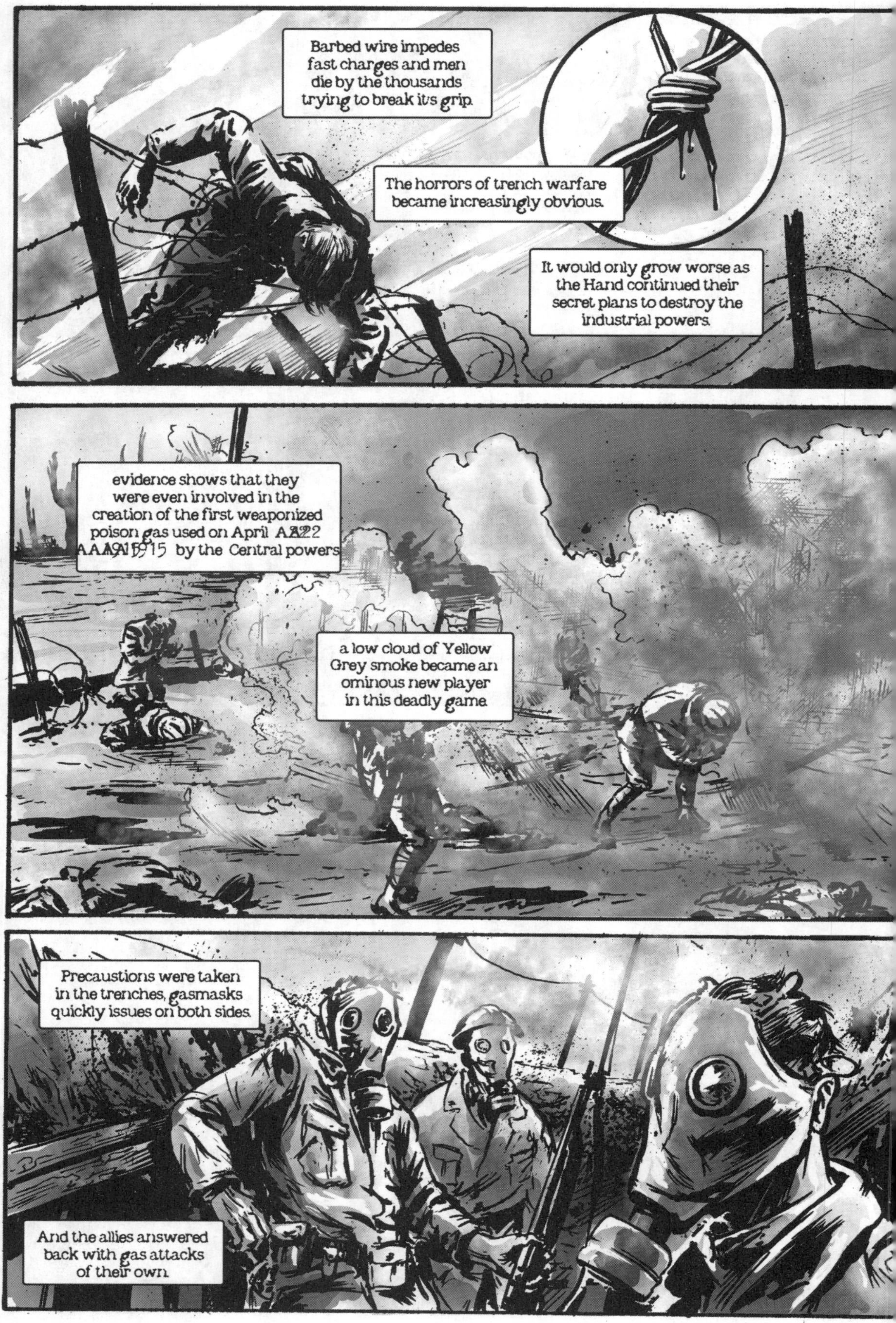
Barbed wire impedes fast charges and men die by the thousands trying to break it's grip.
The horrors of trench warfare became increasingly obvious.
It would only grow worse as the Hand continued their secret plans to destroy the industrial powers.
evidence shows that they were even involved in the creation of the first weaponized poison gas used on April 22 1915 by the Central powers
a low cloud of Yellow Grey smoke became an ominous new player in this deadly game
Precaustions were taken in the trenches, gasmasks quickly issues on both sides.
And the allies answered back with gas attacks of their own

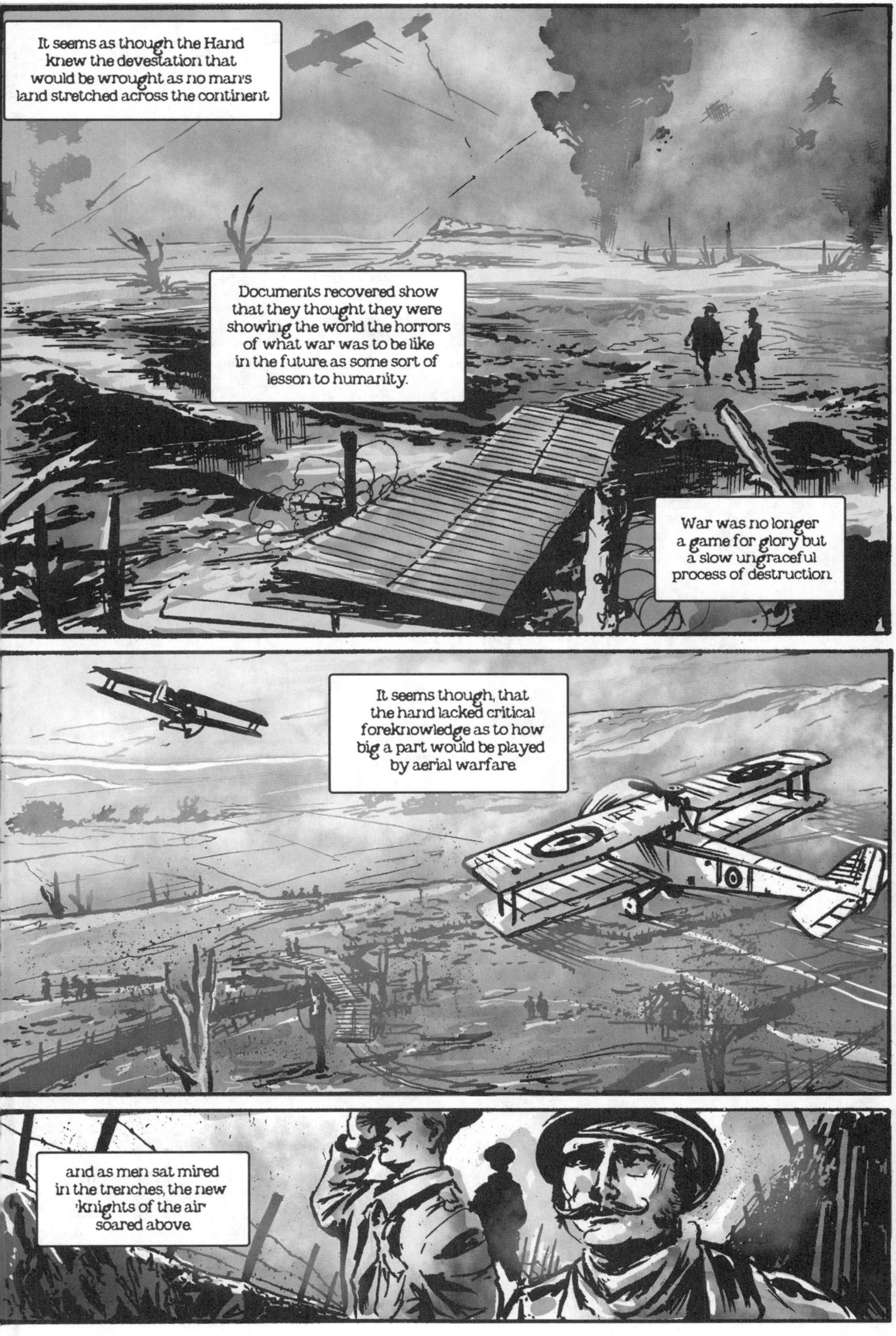
It seems as though the Hand knew the devestation that would be wrought as no man's land stretched across the continent
Documents recovered show that they thought they were showing the world the horrors of what war was to be like in the future as some sort of lesson to humanity.
War was no longer a game for glory but a slow ungraceful process of destruction
It seems though, that the hand lacked critical foreknowledge as to how big a part would be played by aerial warfare
and as men sat mired in the trenches, the new 'knights of the air soared above

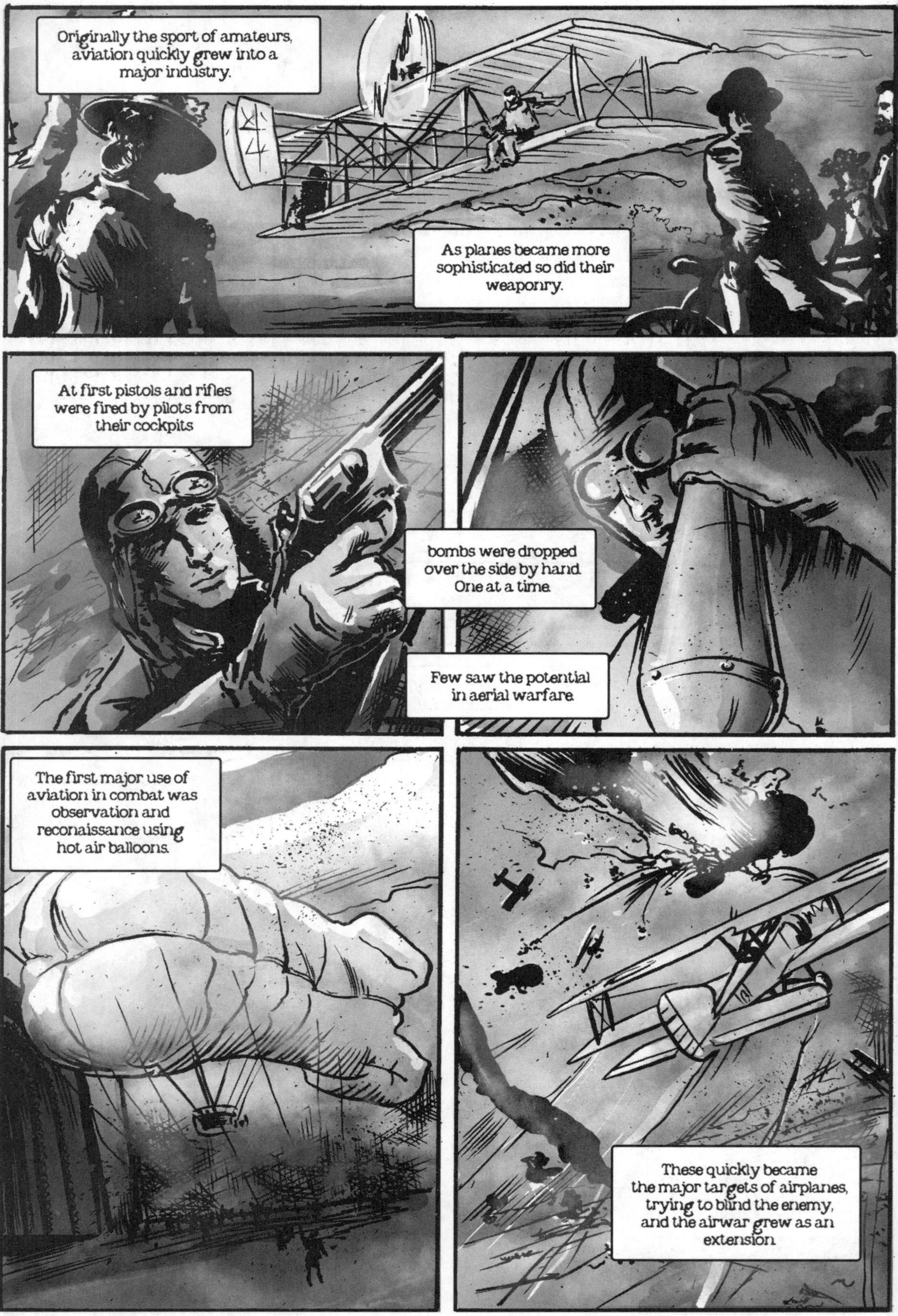
Originally the sport of amateurs, aviation quickly grew into a major industry.
As planes became more sophisticated so did their weaponry.
At first pistols and rifles were fired by pilots from their cockpits
bombs were dropped over the side by hand. One at a time.
Few saw the potential in aerial warfare.
The first major use of aviation in combat was observation and reconaissance using hot air balloons.
These quickly became the major targets of airplanes, trying to blind the enemy, and the airwar grew as an extension.

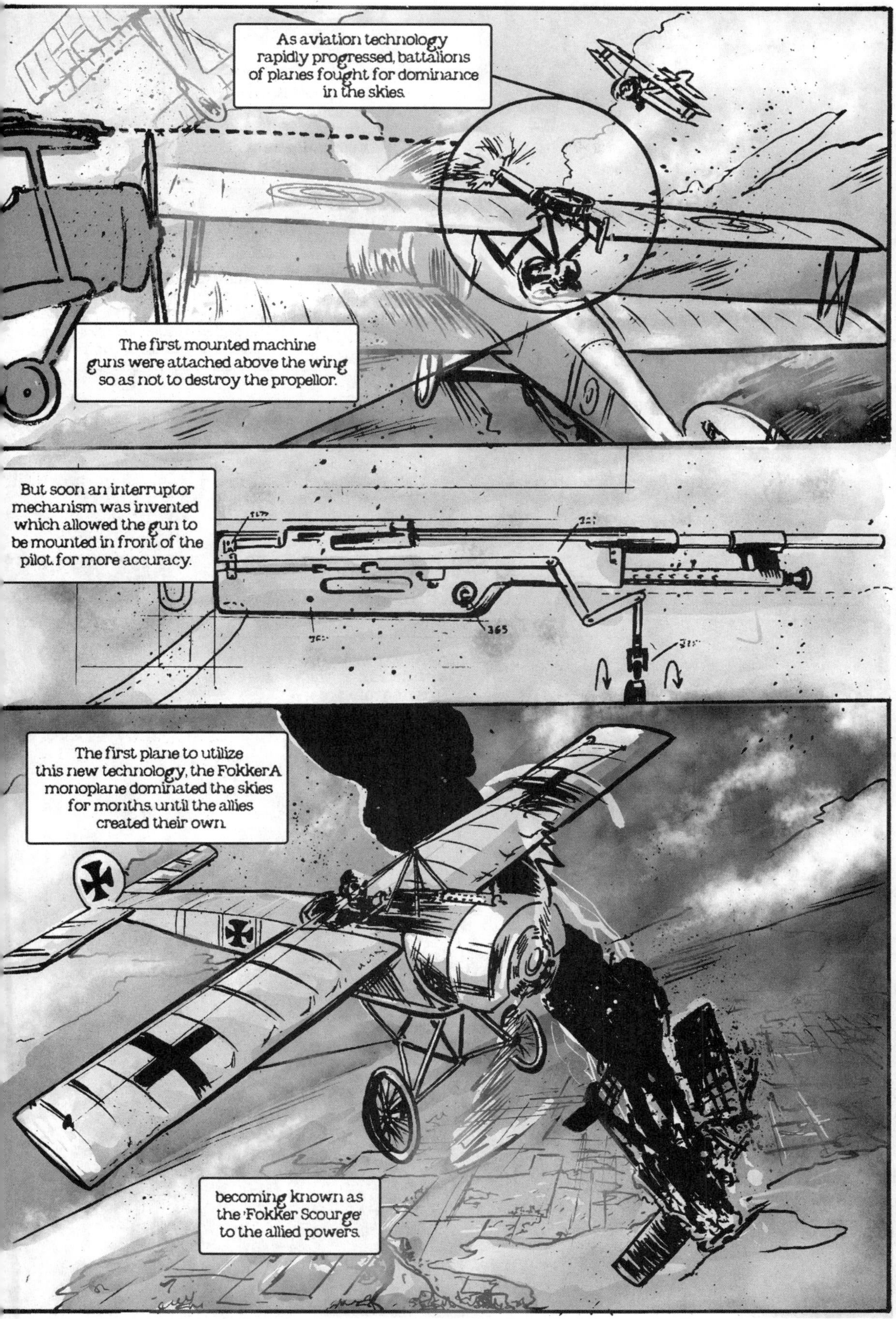
As aviation technology rapidly progressed, battalions of planes fought for dominance in the skies.
The first mounted machine guns were attached above the wing so as not to destroy the propellor.
But soon an interruptor mechanism was invented which allowed the gun to be mounted in front of the pilot for more accuracy.
365
The first plane to utilize this new technology, the Fokker A monoplane dominated the skies for months until the allies created their own
becoming known as the 'Fokker Scourge' to the allied powers.

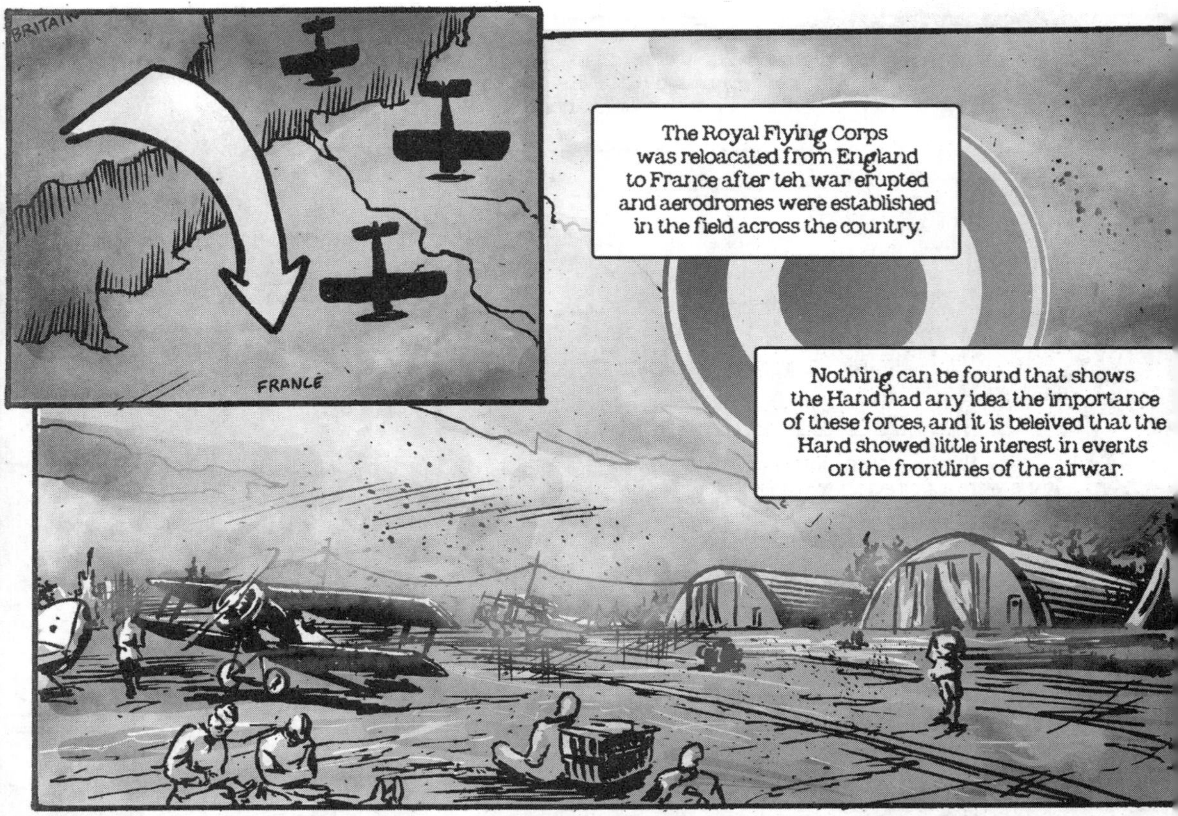
BRITAI
FRANCE
The Royal Flying Corps was reloacated from England to France after teh war erupted and aerodromes were established in the field across the country.
Nothing can be found that shows the Hand had any idea the importance of these forces, and it is beleived that the Hand showed little interest in events on the frontlines of the airwar.

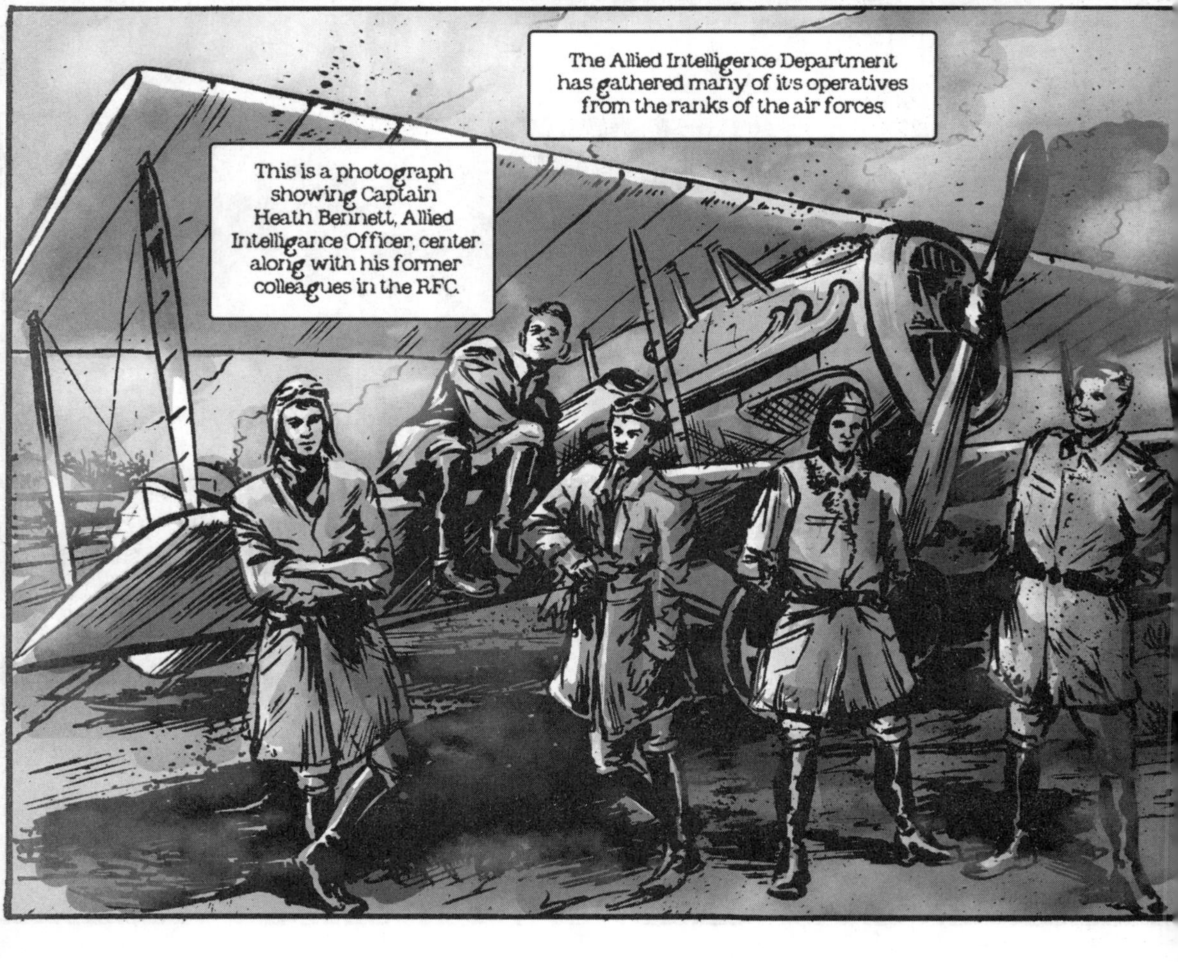
The Allied Intelligence Department has gathered many of it's operatives from the ranks of the air forces.
This is a photograph showing Captain Heath Bennett, Allied Intelligance Officer, center. along with his former colleagues in the RFC.

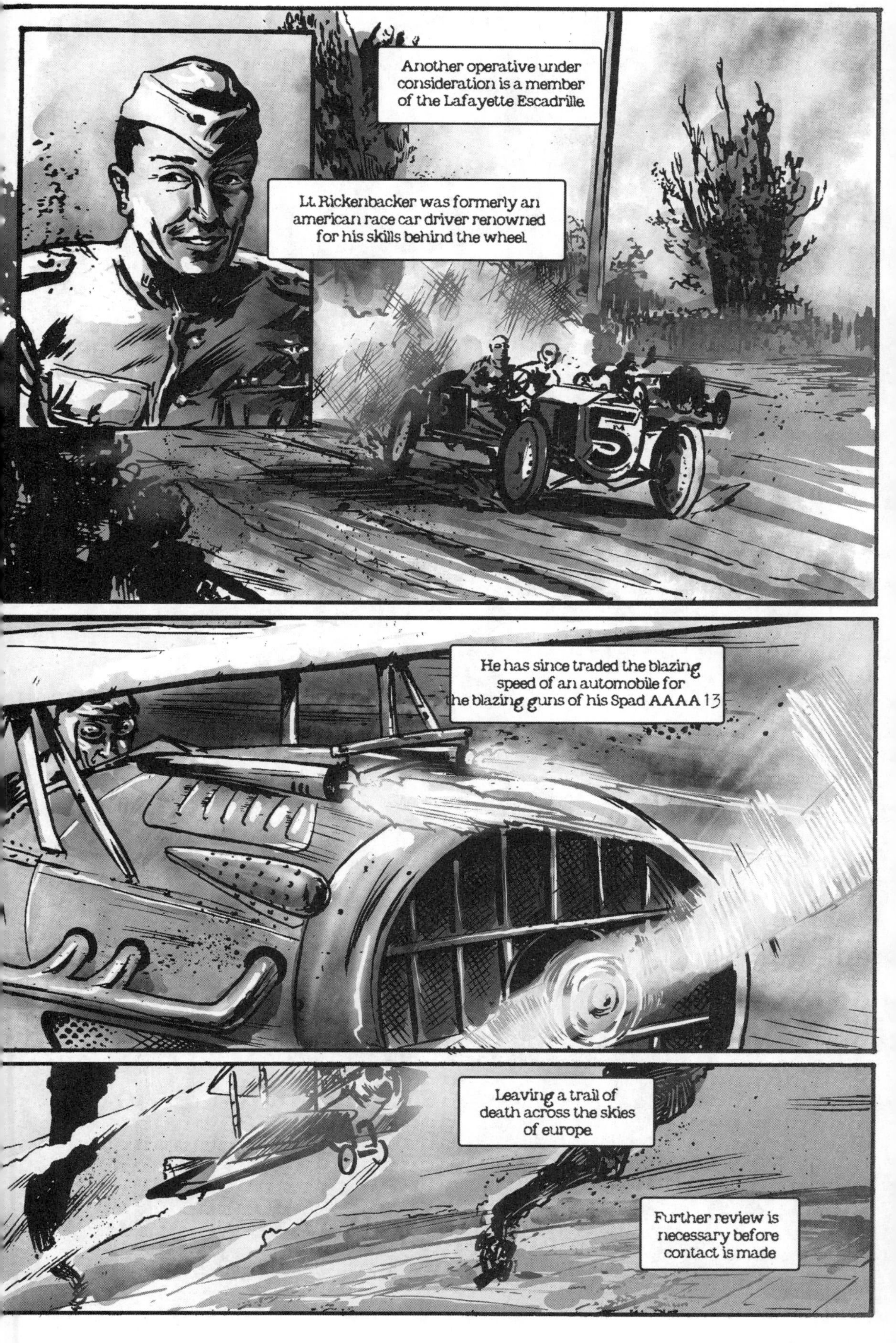

Another operative under consideration is a member of the Lafayette Escadrille
Lt. Rickenbacker was formerly an american race car driver renowned for his skills behind the wheel
He has since traded the blazing speed of an automobile for the blazing guns of his Spad AAAA 13
Leaving a trail of death across the skies of europe
Further review is necessary before contact is made

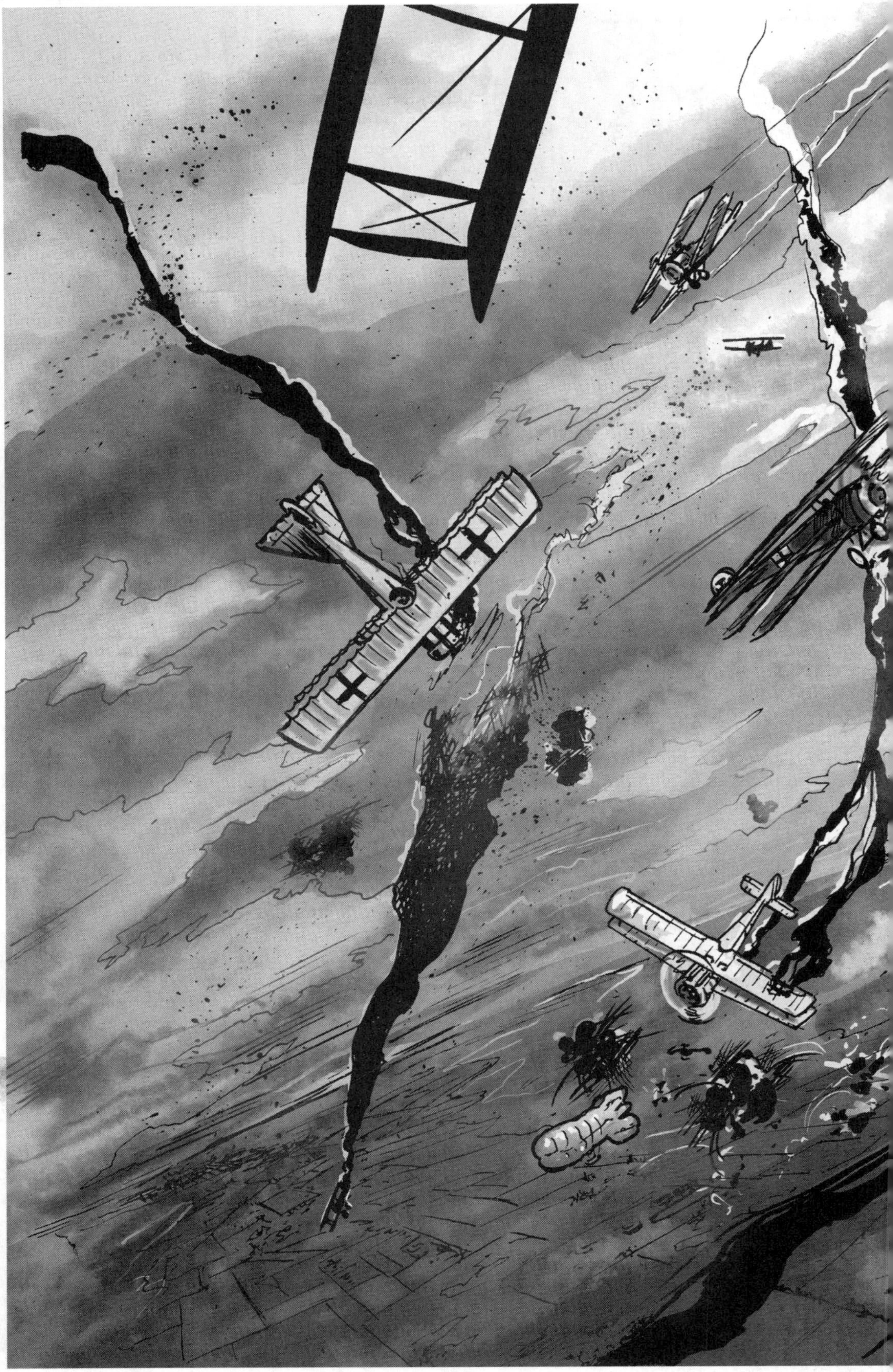

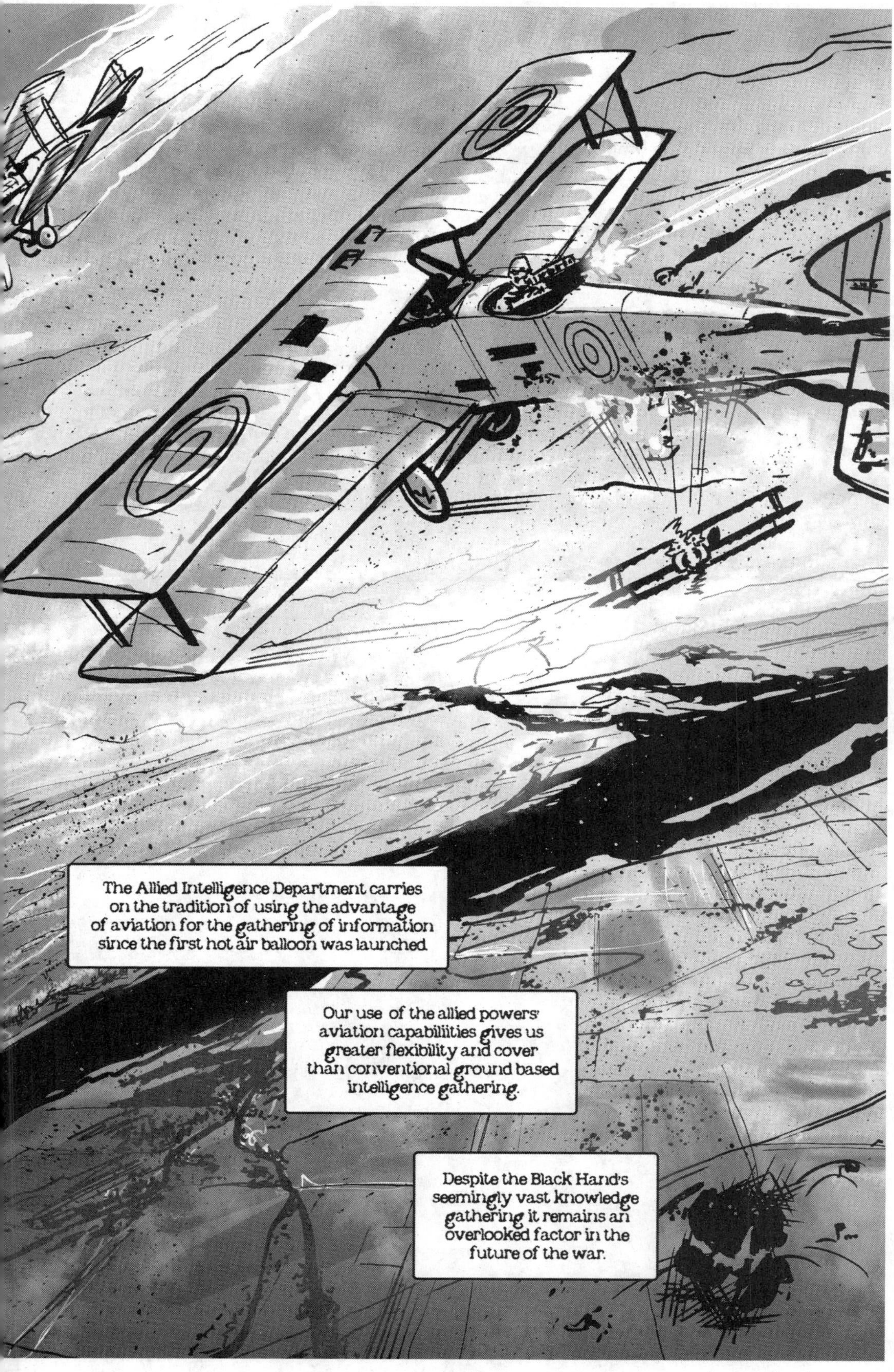
The Allied Intelligence Department carries on the tradition of using the advantage of aviation for the gathering of information since the first hot air balloon was launched
Our use of the allied powers' aviation capabilities gives us greater flexibility and cover than conventional ground based intelligence gathering.
Despite the Black Hand's seemingly vast knowledge gathering it remains an overlooked factor in the future of the war.

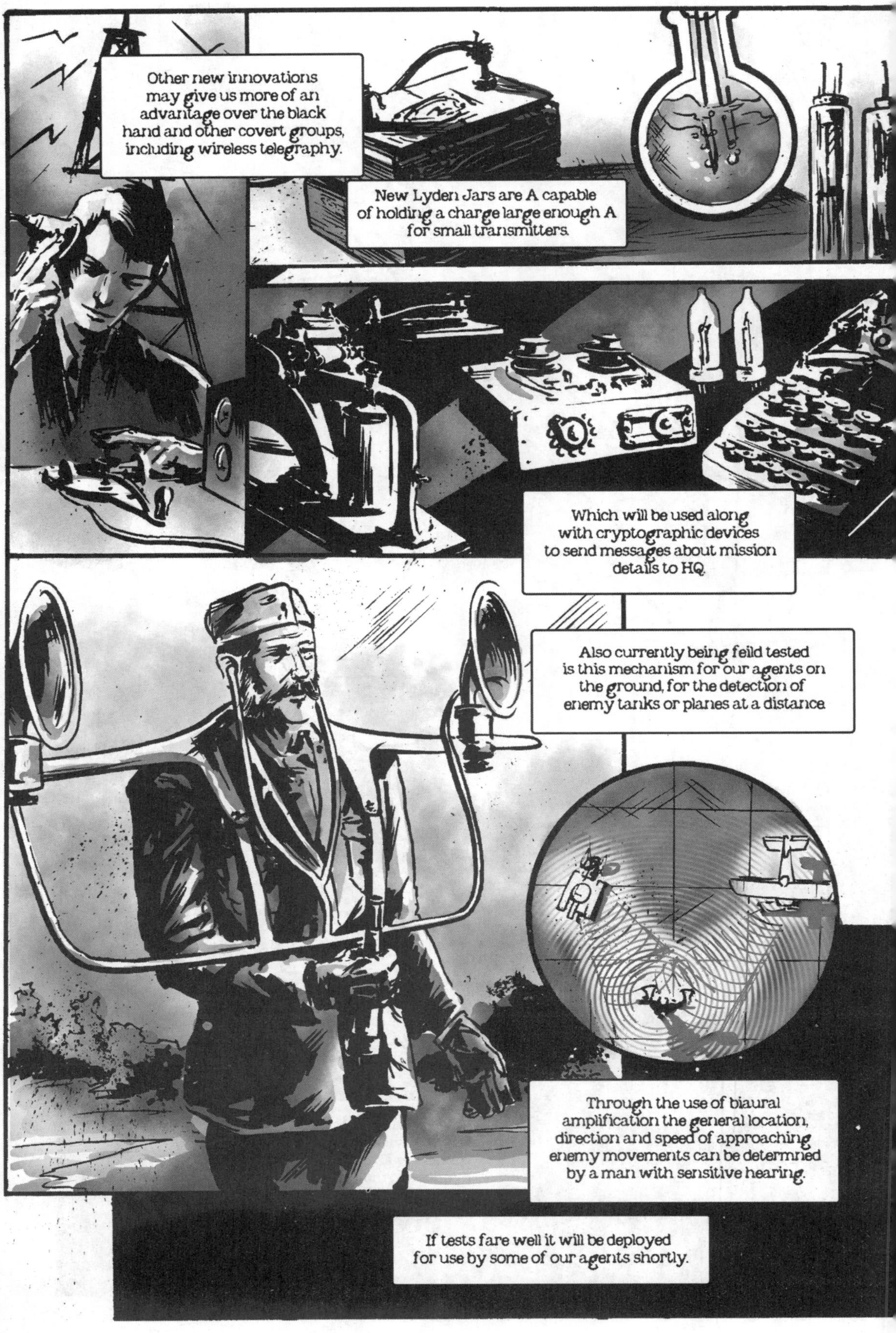
Other new innovations may give us more of an advantage over the black hand and other covert groups, including wireless telegraphy.
New Lyden Jars are A capable of holding a charge large enough A for small transmitters.
Which will be used along with cryptographic devices to send messages about mission details to HQ.
Also currently being feild tested is this mechanism for our agents on the ground, for the detection of enemy tanks or planes at a distance
Through the use of biaural amplification the general location, direction and speed of approaching enemy movements can be determned by a man with sensitive hearing.
If tests fare well it will be deployed for use by some of our agents shortly.

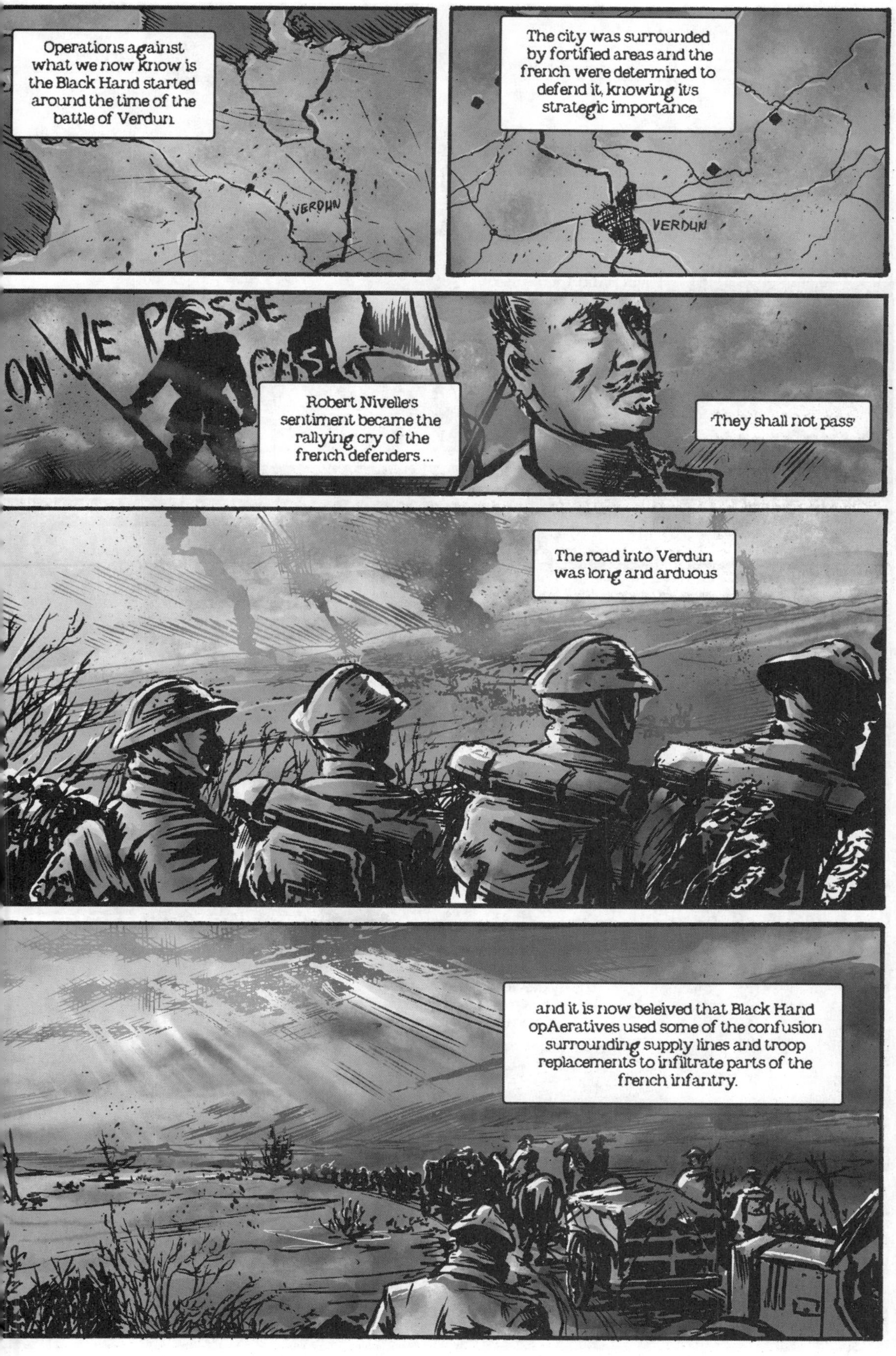
Operations against what we now know is the Black Hand started around the time of the battle of Verdun
VERDUN
The city was surrounded by fortified areas and the french were determined to defend it, knowing it's strategic importance.
VERDUN
ON NE PASSE
Robert Nivelle's sentiment became the rallying cry of the french defenders ...
'They shall not pass'
The road into Verdun was long and arduous
and it is now beleived that Black Hand opAeratives used some of the confusion surrounding supply lines and troop replacements to infiltrate parts of the french infantry.

As the bombinh began Black Hand agents used chaos to steal Allied plans and war documents.

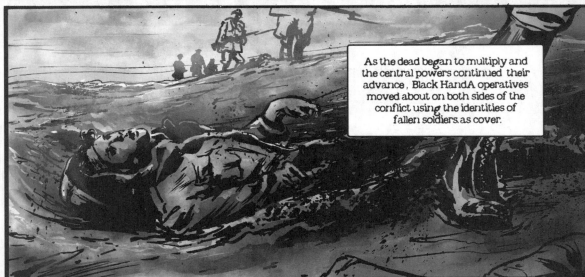

As the dead began to multiply and the central powers continued their advance, Black HandA operatives moved about on both sides of the conflict using the identities of fallen soldiers as cover.

It is still unkown exactly what was taken by the Black Hand, but catacombs beneath the medeivel fortified churches housing french infantry were found looted, ancient documents and original manuscripts stolen.

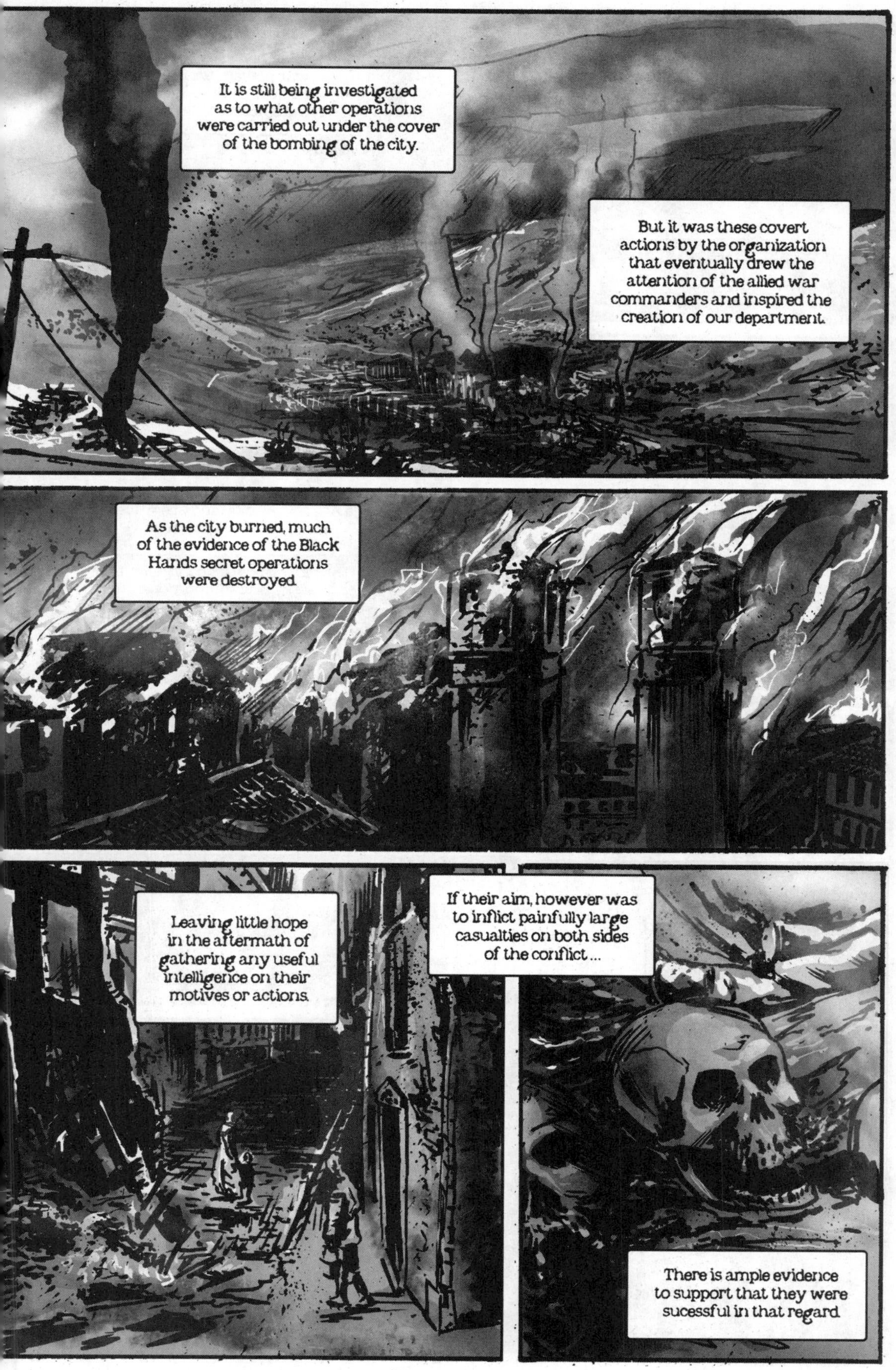
It is still being investigated as to what other operations were carried out under the cover of the bombing of the city.
But it was these covert actions by the organization that eventually drew the attention of the allied war commanders and inspired the creation of our department.
As the city burned, much of the evidence of the Black Hands secret operations were destroyed.
Leaving little hope in the aftermath of gathering any useful intelligence on their motives or actions.
If their aim, however was to inflict painfully large casualties on both sides of the conflict ...
There is ample evidence to support that they were sucessful in that regard.

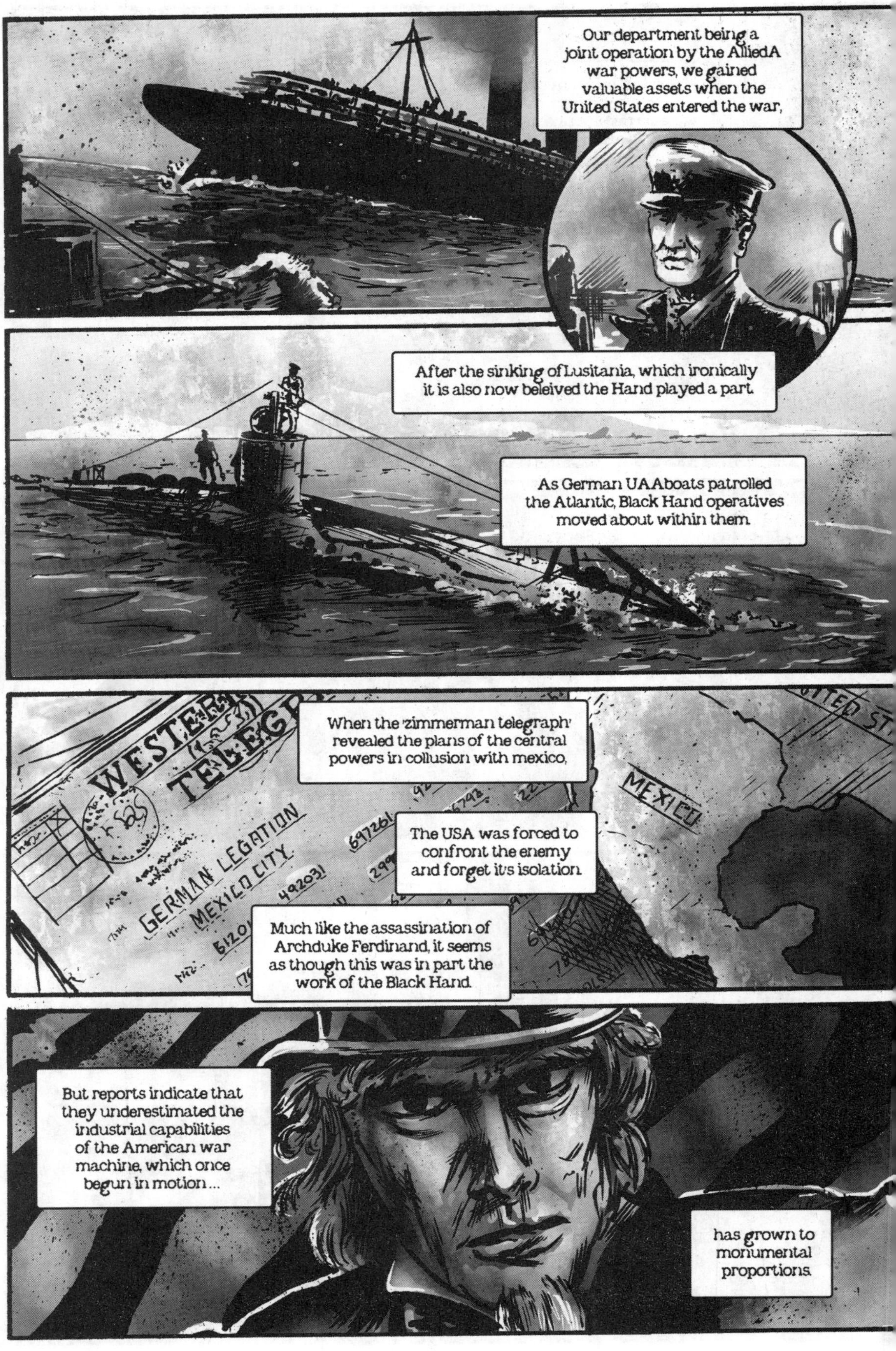
Our department being a joint operation by the AlliedA war powers, we gained valuable assets when the United States entered the war,
After the sinking of Lusitania, which ironically it is also now beleived the Hand played a part.
As German UAAboats patrolled the Atlantic, Black Hand operatives moved about within them.
When the 'zimmerman telegraph' revealed the plans of the central powers in collusion with mexico,
The USA was forced to confront the enemy and forget it's isolation.
Much like the assassination of Archduke Ferdinand, it seems as though this was in part the work of the Black Hand.
GERMAN LEGATION
MEXICO CITY
MEXICO
But reports indicate that they underestimated the industrial capabilities of the American war machine, which once begun in motion ...
has grown to monumental proportions.

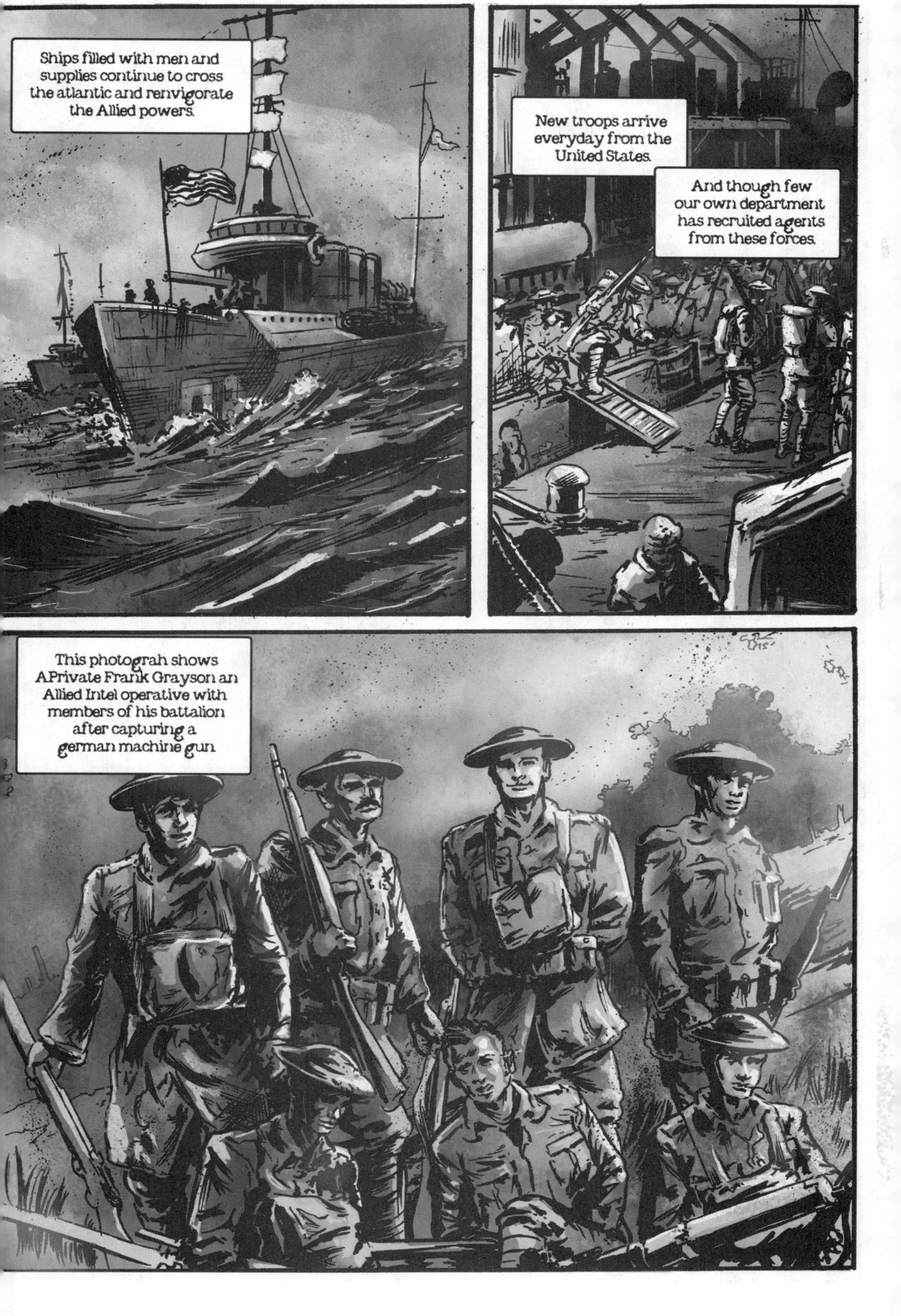
Ships filled with men and supplies continue to cross the atlantic and renvigorate the Allied powers.
New troops arrive everyday from the United States.
And though few our own department has recruited agents from these forces.
This photograph shows A Private Frank Grayson an Allied Intel operative with members of his battalion after capturing a german machine gun

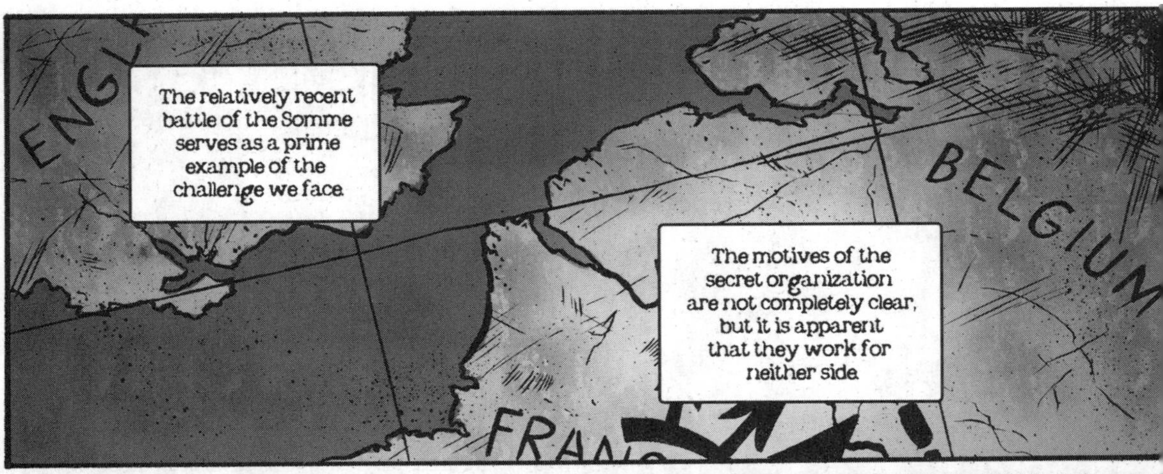
The relatively recent battle of the Somme serves as a prime example of the challenge we face.
The motives of the secret organization are not completely clear, but it is apparent that they work for neither side.
BELGIUM

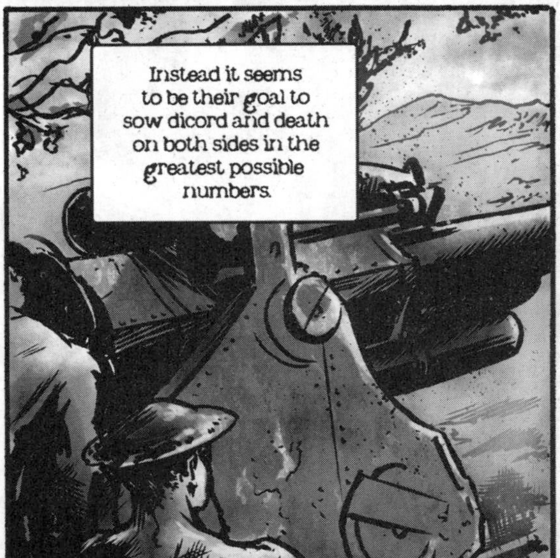
Instead it seems to be their goal to sow dicord and death on both sides in the greatest possible numbers.

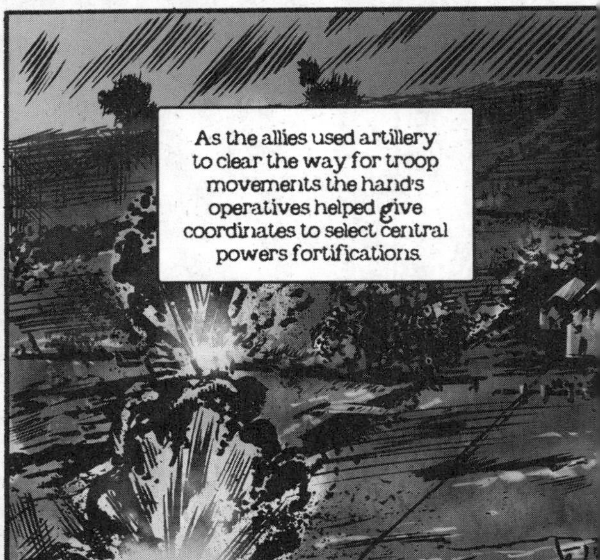
As the allies used artillery to clear the way for troop movements the hand's operatives helped give coordinates to select central powers fortifications.

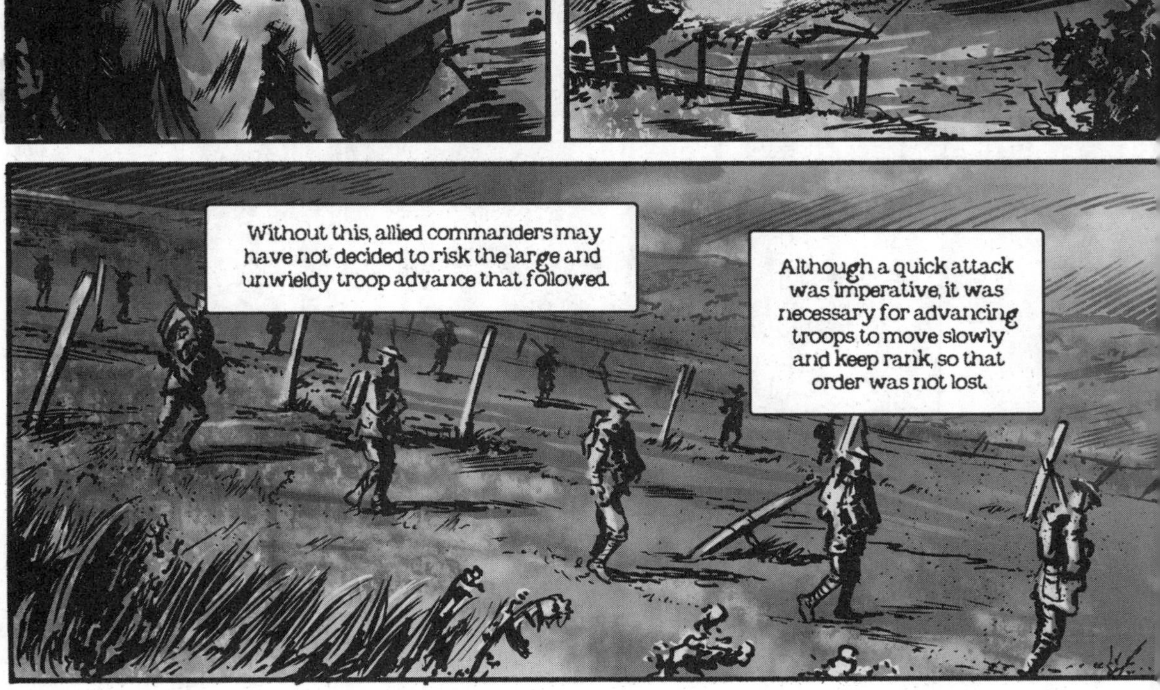
Without this, allied commanders may have not decided to risk the large and unwieldy troop advance that followed.
Although a quick attack was imperative, it was necessary for advancing troops to move slowly and keep rank, so that order was not lost.

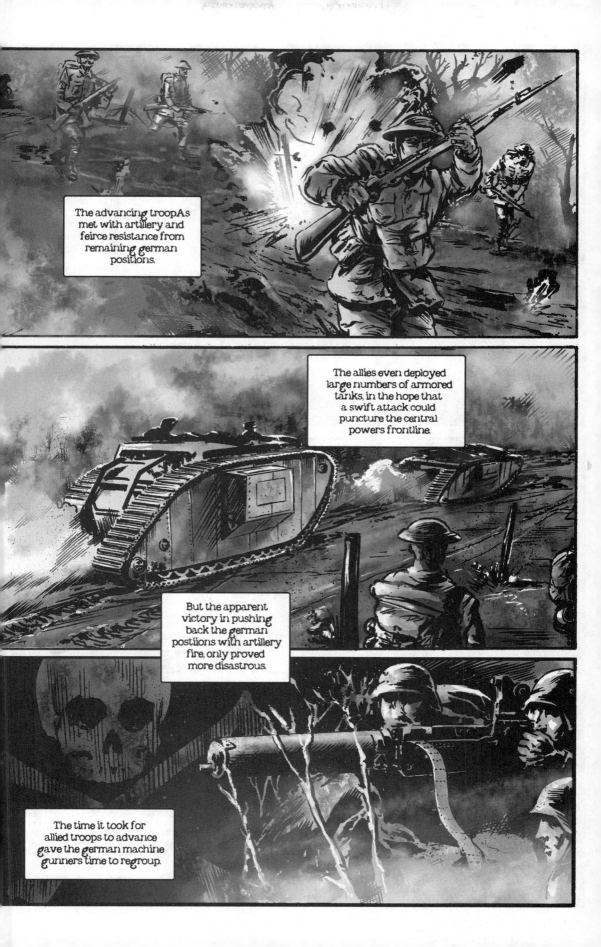

The advancing troopAs met with artillery and feirce resistance from remaining german positions.

The allies even deployed large numbers of armored tanks, in the hope that a swift attack could puncture the central powers frontline.

But the apparent victory in pushing back the german postiions with artillery fire, only proved more disastrous.

The time it took for allied troops to advance gave the german machine gunners time to regroup.

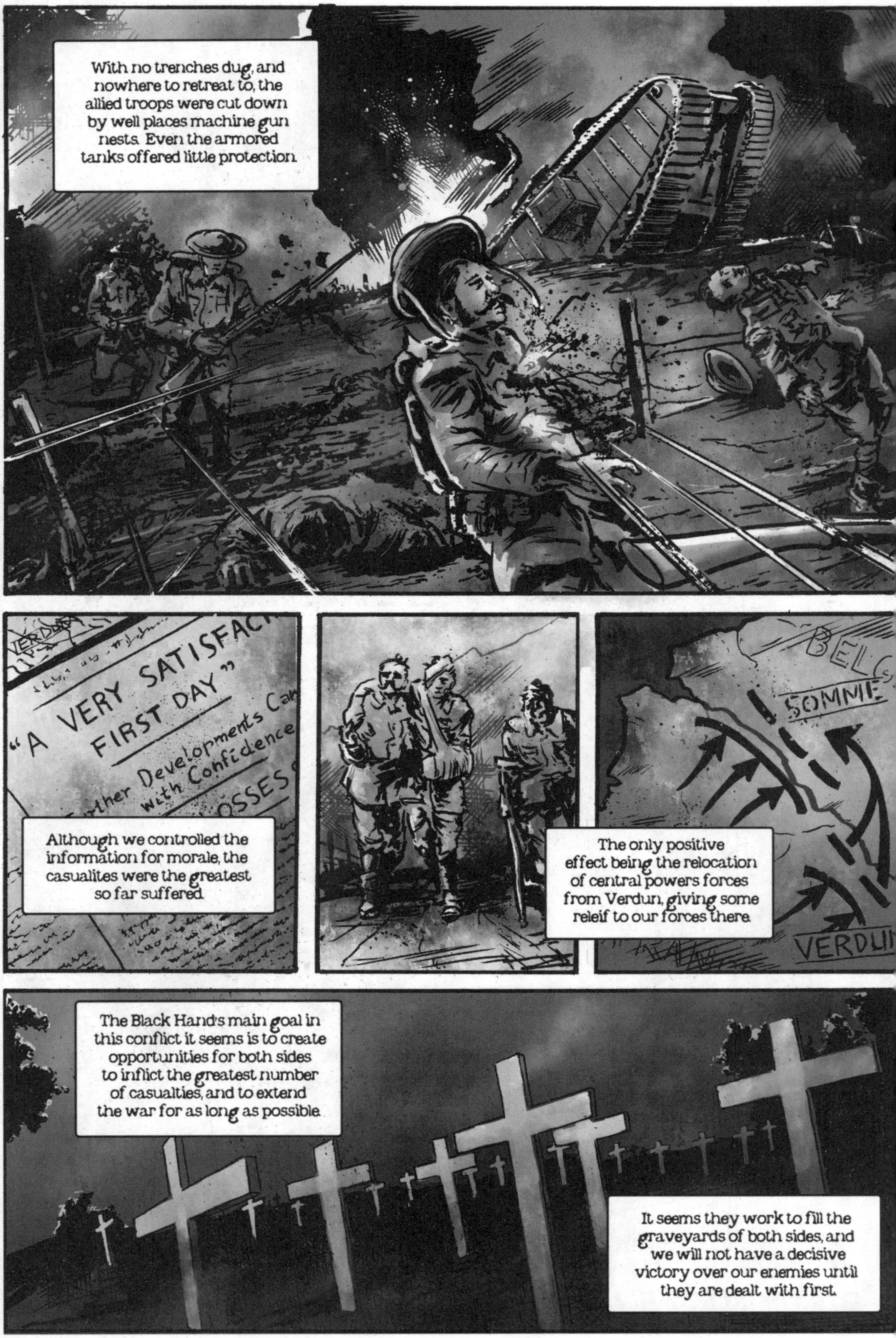
With no trenches dug, and nowhere to retreat to, the allied troops were cut down by well places machine gun nests. Even the armored tanks offered little protection.
“A VERY SATISFAC
FIRST DAY”
with Confidence
Although we controlled the information for morale, the casualites were the greatest so far suffered.
SOMME
The only positive effect being the relocation of central powers forces from Verdun, giving some releif to our forces there.
The Black Hand's main goal in this conflict it seems is to create opportunities for both sides to inflict the greatest number of casualties, and to extend the war for as long as possible.
It seems they work to fill the graveyards of both sides, and we will not have a decisive victory over our enemies until they are dealt with first.

ACES
CURSE OF THE RED BARON

PIN-UPS:

- Christian Duce Fernandez
- Anthony Hightower
- Nima Sorat
- Aaron Sowd
- Will Meugniot
- John Cboins
- Michael Geiger

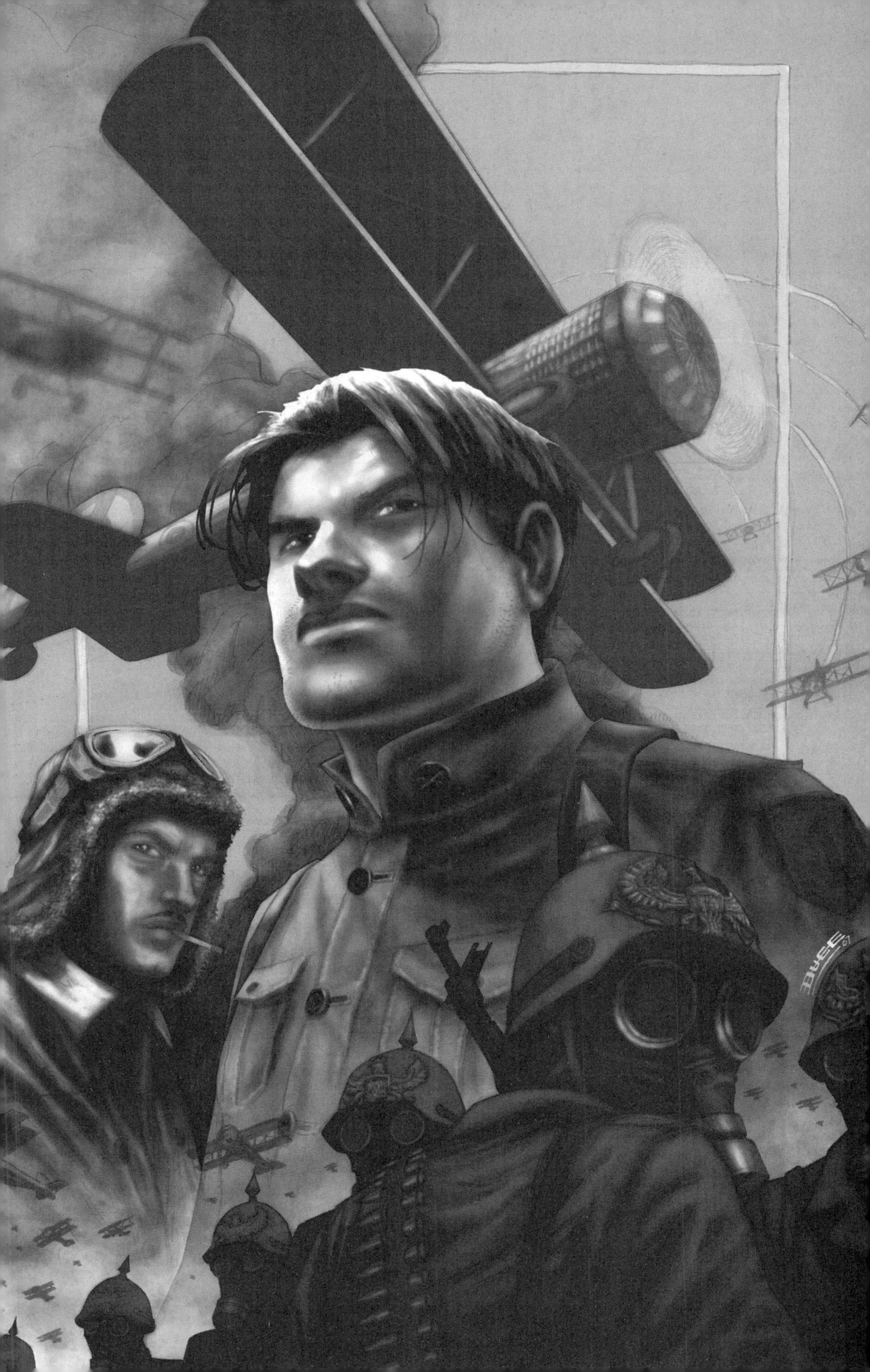

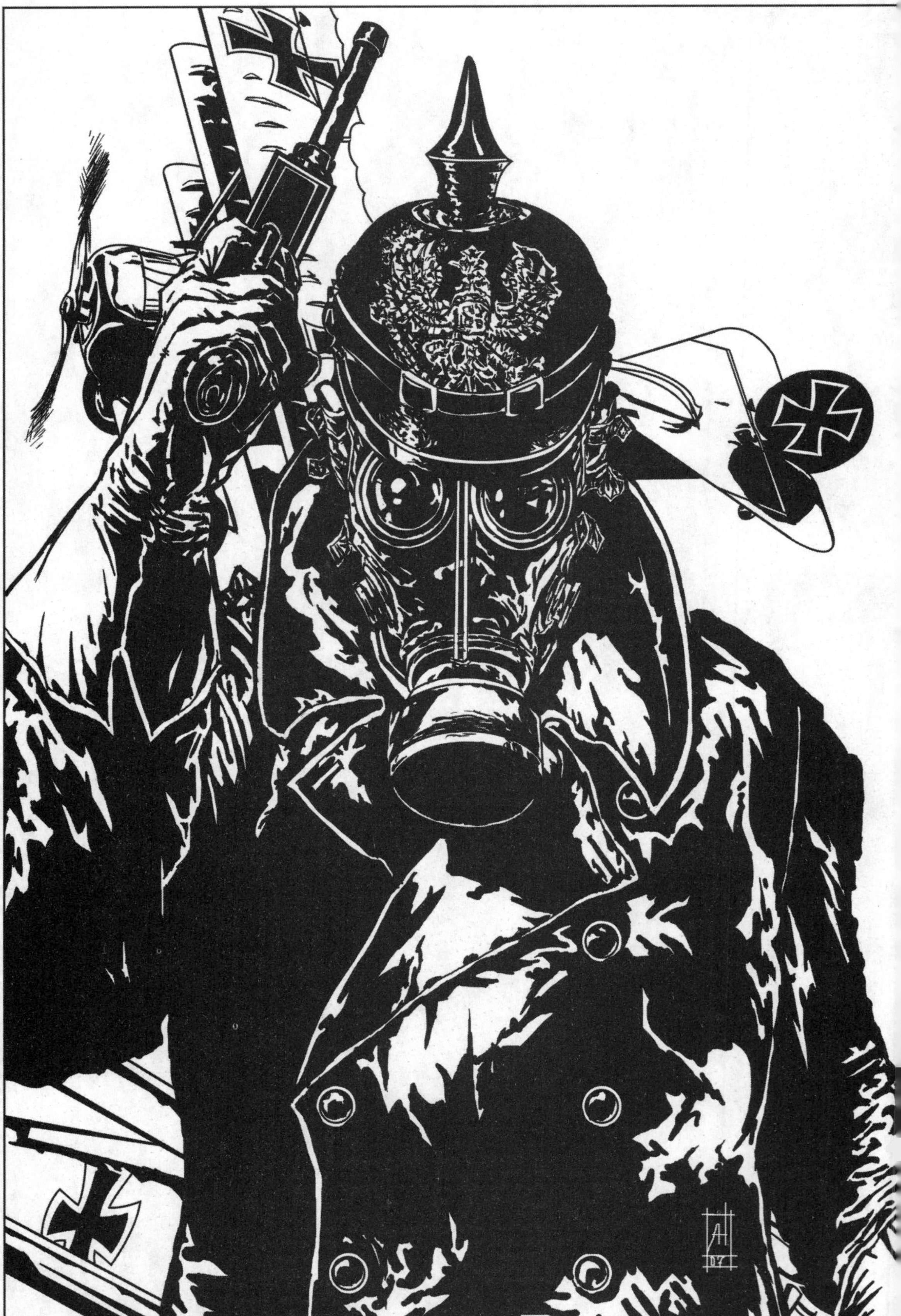

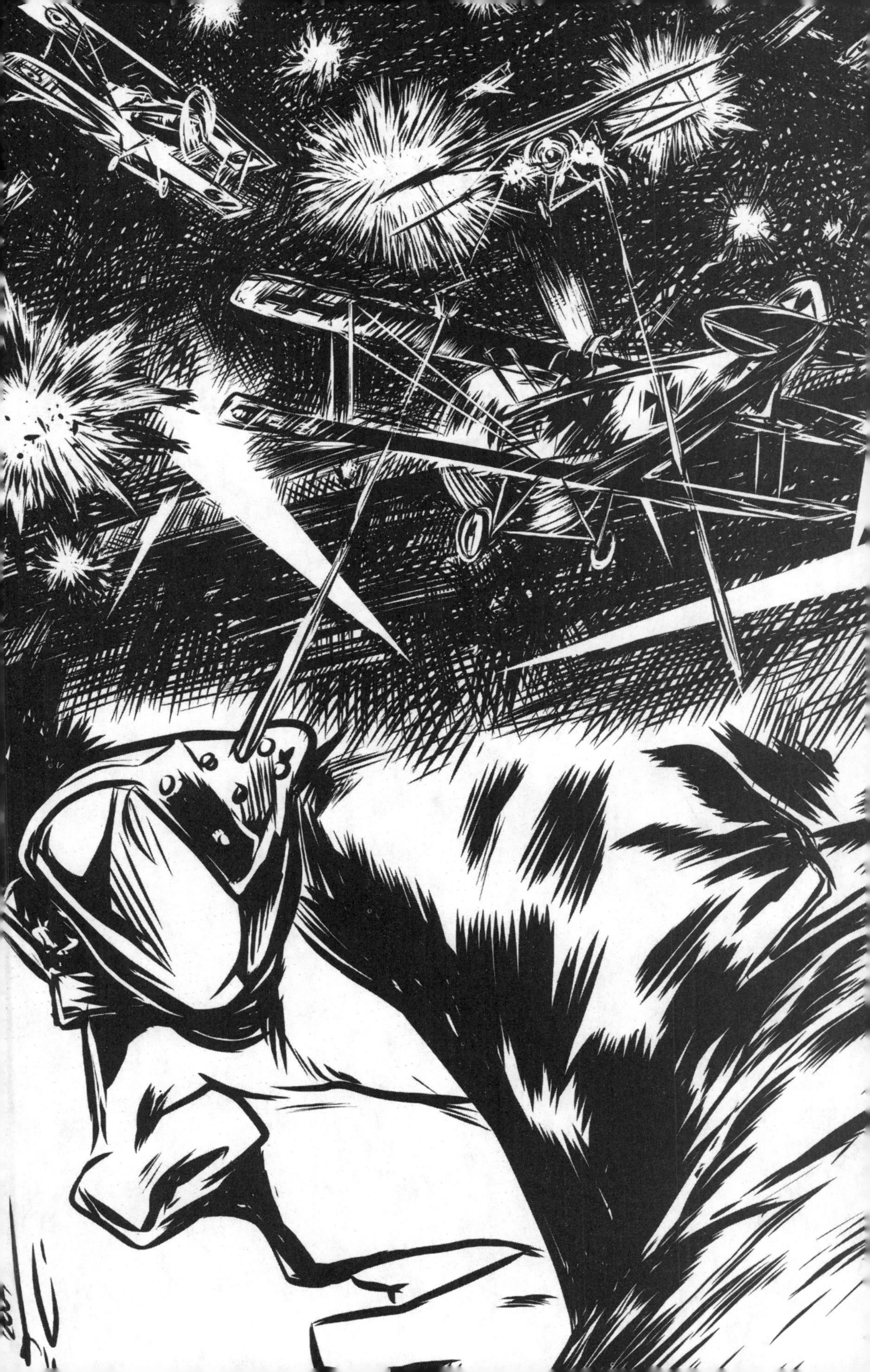

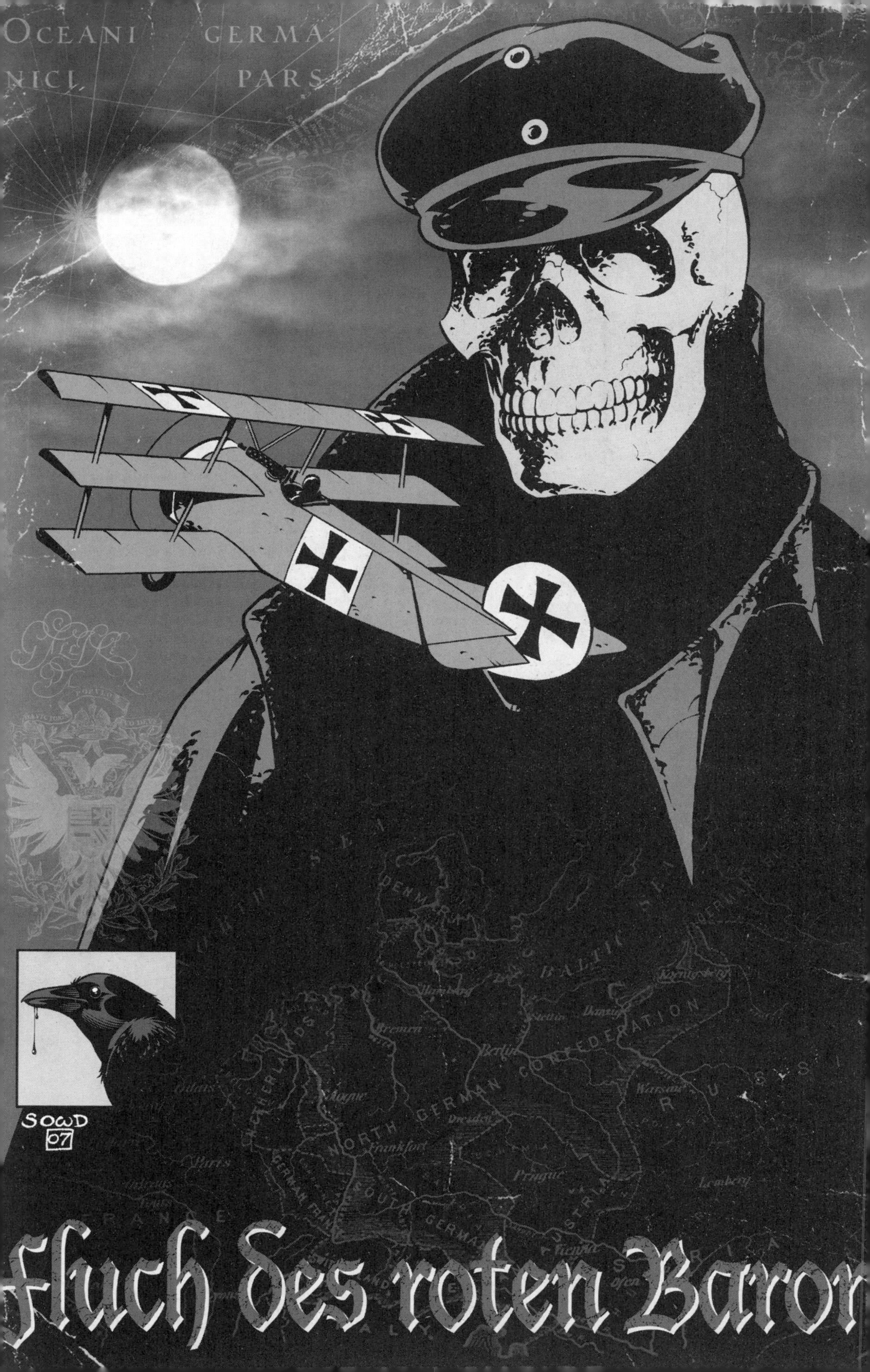
OCEANI GERMA
NICI PARS
SOWD 07
BALTIC
NORTH GERMAN CONFEDERATION
Berlin
Fluch des roten Baron

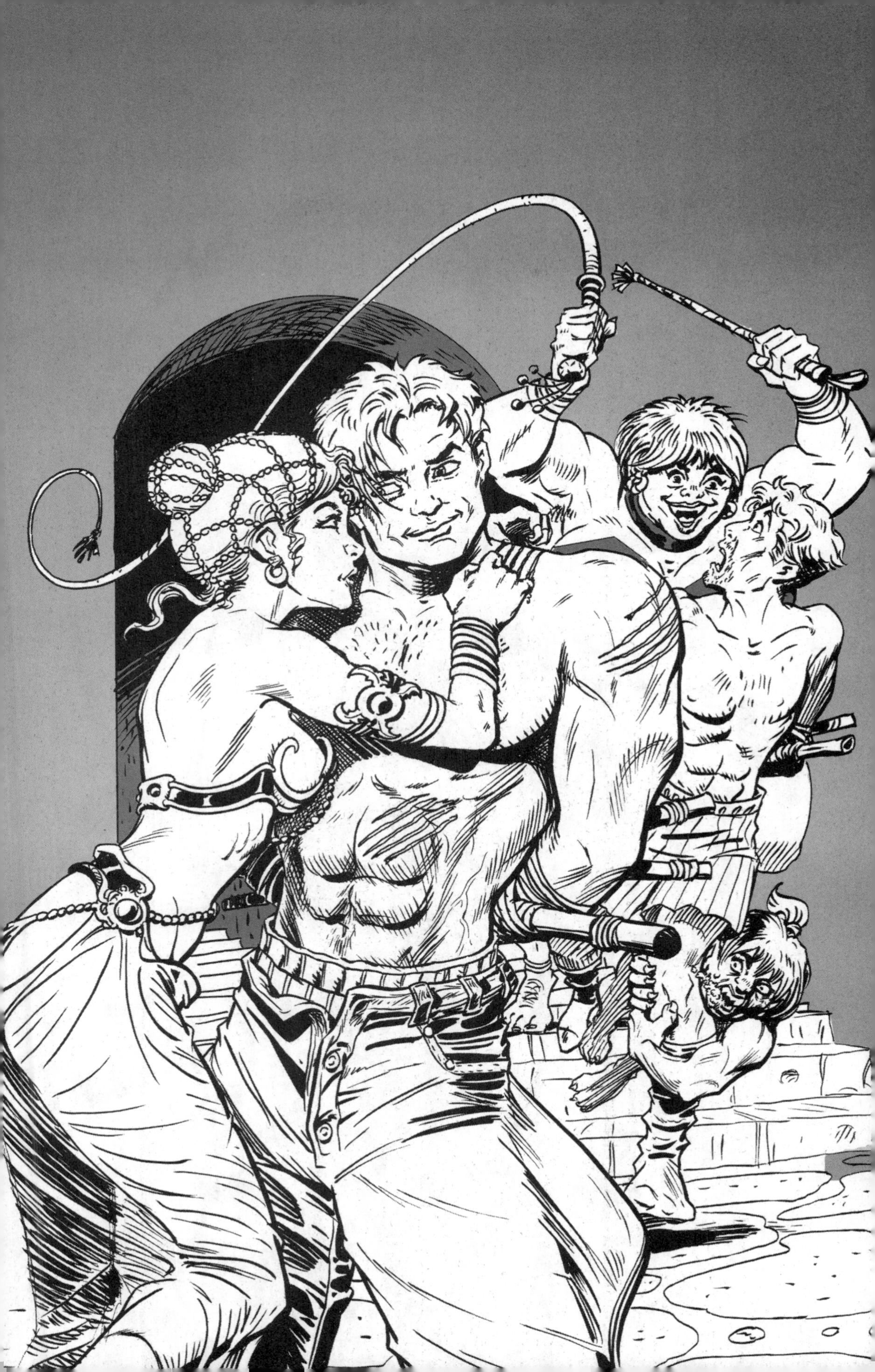

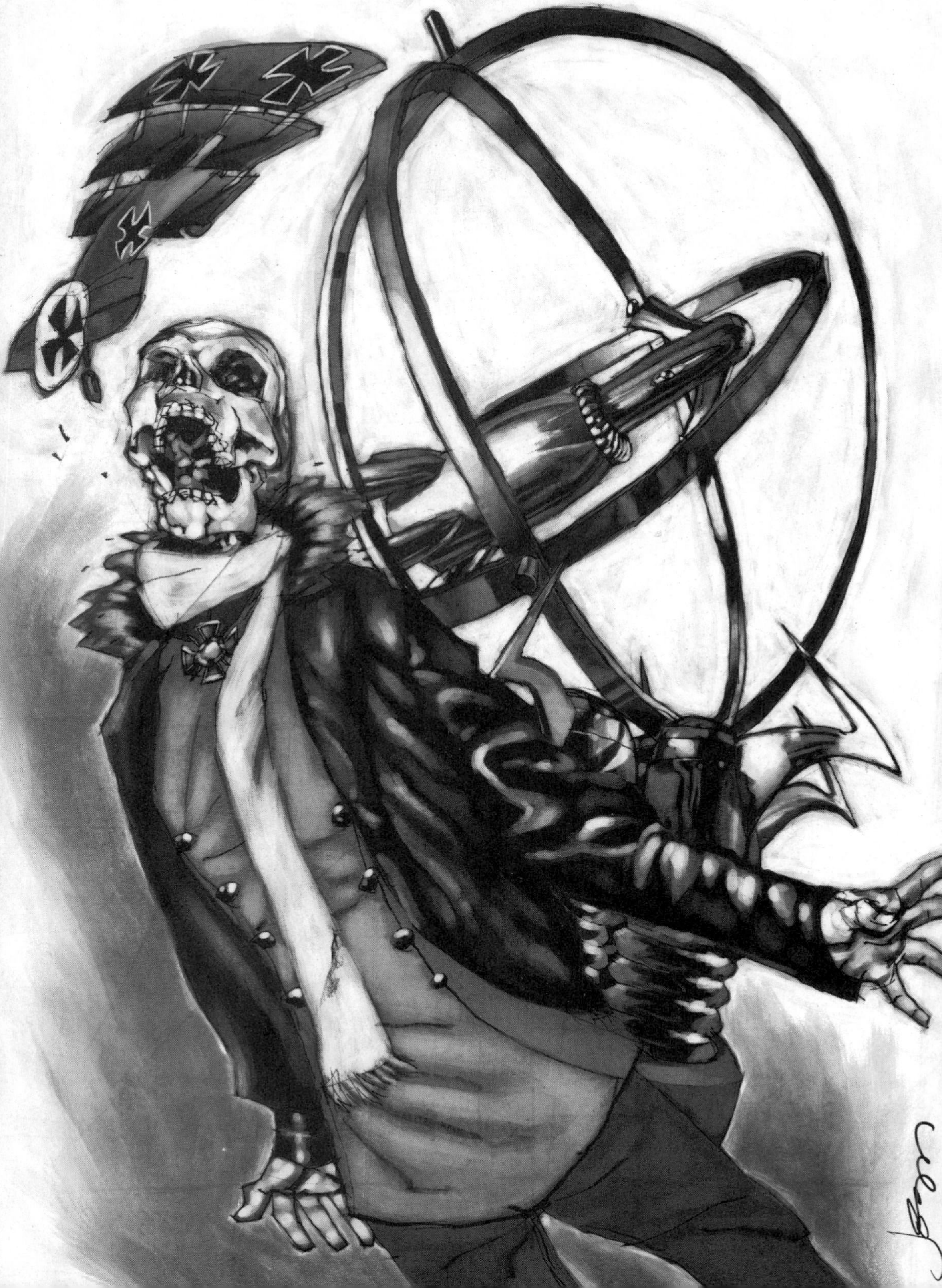

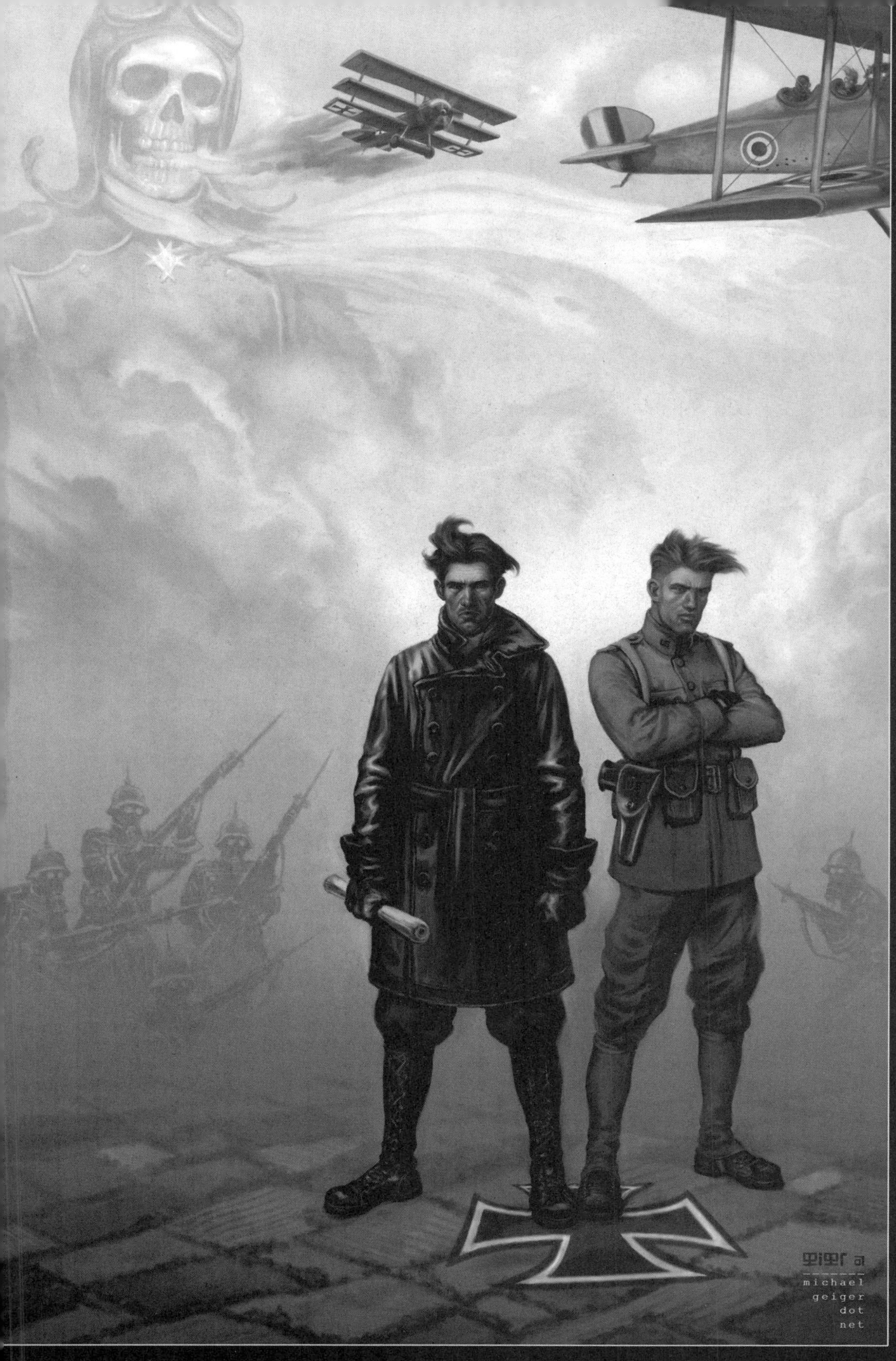
michael
geiger
dot
net

Denton, Shannon Eric

Shannon Eric Denton is a veteran of the comics, video game, film and animation industries. His credits include Cartoon Network, Warner Bros., Jerry Bruckheimer Films, NBC, Disney, Sony, ToyBiz, Marvel Entertainment, FoxKids, Paramount, CBS, Dimension Films, DC Comics, Dark Horse, Tokyopop, Boom Studios, Image Comics, Dimension Films and Nickelodeon. Shannon is currently writing and producing on the upcoming animated series WORLD OF QUEST for Warner Bros., a new line of illustrated children's action books under the ACTIONOPOLIS imprint from Komikwerks, and working for publishers on his creator-owned titles.

www.shannondenton.com

Wilson, G. Willow

G. Willow Wilson's writings have appeared in publications including THE ATLANTIC MONTHLY, THE NEW YORK TIMES MAGAZINE and THE CANADA NATIONAL POST. She has written professionally on titles such as DC's THE OUTSIDERS and her Vertigo graphic novel CAIRO, with artist MK Perker.

www.gwillowwilson.com

Briggs, Curtis Square

'Curtis Square-Briggs is an Illustrator and Production Artist living in Minneapolis with his wife, Valerie. Having a varied background in offset press production, sound engineering, and interactive design, he likes to get his hands dirty creating all kinds of media. He has been in various bands, and his greatest joys in life are playing guitar in stereo through a bass cab and a 4x12 simultaneously, and eating at good but cheap Indian buffets.

www.curtie-pie.com

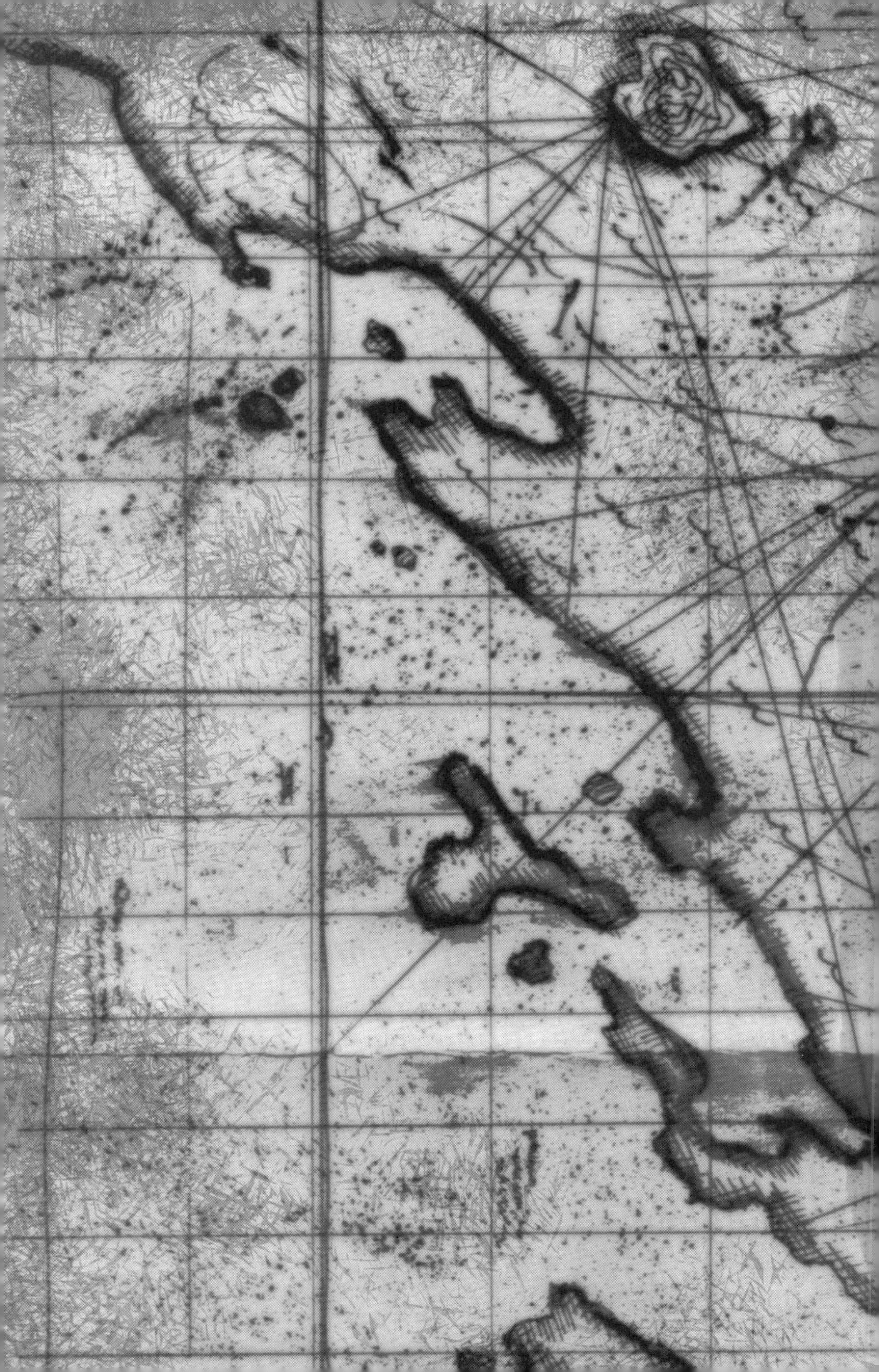